From The Edge

A WAG Anthology

Copyright © 2019 the Authors and Bent Banana Books

From The Edge

Tales from authors of the Writers Anthology Group of Moreton Bay Region and nearby areas of Australia

All rights reserved. No part of this book may be reproduced, stored in a retrieval system, or transmitted, in any form or by any means without the prior written permission of the publisher, nor be otherwise circulated in any form of binding or cover other than that in which it is published and without a similar condition being imposed on the subsequent purchaser.

First published in 2019 by Bent Banana Books in association with the Writers' Anthology Group.

24 Lorraine Court Lawnton, Australia, 4501. 617 3889 2118

Email bentbananabooks@gmail.com

A CiP catalogue record for this book is available from the Australian National Library. ISBN 978-0-6486879-0-0 (paperback)

Cover graphic and design by Ken Armstrong
Cover image: Chris Firth

From The Edge

Short stories of 2019 by members of Writers Anthology Group, based in Pine Rivers district, Moreton Bay Region of Australia

More Contemporary Short Stories
Previous volumes in the Writers Anthology Group collection
Published in conjunction with Bent Banana Books

The Writing on the Wall	2010
Can You Believe It . . .	2011
Sweet and Sour	2012
Serendipity	2013
Alpha and Omega	2014
Inspired By . . .	2015
Redemption	2017

Titles are available as print and eBooks from major on-line books stores.

For a FREE sample of one of our short stories
Email bentbananabooks@gmail.com

Contents

FOREWORD	WAG editorial	6
SHEEP	Jae Salmon	7
TO AN UNKNOWN MAN	David J. Bell	13
ROOM 23	K.J.Sauffs	14
THE CROSSWORD	Kenneth J. Johnson	24
AKERS WINDMILL MOTEL	Raelene Purtill	29
A VISIT TO THE DOCTOR	John R.Nolan	37
THE CAT ON THE SHIP TO THE EDGE OF THE EARTH	Sonya Simonds	46
WAITING FOR MY TEST RESULTS	Vera Murray	56
MISSING	Ronald Holt	57
BEST MATES	Anne Olsson	68
FIVE WORDS ECHO THROUGH TIME	Pauline Davies	77
THE MAY FIRES	Virginia Miranda	82
AN AWAKENING	Ann Lewis	92
THE OUTLIER	Bernie Dowling	93
VISIT TO A NEW WRITERS' CENTRE	Vera Murray	102
TRANSITIONS	Pauline Davies	104
A TURNING WHEEL CONNECTS	Caryn Jacobs	110
A CLOUDED MIND	Bakthi Ross	120
A CURIOUS TALE OF STOLEN BLACK ART	David MacLaughlin	122
BLUEY AND CLIFF'S COASTAL JOURNEY	Lorraine K.Noscova	131
YUSEF BOY	Bernie Dowling	136
DEEP RIVER	Ronald Holt	137
THE HAUNTED HOUSE JACKALS CAUSEWAY	David MacLaughlin	142
THREE KILOMETRES	Jenny Woolsey	145
FINDING ALISHA	Jenny Woolsey	154

Contents

NOT OURS TO SEE	K.J. Sauffs	165
GREETINGS	Karine Dupre	172
THE ONE ABOUT THE FARMER'S DAUGHTERS	Bernie Dowling	174
FROM THE EDGE	Raelene Purtill	191
TREASURE IN THE SNOW	Jeanette O'Hagan	199
RETIRED OFFICERS	David J. Bell	208
FEATHERED HOOVES	Chris Radge	209
YELLOW	Karine Dupre	219
FROM THE EDGE	Vera Murray	224
MISTAKEN IDENTITY	R. William Penshorn	225
DIGGER'S WEAKNESS	R. William Penshorn	230
THE ORPHAN WALLABY	Vera Murray	232
MARTHA'S HEAD	Bakthi Ross	236
KEEPING CALM AND CARRYING ON	Scarlett Reed	241
THE TRANQUIL REALM OF SILENCE	Amy Capstick	258
ABOUT THE AUTHORS		263

FOREWORD BY BERNIE DOWLING

ON behalf of the Writers Anthology Group (WAG), based in Pine Rivers, Australia, I present our 2019 anthology, *From the Edge*. This is the eighth anthology in the series begun by the Arts Alliance Pine Rivers in conjunction with WAG.

This edition includes a retrospective. Along with more than 20 new stories and poems, we include at least one story from each of our previous volumes. Our full complement of WAG editors is back with past editors Anne Olsson and Lorraine Noscova providing retrospective stories. We acknowledge the work of our current editorial panel: Bernie Dowling, Ronald Holt, Raelene Purtill, David MacLaughlin, Vera Murray and Jenny Woolsey.

Some writers, our cover artist, Ken Armstrong, and editors have been with us from volume one; others are newbies; we thank all for their contributions. Authors range from people who earn or have earned a living from writing to those being published for the first time.

Our winners in the Peter Campbell Memorial/ WAG Literary Awards for local high school students are Sonya Simonds and Amy Capstick.

It was more than 12 months ago that we chose our title *From the Edge,* and it was predictive of the zeitgeist, the spirit of our times, the evil soul of which, like a vampire, has no reflection in a mirror, paradoxically revealing its true character to the world. When short stories went out of fashion, we lost great artists holding up a mirror to evil souls, and beautiful souls, and funny ones, and fantastic ones, and mysterious ones. Lost souls, too, to be mourned or comforted or redeemed. In their humble ways, our authors bring us their sometimes unpolished and cracked mirrors.

So, hang on to a life-giving tree as you view the world *From the Edge.*

– Bernie Dowling, WAG editorial committee

SHEEP

Jae Salmon

'I'M AN IDIOT,' he bellowed into the prevailing wind. 'A fat, ugly, idiot,' he continued shouting emotively. The volume and content of these outbursts would normally have attracted attention, but not in this place. In this place no one hears or cares, because no one is here. No one except the sheep grazing nearby. Occasionally the sheep raise their heads from the lush green grass to pass a cursory eye over the young man standing at the edge of the cliff. The sheep do not care why he is here, nor do they care to hear what he is saying. Munching grass is the only preoccupation the sheep give their attention to.

The weather is fine and the wind rising from the cliff face is strong, pushing him back slightly from the edge. The young man's body casts a long shadow across the grass in the afternoon sun. Between the cliff edge and the setting sun lay an expanse of ocean writhing and rolling to the horizon. The tidal flow is about to change from high to low. He has timed his visit perfectly. Debris falling to the bottom of the cliff will be carried out to sea and hopefully lost forever in the swell.

The memory plays fresh in his mind. Her contorted face, her venomous tone, the way his stomach dropped so suddenly, he was sure he would wretch right in her face.

'Why would I go out with you?' she had sneered. The incident happened a few days ago but every detail remains vivid on his cerebral movie screen. 'Surely you know you're not my type,' casting a disapproving eye up and down his full length; from his unbranded sneakers to his long brown hair which bore no semblance to any style.

How he wished a smart, funny comeback had found its way to his lips in that moment, but those kinds of comebacks are the possessions of cool people. Confident people. No, he had no smart comeback. Instead, his chin fell to his chest and the words, 'Yeah, you're right,' escaped quietly from behind trembling lips. As he walked away a chorus of giggles erupted behind him. Her disapproving appraisal had stung, and her words bit hard. He had never felt more pathetic in his life than he did in that moment.

Of course, that incident alone was not the sole reason he had brought himself to the cliff face today. There were so many more moments of torment which had accumulated over the years. He could no longer hold the memories back. Each one crashed through him, taunting him. As each wave crashed against the rocks below him a new memory would come.

The memories began with all the times his mother had asked him in her cutting way, 'What's wrong with you?' Crash. He could never forget her condemning stare. Next came the times his father had said, 'Get away, you're useless,' whenever he tried to help with repairs or maintenance. Crash. His sister had often eroded his confidence with, 'What girl would be interested in you?' Crash. The memories keep coming relentlessly and unmercifully. Too many hurts, too much pain.

Tears begin to pool, blurring his vision. Behind him, he hears two sheep bleat as if in conversation. His self-regard is so low in this moment his brain translates the bleating into vitriolic remarks. 'Oh God, he's crying now. How lame is this guy?'

The second sheep answers in agreement. 'How pathetic.'

Before today he had not considered sheep capable of being derogatory, but today was no ordinary day. His mood turned to anger. How dare the sheep judge him this way? They do not know him. They do not have a clue about his life and what he has endured. He recalls the famous words of Kierkegaard – *Once you label me you negate me.* 'These words spun and whirled, as they came to life in his reasoning mind. He realises a deeper truth in these words. Not only is he negated by the labels others give him, he is equally negated by the labels he gives himself. Ipso facto - *If I label myself I negate myself.*

As he muses he turns his back to the cliff edge to face the sheep. The sheep have no appetite for existentialism, their only preoccupation is consuming grass without care or thought. Now with his back to the wind, his wavy, shoulder length hair rushes to wrap itself around his face. He does not move to scrape it back behind his ears. He allows his hair freedom to choose its own path for a time. Freshly shampooed, he breathes in the fragrance effusing from his unruly locks. The remaining sunlight shines through crinkled tresses, revealing a deep auburn glint. An unexpected sense of positivity begins to emerge, embracing him. He grants himself permission to admit he likes his hair. Yes, he likes his hair.

Shouting more abuse at himself feels wrong now. Despite the flood of endorphins released a moment ago by yelling long-held beliefs and anger to the wind, he no longer wishes to pursue this vein of relief. Observing the sheep and the banality of their lives has brought fresh perspective. The labels, fat and ugly, are in fact just words. This realisation reminds him of a lesson he attended in primary school. Mrs Thompson, who was old and life weary, came in each week to teach Religious Instruction, which he never much cared for. The title of the lesson he is remembering was, *The tongue holds the power between life and death*. He wonders at how memories, most apt to current situations, bubble to the surface when required.

According to Proverbs the wet, muscle which nestles behind our teeth, is a powerful appendage. This may be true, however, his experience atop the cliff today has revealed another layer of insight, which Proverbs missed. His ruminating culminates in understanding *fat* and *ugly*, are only words. The *power* in words is contained in the meaning we give them and not in the word itself. Therefore, it is not the tongue which holds power, it is our mind.

While the words fat and ugly may serve as an accurate description of his appearance, who decided to be thin and good looking was a measure of worth anyhow? *If you label me, you negate me* – those words keep coming back to him. 'You can label me fat and ugly but that does not describe who I am, it merely describes my appearance,' he thinks. Confidence is beginning to tingle through his system.

A positive memory of winning the academic prize for physics shines through the internal gloom. Winning such an accolade must surely mean he is not an idiot as he had proclaimed himself to be only a few minutes before. The weight of these revelations moves him to sit. He lowers himself to the grass and tucks his hair behind his ears. The last rays of the day warm his back as he remains facing the sheep. His brain feels like it is whirring, as if his skull contains actual gears which turn to generate thoughts. His imagination frolics freely through various paradigms of thought. He even dares to wonder *who says academic achievement is the best indicator of intelligence?* He remembers a story he had once heard, of a Professor of Physiology who had caught his foreskin in a zip. He decides this story serves to prove – at the very least – academic achievement is not necessarily a precursor to common sense.

Facing his perceived shortcomings in this way feels good. He decides he still has a legitimate place in this world, despite the value others attribute to appearance and the place he holds on their associated scales of worth. His mother may well think there is something wrong with him. His father may believe him to be useless and his sister may not see what another girl might see when she looks at him. They are all entitled to their view point, he doesn't need to agree with them. He resolves to let their comments slide the next time they speak to him in their usual manner.

As contemplation absorbs his focus, one sheep ambles over to sniff him. He sits very still so as not to frighten it. The sheep breathes in the young man's scent and then blows out heavily from its nostrils, spraying his arm with droplets of sheep snot, and then moves on unperturbed. He feels disappointment, he expected more from the interaction than what transpired. He wonders why the sheep did not take more time to regard him. Was he so easy to dismiss? Recognising the old feelings of self-loathing returning he laughs at the thought of wanting to feel important to the sheep. 'I don't need approval or validation from sheep,' he decides.

The sun is now just a thin shimmer above the ocean horizon. He decides to leave the cliff top, as it seems his original plan could wait for another day, or be cancelled altogether. He prepares to hoist his hefty body into a standing position. He places his right hand next to the wide expanse of his posterior and pushes down firmly on the grass beneath. He has forgotten how close to the edge of the cliff he is sitting. The earth gives way under the pressure of his hand, and it lurches into thin air promptly followed by the rest of his rotund body. Only time for these final thoughts – *What's wrong with me? I'm so useless* – before - crash.

The sheep raise their heads from the grass upon hearing the scream which fades, then abruptly stops. With blank disinterested stares, the sheep briefly look in the direction where the young man had been seated only a moment before, then turn their mouths back to the grass and continue to munch. The grass is particularly tasty at the top of this cliff.

When I wrote the sonnet *To an Unknown Man*, I pictured a man who had spent much of his life at sea during the mid-years of the nineteenth century. I was also influenced by John Masefield's *Sea Fever*, and Alfred, Lord Tennyson's *Crossing the Bar*.

– David Bell

TO AN UNKNOWN MAN
David J. Bell

A man I never knew rests in this place,
a Christian name and date deceased are here
upon the stone. This child of yesteryear
has left no fading picture of his face:
anonymously now he lies, his race
is done. 'Who can recount his love and fear;
or recollections that he held most dear?
What loss or sadness did his heart encase?

Upon the rough hewn slab these words have been
Inscribed, 'Into eternal life he passed.
Who knows what happiness his life has sown!
His treasures were the vast worlds he had seen.
Fond memories encompassed him at last.
As life departed he was not alone.'

RETROSPECTIVE: From the first anthology of 2010:

The Writing on the Wall

ROOM 23

K.J. Sauffs

THE SUN WAS SHINING as Meredith left her house. Summer was not far away and already the humidity was increasing. Normally she would have started getting a few things in for Christmas by now. Trying to summon enough energy for her appointment she started her car and backed out of the driveway. She was on her way to see a psychic.

Her friend Nicki had commented she had nothing to lose; after all she had tried everything else. Perhaps this Chloe woman would be able to give her a clue as to what the problem was. Her best friend Nicki meant well but Meredith was beginning to think that maybe the doctors were right and it was all in her mind.

She found the psychic's house quite easily. It was a basic late twentieth century style brick home with a neat garden that was well looked after. Meredith parked her car in the street, locked it then walked up the front path and knocked on the door.

'Hello dear you must be Meredith. I'm Chloe, come on in. It's a lovely day isn't it? Would you like a cup of tea before we start?'

'No thank you,' Meredith answered the older woman tiredly. She had expected the psychic to be in her thirties or forties because she had sounded quite young over the phone. The gray-haired old lady in front of her was a bit of a surprise.

'I'm guessing that I'm not quite what you were expecting. In my younger days I used to do the whole Gypsy routine. You know long hair, silk scarves and big earrings. I even occasionally used a crystal ball because I thought that's what people expected. I've since discovered that how I look makes very little difference to my ability, but a hell of a lot of difference to my credibility. Come inside out of this awful heat and we'll see if I can help you.'

As Chloe showed the younger woman into a small sitting room that had two comfy armchairs and a coffee table she noticed the lethargic way Meredith moved. As she sat down Meredith let out a weary sigh.

'Now dear if you would give me some item of jewellery that you wear a lot and tell me what's bothering you,' Chloe said.

Meredith took off a silver filigree ring and handed it to Chloe. 'I've worn it since high school. It's not very valuable but I like it.'

'It's lovely.'

The psychic reached over and patted Meredith on the hand. 'Don't be nervous dear. I'm just going to close my eyes and relax and listen to your voice and then I'll explain what I see. Just tell me why you're here without trying to analyse anything and don't worry if it looks like I've dropped off to sleep. I assure you I am listening and tuning in to your vibration.'

As Chloe sat back in her chair Meredith took a deep breath and began to tell her story.

'Well there's not much to tell really. I'm forty-eight years old and happily married to the same man for twenty-eight years. Our daughter is 26-years old and is living and working in London. We're financially secure and up until a few months ago I was working in a florist shop a couple of days a week. I loved my job but had to give it up because I don't have the energy. Most days I struggle just to get out of bed.

'It started almost a year ago when I gradually began feeling weaker. It's not like I want to sleep all the time, it's more a feeling of being drained, like I'm fading away. I've been to four different doctors and various kinds of alternative healers. They all say its menopause or chronic fatigue syndrome. One doctor even suggested it was all in my head but I know it's not. I've always eaten fairly well. I know I could stand to lose a little weight but overall I think I'm fairly healthy and I do a lot of walking. They've given me hormone therapy, acupuncture and a number of different tonics. None of them have worked. A friend suggested I come to you.' She paused before adding, 'If you can't help me I guess my last resort will be a psychiatrist.'

Meredith looked over at the older woman. It certainly looked as though she had dozed off.

Chloe opened her eyes and gave Meredith a gentle smile. 'Well the good news is I think I know what your problem is. The bad news is I don't think you'll believe me.'

'I'm listening.'

'Do you believe in reincarnation?'

'I believe in the possibility of it.'

'You've probably read in the papers that the Ultra Cryo-lab has been having success with reanimating some of their patients.'

Meredith nodded.

Chloe gazed intently into her eyes as she said, 'Your body from your previous life is one of those being reanimated and your spirit, or soul if you prefer, is divided between its two homes.'

'You're serious?'

Chloe laughed. 'I know it sounds preposterous. As I tuned into your vibration I found it going in two directions. I followed the weaker one to a building. The writing on the wall said Ultra Cryo-lab. On the second floor in room 23 there's a young woman, you, in recovery. At this moment in time your spirit is torn between which of its bodies it wants to inhabit. As the body of the previous you grows stronger, your present body grows weaker.'

'Will I die?'

'Perhaps, or perhaps she will. Or one of you may lapse into a coma. It's a fascinating subject and I've done quite a bit of research on it. Ever since I first heard about cryonics I've wondered about the implications for the soul.

'Of course when they started bringing people back the results were so varied. Why do some patients return completely as the people they once were while others remain in a vegetative state, and some don't reanimate at all?'

Meredith recalled what she knew. 'From what I've read some scientists think it might have something to do with the cause of their death or how they were processed after they died. Apparently in the early days some methods were fairly primitive.'

'So you know a little about the subject?'

'Only what I've read in the newspapers.'

'Well I'm sure scientists know what they're talking about but I wonder if they've considered the spiritual aspect. What if those that come back do so because their spirits are free to move on, or, perhaps a new spirit enters? Instead of being born. It may have no need to go through childhood again to learn what it needs to.'

'Then why don't they all come back? There must be spirits lining up to be reborn.'

'I guess that's the question many would like the answers to. From my experience there is no system or philosophy that can explain everything. I think just as there are many sides to a story, there are also many reasons for how and why things happen. Sometimes the answer may be scientific, sometimes occult, sometimes both, and sometimes there is no answer. It just is.'

Meredith sighed again. 'This is all very interesting but how does it help me? Even if what you say is true, how does it help me get my life back?'

'Well I thought the answer would be quite obvious. You must kill your former body.'

'Excuse me?'

'You know it wouldn't be murder, more like suicide really.'

'Somehow I don't think the police would see it that way.'

'I'm sure you're clever enough to get away with it. After all, unless you're actually caught red-handed, there's no connection between the two of you. If you did get caught, I'm sure a competent lawyer could get you off or at the very least you may have to spend some time in a mental institution.'

'You'd be in trouble too.'

'Nonsense, you came to me for a simple reading. It's not my fault if you include me in your delusion. It would even make sense that you would link this visit in some way to try and justify your actions and absolve yourself.'

Meredith shook her head. 'This is too surreal, it's ridiculous. I'm here in this lovely old house, chatting to a nice old grandmotherly lady and she's advising me to kill some stranger to make myself well again.'

Chloe smiled. 'Believe me I do understand. I've been doing this for almost fifty years now and some of the things I say still surprise me. Over the years, experience has taught me not to analyse my readings. I tell you what I see, as I see it. You asked for a solution. I gave you one. What you do with that information is up to you.'

Meredith paid the old woman and left. As she drove home her mind was in a whirl. She needed time to think so she drove to the beach knowing that because it was the middle of the week it would not be too crowded. When she was halfway there she changed her mind and decided to go to the library instead. At the next intersection she turned the car around and headed for her local library to do some research of her own.

As she walked through the automatic doors into the air-conditioned foyer of the library she noticed the other people in the building seemed distant and disconnected from her. This was a feeling that was becoming all too familiar to her. She was beginning to feel more like a spectator of the world around her. It was almost as if she was becoming detached from the rest of society. Taking a deep breath she willed herself to move forward. Ignoring the scientific section she quickly selected an assortment of books on religion and philosophy and took them to a desk along the rear wall. Opening the first book she quickly examined the contents and skimmed through the sections she thought would be appropriate. As she read she realised Chloe was right about one thing. No-one really knows the answers to life's big questions. Scientists employed logic to support their answers and the religious used faith. Belief based on logic or faith was still only belief and she wanted the truth. Meredith had never been a deep thinker. She was fun loving and carefree, even as a child she never was one to question why. She had simply accepted life the way it was. Meredith laughed quietly to herself. Here she was attempting to study philosophy. She put the books away as they were only confusing her more.

Craig would be home in a couple of hours and she still had to pick up a few things at the supermarket. She smiled as she thought about her husband and how good the majority of their married life had been. Of course like everyone else there had been some ups and downs. In the first few years they had even come close to breaking up a couple of times but that was in the past. Just thinking about him could make her go all goose-bumpy like a teenager. Her husband was attractive, sexy and funny. His hair was grey now and he was a bit heavier but then so was she. For a man in his early fifties he was still a good catch even if he did drive her nuts sometimes. As she pulled into a parking space she began to cry. Now that they were finally in a position to enjoy themselves and each other there was no way she was going to sit back and let it end without putting up a fight.

After a few minutes she stopped crying and went into the shop. It seemed to take ages to get around the aisles and through the checkout. By the time she got home her good intentions of making a nice home-cooked dinner from scratch had gone out the window. She went to the freezer to select a frozen dinner. Before her last reserves of strength were gone, she decided to update her diary and then have a nap until Craig came home.

What a day it had been she thought as she wrote down every detail including Chloe's crazy suggestion that she should murder some unknown woman who had once supposedly been herself. Meredith shook her head, there could be no excuses, murder was murder. But if it gave her back her vitality so that she could once again enjoy her life? Anyway how could it be murder if the woman was already legally dead? This was absurd, she could never kill anyone. She closed her diary and went to lie down.

Craig came home at his usual time and as usual he was just as caring. He was beginning to really worry about his wife's health. He had watched her growing weaker and he knew there was a genuine problem. Meredith was not the type to develop a psychosomatic illness.

'Sorry about dinner. Again,' she said softly.

'That's all right, Love. On Saturday I'll cook us up something nice, you can supervise.'

'You're a sweetheart.'

'I know.' He cupped her face in his hands and kissed her tenderly. 'Go and sit in the lounge and I'll make us a cuppa.'

Craig brought her a cup of milky tea and sat in his chair next to hers to read the evening paper while she tried to concentrate on watching a favourite TV show. She was drowsy as her energy was in limited supply and she had used up her daily quota.

Craig looked up from the paper. 'Says here that cryonics place is having an open day tomorrow. Pity I have to work.'

'I didn't know you were interested in that sort of thing,' she said.

'I think it's very interesting, although I wonder if people should be brought back to life.'

'Why do you think they shouldn't?'

'Well they've had their turn haven't they? It's our turn now and our resources are limited. We're having enough trouble looking after the current population as it is. I know they say the Mars colony will help ease some of the problems but I honestly don't think that resurrecting fossils from history would offer anything other than curiosity value. Besides, most of them have been dead for over sixty years. They won't know anyone and the media will probably turn them into sideshow freaks. I don't know; it just seems selfish to me to even want to have another turn. What do you think?'

'I haven't really thought about it all that much. Still you've given me something to sleep on.' Meredith leaned over to kiss him. 'I'm going to bed. Goodnight, Love,' Meredith said.

'Night, I'll be in soon.'

The next day Meredith got up two hours after Craig had left for work. Every day it was getting harder and harder for her to force herself out of bed. While eating breakfast she made up her mind that once she was dressed she would pay a short visit to the Ultra Cryo-lab. Chloe had told her what room the other woman was in. She laughed quietly to herself; this was not what most people had in mind when they heard the term 'the other woman'. She was only going to have a look to appease her curiosity.

    Driving along Main Street she was looking for the street numbers when she saw the truck out of the corner of her eye come hurtling towards her from the right. Unknowing, Meredith had run a red light. There was no pain as she was enveloped by darkness. In the distance she saw a white light emerge. As she floated towards the light she was unexpectedly tugged away in a different direction. Consciousness returned and her eyelids fluttered open. She was staring at a white ceiling. She knew exactly where she was: Room 23, on the second floor of the Ultra Cryo-lab.

    She felt amazing, still Meredith but with her old vitality back. Her muscles were a little weak but she felt absolutely fantastic. Getting out of bed, she went into the adjoining bathroom and looked at her new reflection. She was gorgeous. This was a middle-aged woman's dream come true. As Meredith she had been good looking in an ordinary sort of way. This prior face and body was stunning. She was taller now with long red hair and green eyes and a figure that was curvaceous without being overweight at all. Running her hands down her new body she noticed that her stomach was flat and that her breasts were firm again and up where they used to be. Denise. She remembered her name had been Denise and that she had died from a heart problem which, judging by the scar on her chest, the present day doctors had fixed. She had been twenty-four when she died. Even though she was extraordinarily good looking, she had rejected modelling offers to study landscape gardening. At the time of her death she had been madly in love and she guessed that it was Mark who had paid to have her body frozen. She wondered if he was still alive as he would be in his eighties by now.

Meredith shook her head to clear it as she went back to sit on the bed. She had a new body now but also the burden of all the memories, good and bad, from another life. What about Craig? Would he be able to accept her like this? She was now two years younger than their daughter. Maybe it would be better if she let him believe she was dead and she could go on and build a new life for herself. How much should she tell the doctors? She could give them some valuable insight into the mysteries of life and death, although the sceptics would probably say it was all an hallucination or something.

Footsteps were approaching her room, the door opened and Craig entered.

'How did you know to come here?' she asked him with a voice that was still a little raspy from not being used.

'I read my wife's diary. I've been reading it ever since she became ill. I thought it might help me understand what she was going through. You're very beautiful.'

'I know. 'Isn't it great?'

Meredith looked at him lovingly. She should have been angry with him for invading her privacy but if the situation had been reversed she would have done the same thing. Especially as she had not had the energy to talk to him much about what was happening to her. As she looked at him she knew that she would stay with him because she loved him. It was as simple as that. Her face and body might be different but her thoughts and feelings were the same and she would deal with the old memories as they resurfaced. In time they would probably fade.

For his part Craig saw a beautiful young woman who bore no resemblance to his wife. He did not yet know that Meredith had been killed in a car accident. He had been sitting at his desk at work when his curiosity got the better of him and he had decided to check out the Cryo-lab. Meredith's diary was very detailed. She had written down everything including where Chloe had said this woman was. He had read it again last night before going to bed.

Meredith crooked her finger at him, beckoning him to follow her into the bathroom. He stood behind her as she stared at her reflection.

'I bet you can't wait to make love to this body,' she said as her eyes sparkled with excitement.

'I want my wife back,' he said as he brought the gun to the back of her head.

Her eyes opened wide in terror. 'Wait Craig, you don't understand!'

As he squeezed the trigger their eyes met in the mirror and he recognised her. Her body slumped to the floor and as he realised what he had done Craig began to cry.

A tall distinguished old man in his eighties was standing in the doorway.

'Why did you do that? She was the love of my life,' said the old man.

'Mine too,' said Craig as he let the gun fall from his hand.

THE CROSSWORD
Kenneth J. Johnson

THE CROSSWORD CLUE read, 'Classic horror dissect personality (13)'. I was struggling with the cryptic wording while enjoying a peaceful coffee on the veranda outside my hospital room, when a woman peeped around the door and asked if she could join me.

'Yes, of course,' I said, silently resenting the intrusion but feeling I had no right to object to her utilising the joint facility. She looked to be in her mid-forties and had a darkish complexion. Her hybrid appearance defied my attempt to associate her with a particular ethnic group and she spoke perfect English with only a trace of accent. She might have been Asian or an Islander. I'd had a chat to her husband in the bed next to mine after he was admitted and knew he was as Australian as they come.

'My husband's in the bed next to you,' she said, sitting down heavily on the chair beside me. 'He's with the doctor now, getting an injection,' she continued. 'I hate needles, have a real phobia about them.'

'That's a useful fear to overcome,' I said, keeping my eyes on the crossword to discourage any further conversation,

'Yes.' She agreed, deliberately ignoring my body language. 'Especially as we get older and are subjected to more and more of them.'

I grunted discouragingly, but she was determined to hold my attention.

'Unfortunately,' she went on, 'I've already passed the fear on to two of my grandchildren.' She opened her bag, took out a ball of wool and began to crochet. 'I had to take them to the doctors for an immunisation jab a few weeks ago when their parents and my husband were away. The doctor prepared for the eldest and I cringed. When he brandished the needle, I couldn't stop myself from crying out. Naturally, the child played up and he couldn't get the needle into her so we had to leave.'

'Unfortunate,' I agreed, taking care not to lift my eyes from the paper.

'Very,' she went on. 'My younger granddaughter is thirteen. She said she didn't have a problem with needles.'

I gave up, lowered the paper onto my lap and lifted the coffee. 'A cocky teenager, eh?'

'Cocky! Full of bravado and swagger until *her* name was called. 'Gran, come with me,' she pleaded. Oh-oh, I thought, here we go again.'

'Did you go in with her?' I asked, feigning interest.

'Well, I had to, didn't I?' The question was rhetorical. 'The doc produced the needle and I couldn't help myself. Like a Pavlovian dog, I am. Scream whenever I see a needle. Well, that did it – no injection for her either.'

Having acceded to a conversation, I felt obliged to offer a continuance. 'What's your husband in for?' I asked, expecting a brief response that would elicit a similar enquiry of me.

'He's working down here temporarily – been put up in a hotel by his work. I flew down from Townsville on Thursday for the week and found him asleep in the middle of the day when he should have been at work. That's not like him at all. I woke him and gave him some food. Within half an hour he was asleep again. I woke him again for dinner and he went straight back to sleep afterwards and slept through the night. After breakfast next day he started to nod off again saying he didn't feel right so I took him to the doctor. We were told to come straight to the hospital for tests and they've found a virus infection in his bowel.'

'That doesn't sound good,' I lamented, wondering if I was in danger of catching it.

'No,' she agreed.' And our children are all over the place; two sons in Perth, a daughter on the Sunshine Coast and another in Sydney.'

Sensing a point of contact, I told her we had a daughter who had immigrated to New Zealand.

'What part?' she asked.

'Lumsden; not far from Queenstown on the South Island.' I said, abandoning my paper onto the coffee table.

'I'm from the North Island—Auckland,' she said.

I recognised her physiognomy then, as part Maori of Polynesian decent. Not wishing to let the conversation lag, she went on, 'I've just been back there to see my parents. They've just separated after fifty-four years together.'

I must have looked mildly surprised because she nodded conspiratorially. 'Yes. I know. How stupid's that? I got a phone call from my eighty-five-year-old dad. 'Your mother's just walked out on me, Girl. You've got to come home and bring her back,' he said. 'Where is she?' I asked. 'Moved into a flat down the road,' he said. 'I told her she's stupid paying rent when we own our own home, but she's as stubborn as a mule with no legs. Come now before she gets too settled.' I told him I was in Townsville with things to take care of, I couldn't jump on a plane just like that. It'll take a few days, I told him, but I'll see what I can do.'

'Did you go?' my curiosity piqued despite my reluctance to get involved.

'Well, I had to, didn't I?' She stood to peer through the screen door at her husband's bed. 'Doc's still with him,' she said, backing into her seat.

'What happened next?' I asked.

She saw she had me hooked so felt at liberty to go into more detail. 'I went to Dad's place and asked him what had happened. 'Your Ma's gone mad,' he said. He gave me her address and I went to see her. She opened the door quite casually and ushered me inside. There was a slight glint in her ancient eyes and I noticed she'd had her hair done and was wearing new clothes.

'What's got into you?' I said, 'Get your things, you're going back home right now. She looked at the floor and told me she couldn't do it anymore. Said she just couldn't live with him any longer.'

'Did she say why?' I asked, intrigued despite myself.

'That's what *I* asked. 'What's wrong?' I demanded angrily. 'I can't take his swearin' and demandin' ways. He's messin' with me 'ead,' she said, tapping her grey hair as if it was his fault.

'Did she go back?'

'I left, not knowing what to think, and went back to Dad's. He was in the garden, so I made him a meal and went out to call him. 'What time is it?' he demanded. Ten past five, I told him. 'I 'ave my @$#&*ing dinner at five-thirty, Girl. Get your black ass back in there and shove it where the sun don't shine.'

'He really said that?'

'He surely did. 'What did you say to me?' I asked in utter disbelief. He repeated himself word for word.'

'How odd.'

'Don't you dare talk to me like that,' I said, and stormed back into the kitchen. I picked up his dinner, took it outside and threw it in the bin right in front of him. He lifted his walking stick and shook it at me. 'What do you think you're going to do with that?' I shouted. 'I'll beat you around the head with it if you're not careful.'

'I stomped to the front gate leaving him tottering on the porch waggling his stick. I went back to Mum's and told her what happened. 'What did you do with his dinner?' she asked. 'Threw it in the bin,' I said. 'Ooh! You shouldn't have done that, Dear. Last time I did that he made me drive in to Auckland because he fancied fish. When I brought it back, he didn't want it and swore at me somethin' awful.'

'How long's he been like this?' I asked in disbelief. 'About ten years,' she said.

When she paused for breath, I said, 'I guess she was justified in moving out.'

'Oh, yes, I completely understood. I thought Dad must have had a brainstorm or the beginning of Alzheimer's or something. He never behaved like that when we were with him.' She got up again to peek in at her husband. 'Still there,' she said, with an impatient tut.

'So where is it at now?' I asked.

'Mum's never looked better. She's lost heaps of weight and has a job volunteering. She comes over to see us regularly and is healthier than ever.'

'And your Dad?'

'Oh look – the doctor's just left. I'd better go and see what that was all about.' And with that, she packed up her wool. 'We don't see him anymore. Well—he had seven daughters, three of them are on his side and the other four are with Mum. I'll let you get back to your paper. Nice chatting with you.'

She picked up her bag and wandered inside leaving me up in the air and wondering why I should be interested in anything this woman said.

I picked up my paper, looked down at the crossword and wrote PSYCHOANALYSE in the appropriate squares.

RETROSPECTIVE: From the 2017 anthology:
Redemption

AKERS WINDMILL MOTEL

Raelene Purtill

ELISE tucks a stray hair behind her ear. 'There's no need to speed, Sam.'

'I want to be there before dark.'

She turns her blonde head away from me. Beyond her, the paddocks skim by and the trees cast long shadows across the vanishing road. Her profile has turned amber in the light of the departing sun. When she moves a hand up and across her face, I detect tears and I turn my attention to the road against them, increasing the pressure of my right foot.

At the turn-off to our destination, a boy is playing on the sign post. He swings around and around, one arm held out. Another boy inspects the painted rock where he sits. Elise waves and the boy on the pole stops spinning. The other slides from the rock and stands to attention as we crunch up the gravel road.

A large blue arrow marked 'Office' in solid letters points us around an extensive veranda. Behind the counter is a girl with dyed hair and pierced nostrils with her name embroidered at her left breast pocket. She passes me a shabby leather tag with '6' burned into it. Attached is a single key.

'There you are Mr. Jameson. Your room is just here.' She points behind her. 'Dinner's at seven.'

Elise says, 'Thank you, Karen.'

The dining room is decorated with a variety of memorabilia. In one corner, an early Singer sewing machine hosts a vase of wild flowers. On the shelf above sit Arnott's biscuit tins, original Vegemite jars and a Bushells tea container. One wall is crafted in corrugated iron.

At our table, one of the boys is standing at Elise's elbow.

'Hello. Hello,' he repeats as he rocks back and forth to his internal soundtrack.

Karen arrives with her tray of home-cooked offerings and I breathe in deep the aroma of steak, gravy and fresh vegetables.

'Go away now. Go on,' she says to the boy. He departs reciting in a lilting echolalia, 'Go away. Go now. Go away.'

I watch him head toward the veranda where an older woman is standing with her arms out. She gathers him and ushers him away. Her breast pocket reads 'Janine.' She leads him down the veranda and out of sight.

Karen serves us. 'My brother, Mickey. Don't mind him. He always says hello to new folk.'

'We saw him at the turn off,' says Elise, placing her napkin to her knee.

'That's his favourite place to be.'

'Who was the other boy?' I ask.

Karen frowns. 'Just Mickey,' she replies, completing our plates and moving on.

The night comes in hot, without relief from the day. We are lying together watching the blur of the fan above us and listening to the distant rumble of the highway when we hear a scream followed by a thud.

Elise says, 'Don't get involved.'

But I am already pulling on a tee shirt, and soon out the door.

In a room behind the office, Karen sits on the floor crooning as she strokes Mickey's forehead. Around them is the debris from their altercation, forgotten now as his head lies across her lap.

Janine stands behind them. 'Sing to him, Karen. That's right. He likes that.'

Mickey is pulling at his ears and emitting a low groan. Karen moves to hold his hands in her own, away from his head, without interrupting her song. When the tension leaves his body and he is breathing evenly, she slides from beneath him and sees me.

'Oh, Mr. Jameson, I am sorry to disturb you. He'll sleep now.'

'You are very good with him.'

'Thank you.' She smiles and ducks her head. 'It's nothing I can't handle. Really Mr. Jameson, you should go back to your room.'

I retreat but the night invites me to linger outside and it is then I see the other boy peering in the office window.

'Hey.' I call to him but he dashes away into the darkness of the paddock. When I enter our room, Elise is lying awake, watching me with a disapproving frown.

'Come to bed, Sam. It's late.' She turns over and is asleep instantly. I envy her. I stand at the window looking into the motel carpark for a long while before sleep sends me to bed.

During breakfast we are trying to ignore the raised voices coming from the kitchen. I cannot bear it and rise to investigate, Elise's protests following me to the source of the disturbance.

'Karen?'

'Mickey didn't want his Weetbix this morning,' she informs me. The rejected cereal is splattered up the wall and trails across the floor to an overturned bowl, confirming her statement.

The boy stands shaking his head. 'Bad boy. Bad boy,' he repeats.

From the sink, Karen takes a wet rag and leads Mickey to the wall. 'You must clean it up.'

She guides his hand until the motion is transferred, then she uprights the chair to the table. Janine stands beside him and watches with a compassionate smile on her face.

'That's right, Mickey. You are a good boy.'

'I am a good boy,' he repeats.

Karen turns with a frown. 'Just clean it up, Mickey.'

'We saw two boys at the junction. Who's the other?' I ask, watching Mickey, his face close to the wall where he is cleaning a particular spot. He ignores the rest of the soggy mess up the wall. Janine remains supervising.

'No other kids around here for miles.' Karen shrugs in such an offhanded way that I am rejected and turn to leave. From the corner of my eye, I see movement across the window. A chill travels through me.

Our sightseeing is welcome. For a brief, sunny afternoon, that which is unspoken between us is displaced and retreats, allowing us to glimpse hope. We return to the motel with the radio thumping and us singing along with it. Even the threat from the horizon does not alarm us. Those dark clouds bring the promise of a cooler evening. I am looking heavenward, indulging in the towering formations, when Elise screams. 'Look out!'

Mickey is standing in the middle of the road, the other boy calling him from the edge. I swerve, sideswiping the sign and spinning in the gravel before bringing the car under control. Elise is out and running to the junction.

'Where did he go?' She turns to me arms wide. 'I can't see him.'

She brings her arms in close then, hugging herself. 'Oh no.'

She collapses into my arms.

The first large drops of rain begin to darken the grey gravel as we cling together in our grief. The rhythm of her sobs ends and she takes in a sharp breath sucking the tears back inside her. I pull away. The other boy is standing close beside us and the hairs on my neck rise.

Mickey paces up and down the road. His arms are flailing in small circles and his fingers jitter. Elise watches his rain dance for a moment then goes to him.

'Mickey, you must not stand in the road like this. You could be really hurt.'

She places her hands on his shoulders looking into his face. His rocking ceases and he yowls, pushes Elise to the ground, and bolts up the driveway. As I gather Elise back into the car, there he is again. The other boy is watching us from the front of the car.

The rain trickles down my back, cold fingers reaching for my bones.

Later, Elise and I sit dry and comfortable in our room. Our time together has connected us and our moment at the turn-off has sealed us. We are united against the elements of grief threatening to destroy us.

'Where do you suppose Mr. Akers is?' I ask.

'Men don't stay around when there's kids like Mickey. I suspect he's long gone.'

The boy's screaming can be heard now above the steady rain. There is a crash that is not of the storm, followed by the sound of breaking glass. I am at the residence in the seconds between lightning and thunder.

'Mickey, you must stay in your room.' Karen is standing at the doorway and before she closes the door I can see Mickey sitting on the floor. 'And stop that rocking,' she says as she shuts the door on the turmoil.

Janine slips out as the door is closed. 'He is safe. Get yourself cleaned up.'

Karen is holding her bleeding hand as she follows Janine to the nearby bathroom.

And then he is standing in the hall. I move toward him, my palm extended. 'I'm Sam Jameson.'

'My name's William,' he replies, but he makes no move toward our greeting, just stands, eyes cold.

'Did you come from in here?' I ask, but the room is locked. My hand is cold and I cling to the door for support as my knees release from under me. Then Karen is there. 'No. Mr. Jameson. You mustn't.'

She takes my hand from the door, her warmth melting the icicles possessing my fingers.

The boy too has drifted away.

The new day arrives fresh and clean following the storm. I am infused with new beginnings and keen to be on the road. I stow our luggage, stepping back and forth through the puddles dotting the carpark. On the surface of each is a liquid rainbow. It is a sign: the river of our sadness runs together with the oil of healing to form this spectrum for us.

Voices from behind the house are calling and yelling. I follow them to see Mickey climbing the windmill.

William is above, bidding him up. 'Come on Mickey. Come see the view from up here.'

Karen is calling him down, Janine beside her. 'Karen, get him down. How did he get this far?'

Mickey's laughter is high above us as I join Elise.

'Oh Sam. Help him.'

Karen echoes Elise's pleading and I am compelled. I climb the wooden frame. Mickey has almost reached the platform where William is perched beneath the sails, still calling him. I am engaged by open paddocks dotted with cattle and sheep. A distant line of green trees marks the path of the river and I can see the highway coming to life. Another time I would have appreciated the view, but now I am concerned for Mickey's safety. There is a memory of another time, another child whose safety I could not secure. I remember the football field in the suburbs, a runaway ball and a speeding car, and Joshua.

Today I have the power to rescue. I climb further with new determination.

'Stop, Mickey.'

He is laughing now and William is pointing. 'From up here you can almost see the city. Look, Mickey.'

'What are you doing?' I call.

'We're climbing the windmill tower.'

'And you think Mickey will understand the experience? It's so dangerous for him.'

The boy's eyes darkened. 'He's done it before. You remember the last time we were up here, don't you, Mickey?'

Mickey sits on the small platform, still and quiet, as if this spot is where he understands the world and he is in his right mind. I cling to my own position below them. 'It is time to come down now. Come back to Karen and your Mum.'

Now it is William who disturbs me with his unhealthy laugh. The shiver running through me threatens to remove me from the tower.

'Mickey, follow me back down, okay?' I say. Mickey looks down. 'Karen,' He waves in his uncoordinated way and then he slips. I catch him and when I hold him it is our son I am holding and I have saved him. The red Ford does not collide with him. 'It's okay. It's okay.'

I glance up to see if William is following but he remains in his unmoving petulance.

On the ground, Karen confronts Mickey. 'Why did you do that?'

I look at her. 'William. He died.'

'That's right, yes.'

Elise gasps beside me. When I squeeze her hand, I am passing on the closure I experienced. 'I saved him. It was Josh I was saving.'

We hug.

Karen ushers Mickey inside the house.

'I should be there,' says Janine, watching them leave.

'William?' I go to the boy who has descended and is standing before Janine looking up at her.

'She still doesn't see me. She never looks at me.'

'Janine, why do you not acknowledge William?' I ask.

'William fell from this windmill two years ago. He's dead, Mr. Jameson. My son is dead.'

'Why can't you see me? Why don't you look at me?' William is searching her face for answers.

Then he says, 'Come on,' and we follow him across the paddock.

Under the wide branches of a large tree there are graves. One marker bears William's name.

'See.' William points to the second grave and I am paralysed: 'Janine Akers'.

Janine stands with her back to the stones watching the house. 'How will they survive without me? I am the only one who can manage Mickey.'

'You don't have to anymore, Janine. William needs you now.' Elise's empathy and compassion break through Janine's denial.

'William? Where is he?'

'I'm right here, Mum. I've been here all the time. Do you see me now?'

Behind us, the dead look after the dead as we remove ourselves from their reunion.

Elise takes the car keys. 'I'm driving.'

The sun is high and hot and the highway ahead of us is clear.

A VISIT TO THE DOCTOR

John R. Nolan

I PARKED THE '47 FORD ELEPHANT near a savage wild-rose bed. On the front of the Elephant was a long trunk, containing a supply of liquid refreshment which in my haste, I ignored. The trunk could also be used for long distance calls and I might need that service later.

The Ford backfired, dropped a small offering on the bed beside the roses, to cover the cost of parking. The backfire introduced a funky tone to the garden.

Decorating the entrance was a winding white marble staircase leading to dark double doors. The doors hung ever so slightly ajar before me: inviting, challenging, threatening.

I crept forward, alert for any sign of movement, the tension parching my throat. I thought of the stash in the Elephant's trunk, but there was no time. This is it. Confrontation, no more procrastination.

With due care and attention I gingerly tested the large, teak-panelled ever-so-slightly-ajar doors that seductively questioned my resolve.

Ever so delicately I pushed, slinking into the dark before me, like a spiteful cur. I stepped through, my heart pumping faster, the adrenalin coursing through my veins, preparation for fight or flight.

Lying on the floor was a rug.

It was Indian, like the Elephant, and I knew there had to be more to it than first met the I. 'Aye, aye,' I replied to myself, before realizing I was alone, in the deep pitch of night, with limited internal light.

A corridor beckoned, weaving to the inner depths of the mansion.

In the chaotic light of a passing storm and repeated strikes of Federal matches, I saw walls draped with paintings of different shaped and sized frames, some large, some miniature. The curtains were drawn – with indigo ink – on the windows.

Dull light revealed antiquated furniture and corners of the room covered in thick dust and reeking of mustiness, suggesting many moons had passed since the regular attendance of a maid or any caring dust-averse hand.

Somewhere, deep within the outer reaches of my socks, were my toes which I put there before leaving home, to prevent misplacing them. They were hardly moving, but I knew they were there by the length of my feet. Thanks to my sock diligence I was able to tiptoe forward, like a wild banana adjusting to a new bunch.

Carefully examining the surrounds I moved deeper into the labyrinth, ready for anything. The tension stretched, like wet dough, the kind that doesn't break, across the half moon, etched by night on the floor.

A lucid idea leapt into my head, an escapee from a marauding band of Thought Police. The plan plunged deep into my psyche, seeking refuge, a place to hide from the dominant painfully throbbing thoughts.

I dragged it back out, unsure if it was one of mine or a stranger's. I put it in the in-tray, so, when my mind got in, I could look at it. It's very difficult to look at things in the in-tray when your mind is not in. I turned the new idea over a few times, like a favourite record, without playing it all the way through.

Clinging to the wall I found a light switch. I clicked it down; soft light crept through the room, destroying all but impenetrable darkness. I looked around, searching for some clue as to my location. Quickly I determined I was inside.

I examined the room, straining in the dull light, to detect any sign of movement, any trace of occupation. I closed my eyes, to adjust to the lack of light, but couldn't see any better, though, when re-opened, there was sneaking intuition, suspicion of rapid movement escaping my watchful orbs.

Outside the storm was getting more in-tents. Easier to get into tents than into the white walled room where I was trapped.

MANY FIND WHITE WALLS go well with matching, long sleeved white coats. Nurse O'Grinner grinned gleefully.

Nurse O'Grinner is very helpful; she always likes to help people get on with their medication and the side effects, with the least amount of stress, trauma, suffering and confusion – for herself.

We all liked Nurse O'Grinner, even when she lost the plot, as is obviously happening right now. She always wore a Clockwork Orange suit, of pristine white; she almost always wore an Alex-inspired smile, hiding a brutal mentality. Looking like Venus, but with skin as hard as a pearl, nurse O'Grinner stood as a Roman goddess of terror.

Rumour had it she fell from the chaste path of mindless commitment to serving the ill, after a torrid session with a psychiatrist who thought he was sane. No patient dared bring up the rumour for fear of an evening overdose or suffering a fatal pillow- over-face attack during Nurse O'Grinner's night-time vigils.

SURREPTITIOUSLY, I OOZED OVER the polished wooden floor. A reflection of myself grinned back in a bewildered manner. This was a relief. I hadn't been expecting anybody else and I quickly identified myself with the secret sign.

A door crashed open. I all but passed out with fright.

'What are you doing here?' a powerful voice thundered from the black hole in the wall.

'I'm looking for my mobile 'phone.'

The voice spoke again, with a less threatening tone. 'Oh, that's okay. At first I thought you were some sort of a weirdo who's snuck in to get out of the rain.'

'Is it raining? Sorry, I must be off. Have to wind up the windows in my Elephant. Could you call me if you find my mobile 'phone?' I moved quickly toward the hole in the wall through which I'd entered.

'Not so fast, Neddy.'

'How did you know my name's Neddy?'

'Is your name Neddy?' asked the voice.

'No, but I won't argue about it. I'm flexible when it comes to names.'

'That's good,' said the voice.

'Well. Now that we don't know my name, maybe I could have yours?'

'Why, do you collect names?'

'Not really, I just like to know who I'm talking to when I'm not talking to myself.

'It gets very confusing, not knowing who I am or where my mobile 'phone is. I can't ring myself up to see if I'm in or out, or who's answering the 'phone.'

'That makes sense,' said the voice.

'That's great. Is there anything else before I go?'

'No, just leave your card so I can get back to you, if I don't see you again.'

I gave the Voice my mobile number and retreated backwards, imagining myself passing through the black hole of a Celestion speaker, fading like a song to which a coda could not be found.

RUMOUR HAS IT that Dr. Freudrickson is having an affair with Nurse O'Grinner, though such talk is not allowed during working hours, as the THOUGHT POLICE are everywhere, even in here, as far as we know, so be careful.

Dr. Freudrickson's written about another infatuation in a little ditty, that someone saw and copied to put on the dining room wall. He never admitted he wrote it and Nurse O'Brien swore she would kill the author when exposed. Dr. Freudrickson was really keen to expose himself, but not necessarily in that context.

Nurse O'Brien is really cute,
A buxom wench, who carries a wrench,
In her white flak jacket and hobnailed boots
To tighten up nuts or her wrath to rent.
With a smile t'would make a crocodile drool,
With her pills and shots for those who think,
She lies in wait by the hospital pool
With an overdose for whomsoever she'll choose.

Some of the residents believe Nurse O'Grinner needs a lot of help, so they smile at her and try to give her a dose of strychnine or deadly nightshade, but she is, it appears, immune to both.

The clients all hoped she and Dr Freudrickson would elope but knew Nurse O'Grinner's dedication to unbridled control and mayhem would never allow her to depart her ivory tower of power.

'HOW LONG HAVE YOU BEEN HAVING these sorts of dreams?' 'Doctor Freudrickson Jr. asked, 'Here, have another pill.'

'They've only started since you began treating me. No thanks doc., I've just had a vasectomy.'

'What's that got to do with the pills?'

'You'd better ask my psychiatrist about that.'

'What pills are you taking?'

'I take three Zeropax, two Trimortazone, four Zonkyabrian and two and a half Killsemall and one Knoxemout.'

'Do you believe they are helping you?'

'Depends who's taking them. Would you like some?'

'What are you taking them for?'

'The Zeropax are to prevent me sleeping, which is reverse sedation; the Trimortazone change the voices I hear into assorted ring tones; the Zonkyabrian are for inverse psychosynthesis, the Killsemall are suicidal-thoughts stimulators. The Knoxemout is to keep me awake when I'm sleeping.'

'Did you ever think everybody hates you?'

'Not everybody. Only my father, mother, sister, all my relatives and everyone else I know,' I replied.

'That's good to know. It means there's still lots of people out there who don't hate you, doesn't it?'

'I guess you're right. I'd never thought of it from that angle. Thanks, Doc. I feel better already.'

'Have another pill.'

'Which colour this time?' I asked.

'Doesn't matter, you pick, they're all the same, they only look different.'

'Now, that makes sense,' I observed. 'Hey Doc, I just had a great idea for us to make lots of money.'

'Now that interests me.'

'What about we go into business making straightjackets?'

'Why compete with the corporations?' asked the doctor.

'Well, everyone is on about cost cutting, reducing staff numbers, improving the bottom line, though, one must admit, Nurse O'Grinner has a great bottom line. I came up with a great idea to design and make DIY Straightjackets.

'With these, the clients put the long sleeved white coats on themselves, when they feel an attack coming on and take them off later.

'It would improve Workplace Health and Safety standards. No nurses would need take risks trying to restrain a raving psychotic. Think of the staff reductions this could produce.'

'I think we'll have to work on that one a bit,' Dr. Freudrickson said. 'But it sounds viable. How do you intend to get the clients to tie themselves in to the coats?'

'Velcro. Stick yourself up Velcro. It's great, flexible, waterproof and user friendly.'

Dr. Freudrickson is a man of indeterminate taste, especially when it came to clothing. He tried everything together. Oft he looks like a passing rainbow or a deserted tropical island, though there is no evidence to suggest he doesn't know what he is doing.

He lives in an expensive mansion on Thirty-Fourth Street, near the corner and opposite a vast expanse of natural calamities.

His mother left him this house in her will, though not of her own choice. He became a psychiatrist to avoid national service and the dole queue.

'My previous girlfriend was very musical,' I told the doctor, 'She was a chorus girl.'

'That's a tough way to earn a dollar, how did she cope?'

'It was good for her. She was secure. Always knew to come in after the second or third verse, unless it was a ballad, or there was a bridge. Her life was arranged.'

'Have another pill.'

'No thanks, Doc. I'm told they're habit forming, and I'm not planning to become a monk.'

'You don't mind if I have one, do you?'

'What colour are you having?'

'Oh, it doesn't matter; they're all the same, they only look different.

'It is getting easier and easier to see that the who/ where/ when/ how and why of the situation is getting ever more elaborate,' the doctor said, swallowing three pills of different colours, just in case they were not all the same. 'There is a serious need for you to get help.'

'That's why I was referred me to you,' I replied.

'Did you ever discover who it was that referred you to me?'

'Yes.'

'Would you tell me, please, it's important I know what sort of people are referring people to me as I'm not sure if they can be trusted.'

'There are all sorts of people out there, who bring in psychoses, and stimulating thought-provoking dreams. This is having a debilitating effect on my general state of health.'

'I'll tell you if you'll tell me why I'm here. This is the three hundred and thirtieth time you've wanted to see me. My Medicare card is getting thinner and thinner with each visit, but I don't know that I've seen any progress.'

'Maybe it was your mother?'

'Hey, I'm not into any of that Freudian stuff, I'm a clean-living bloke.'

'Maybe it was my mother?'

'Look Doc, this needs to end, quickly and painlessly, for both of us. You could simply certify me. Then I'm out of your space, and you can eat all the pills yourself. I'll leave you a referral note to a good psychiatrist.'

'Where would I find one of those; is there any such thing? I thought we were only in it for the money.'

'There has to be a resolution to this inane consultation,' I continued.

'Oh, so that's what it's about. You're simply looking for an easy way out of this plotless nonsense and you expect me to bear responsibility for it all?' he declared indignantly.

THE RUG STILL LAY AGAINST THE FLOOR. I knew there was no escape but I had to try.

To flee. Flee from the mind-chilling grip of the voice's invitation to dinner.

I couldn't see any option but to run for it. I turned.

'How do you take your herbal tea?' It spoke from the dark void.

'Black and white, thanks,' I carefully replied.

'One lump or two?'

'Don't hit me. I bleed easily.'

I ran, adrenalin stoking the fires of my flight, in desperation, through the wall's black hole which was like a Celestion speaker. Leaping ecstatically into the arms of the men with the white coats, I fell into peace.

'Do you want to make an appointment for next week?'

'No Doc. Thanks anyway. For years I've had psychiatrists asking me to come and talk with them. They need help and I try to support them the best I can. To help them see themselves in a different light.'

'Oh, how do you do that?' he asked

'I just turn it on.'

THE CAT ON THE SHIP TO THE EDGE OF THE EARTH
Sonya Simonds

THE CAT STOOD ON THE MAST of the ship. His name was Salmona, and he was a mostly grayish-blue speckly colour, with a misshapen patch of rough white fur just above his left eye.

He was on the Captain's ship, and they had been sailing out here for weeks.

They were sailing to the edge of the earth.

Salmona had first learned this when he climbed up on a wooden box beside the Captain, who was steering the ship, and looked at him exactly like he wanted to know where they were going. And the Captain's response, in his usual pleasant, enthusiastic tone, was, 'We're sailing to the edge of the earth, my friend.'

Salmona had first joined the voyage because the Captain thought he could help with the mice. Salmona didn't catch the mice; instead, every evening, they reported to him below deck, usually six or more of them, and stood up straight on their hind legs in a row. Then the cat would share with them the small leftovers from his meal, and listen to their exploits of the day. He'd promised them they'd be safe so long as they stayed out of sight of the people and didn't take what wasn't theirs, and this way, everyone was satisfied.

Later he would sit on his box, keeping the Captain company while the ship was being steered. The Captain had one other friend too, whose name was Lars. Lars thought the entire expedition was all for naught.

'For instance,' Lars had said, 'If the earth had an edge, wouldn't all the water spill over? Wouldn't the earth eventually run out of water altogether?'

The Captain's answer to this was rain. It rains a lot around here, so perhaps it fills up the oceans again? But even he seemed to have doubts.

Lars had laughed at the thought of all that water drifting around space.

Lars often found humour in those sorts of things.

So on the conversation would go, and when it was fully night-time, Salmona would go down to his pillow underneath the Captain's bed to sleep. He'd wake up the next morning to go upstairs and climb the mast and stand high on his perch in the basket at the top, to watch the ship move elegantly over the waves in the early morning, the water tinged pink and orange like the sky above. He sat there now, feeling the wind blowing around him and watching the birds, dabs of white and grey with long arching wings, fly by overhead. Sometimes the Captain or another sailor would stand here with a telescope, looking out to the continuous ocean ahead for some sign of a destination.

It often rained while they were on board the ship, just as much as what the Captain recalled from back at home. Everyone but the Captain, who just went on steering the ship, had to go below deck and in the cabin when this happened. The mice were especially inclined to mischief in damp, wet, soggy weather, so Salmona had to keep them in line, which was particularly tricky when the people were so close by. Thus far, however, it hadn't stormed—that would be a disaster—so the rain had never yet reached a point where they were powerless against it. That suited the Captain—and Salmona—just fine.

But today the skies were almost spotless; the only clouds as far out as Salmona could see were streaks of white mist that painted the sky. There would be no rain today.

In fact it looked less like it would rain then it had in a long time. Maybe the Captain was right, and they were getting closer. The weather was changing; maybe that was a sign they were reaching the edge of the earth?

'Or a sign we're just getting further from home,' Lars had offered.

SALMONA WAS STILL UP IN HIS PERCH when the Captain got up, but he made his way back down when the Captain called his name. He sat on his box beside him while the Captain peered through a telescope.

'I don't know about this ocean, Salmona,' the Captain said, putting down the telescope on the box beside Salmona. 'It seems to go on forever.'

He continued to steer the ship on through the apparently endless ocean, with no particular idea of where to go except some general western direction, to nowhere.

Salmona leaned toward the telescope and prodded it with his paw, then stuck his face down behind it to peer out at the magnified ocean. He saw a flicker of movement in the waves, just for a moment. A giant tail burst up through the waves, then vanished below.

A FEW HOURS LATER, everything changed.

'I see something!' the Captain was shouting, unable to contain his excitement. 'There's something out there. There's a *thing* out there on the water! A *thing*! What could it be?!'

'Probably pirates,' Lars remarked.

Their Captain darted around the ship, just to make sure that everyone on board knew. Even the mice knew that something interesting was going on, and they all came out from hiding and stood scattered atop of Salmona's box. If the Captain had seen them, he was too excited to be bothered.

'What's this happening, Mr. Cat?' asked one of them, whose name was Ellie.

'The Captain's seen something,' Salmona explained.

'But why is that remarkable? Was he blind once?'

'No, but he's seen a thing out on the ocean. That's the unusual part.'

'I can't wait to get up close and see what it is,' the Captain was saying to himself. Salmona, can you—'

But that's when he saw the mice. And, in fact, he was not happy at all.

'Mice?!' he exclaimed. 'There shouldn't be *mice* on my ship!'

The mice went nuts at being discovered and scurried trying to get away. Salmona backed away, trusting them to save themselves. The Captain tried to grab at them with his hand. Most of them raced out of sight, but one didn't get out of the way in time. It collided with his hand and flew out of the ship.

Salmona darted to the edge. He saw the mouse in the water, struggling to stay above the surface. The Captain stared down too. But Salmona was a guardian to these mice, and he had to do something. So he plunged down into the water after it.

'*Salmona!*' shouted the Captain. 'What are you *doing*?'

Salmona's fur stood on end in the freezing water, but he reached toward the mouse, ducked his head underwater as it lost its upward momentum. For a brief moment, he saw the world of underwater, all the brightly-coloured fishes and silver ones alike, all the colours of the plants and coral and pebbles deep below. But he grasped the mouse, its back legs kicking but slowly sinking down, in his mouth, and thrust himself toward the ship, his claws out to latch onto the wood. They missed, slipping away, and he fell back into the water.

'Grab the rope!' the Captain exclaimed, hurling one into the water. Salmona gripped his claws onto it and held, the fur on his head and neck and paws above the water bristling from the coldness. The Captain pulled the rope, and Salmona was brought back up toward the ship, and he ducked through the railings back on board, fur clinging to his body so he looked half his size, and laid the mouse down in front of him.

The other mice slowly emerged from hiding places to see their fellow mouse and their cat friend. The Captain didn't touch them. He just watched with the same astonishment that had stayed with him for the last several minutes, and then he carried the soaking cat and mouse down to where it was warmer, and the other mice followed.

SALMONA SLEPT FITFULLY for much of the night. The mouse he'd saved slept against his paw on his pillow, and the other mice stayed with them, holding vigil through the night. When Salmona at last got into peaceful sleep, he dreamed he was an ocean cat-thing, half fish, swimming among all the other fishes in their underwater kingdom. The Captain left hot drinks for him and tried to make him comfortable while he recovered. They still had not reached the thing in the middle of the ocean, but the Captain thought they could get back to it in the morning.

Salmona woke refreshed that morning. It seemed to be a normal morning—he'd almost forgotten what happened the day before, until he saw the mouse at his paws and the others gathered around him. When he got up and looked around the area below deck, he saw just how *abnormal* this morning was.

There were no sailors to be seen anywhere.

Maybe they were upstairs.

But when Salmona went up, the area appeared completely vacant.

'They might have vanished from those men with funny hats coming here,' the mouse named Ellie piped up then.

'What men with funny hats?' Salmona asked.

'They came out of the thing on the ocean,' the mouse added helpfully.

'*Probably pirates.*' Lars's remark came back to Salmona. He frowned. Could it be? Was it pirates, after all?

'Come see the thing,' the mouse invited him.

Where are all the sailors? Why is the thing on the ocean over here now? Salmona thought as he followed the mouse.

She led him to the front of the ship, where Salmona's box and the helm were, and pointed at a ginormous object obscuring the ship's path.

It was another ship, with the words *The Pirate's Delight* engraved across the side.

Oh, Salmona thought. *That explains it.*

'They're all gone?' Salmona asked. 'The Captain and Lars and everyone?'

'Well, some of them got locked up in the cabin,' the mouse explained. 'The Captain and Lars, they were taken.'

The cat clambered up onto his box. A makeshift bridge of wood planks and rope lay across the space between this ship's railing and the pirate ship. Chaotic voices, singing and talking rowdily, came softly across from the sides of the ship, and on the deck, Salmona could see people walking around. Two figures stood against the mast, moving and struggling.

It was the Captain and Lars, and they were bound hands and feet while the pirates sauntered around and tried to find out where the treasure was.

It didn't matter whether they had it or not. The pirates just wanted *the treasure*, and they were going to get it, even if it didn't exist. This was their specialty, apparently.

'We don't have any treasure!' the Captain tried to explain again. 'We're just simple sailors going on a quest.'

'A quest means finding things,' the Head Pirate sneered. 'You be finding treasure, that be what quests are for.'

'That *not* be it,' the Captain sighed. 'If you must know, we're sailing to the edge of the earth.'

'Huh!' The Head Pirate's eyes widened, and he fixed them on the Captain's ship. 'The edge of the earth?' He bent back and laughed and said in the midst of laughing, 'That be ridiculous.

Who's ever heard of sailing to the edge of the earth? That's— that's—'

'But, H.P.,' interrupted another pirate, 'isn't that what we're doing?'

'Uh . . . n-no?' the Head Pirate spluttered, looking at the other pirate. 'No, course not, uh, where'd you get an idea like that?'

'Riiiight,' Lars muttered. 'Ridiculous, is it?'

'Quiet!' the Head Pirate exclaimed. 'Don't listen to him. He be talking nonsense.'

'But H.P., you said there be treasure at the edge of the earth so get going,' the other pirate put in.

'W-What? No,' I said, 'um . . . there be treasure with the people going to the edge of the earth, that's what it was. So where is it?'

'Where's what?' the Captain asked, with mild confusion.

'The treasure!' the Head Pirate exclaimed.

Back on the Captain's ship, Salmona was watching all this intently. The mice all stood in a row beside him.

At last Salmona turned to the mice and whispered, 'I think we should rescue them.'

'Rescue them?' the mouse named Ellie whispered back. 'Are you thinking of a plan?'

'I have one in mind,' Salmona said thoughtfully. 'Who among you can chew through ropes?'

Five mice raised their paws.

'Good,' Salmona said. 'That skill will be vital to our rescue mission.' He glanced at the mast where the Captain and Lars were tied. *How threatening do those pirates seem right now?*

The Head Pirate was getting rather annoyed. 'If you don't tell me where the treasure is soon, I'll . . . I'll . . . I'll be making you walk the plank!' he announced.

'Okay, follow me,' Salmona said. He headed toward the bridge. The mouse he'd saved rode on his back, clinging to his fur.

He crept along the bridge, the trail of mice following after him. The bridge swayed above the deep blue water, wobbly under his paws. As he reached the other side, he got down low and clambered onto the pirate ship. The mice dropped down after him.

He flattened himself against the wooden planks and snuck forward. Footsteps sounded around the corner, and a mouse grabbed Salmona's tail, and all the others grabbed the tail of the one in front of them, and he leapt behind a barrel against the wall of a cabin.

Salmona watched as the feet trundled past, then turned to the mice. 'Where's the five who can chew through ropes?' he asked. 'Could you sneak around the corner, come up to the mast on Lars's side, and climb up to chew them free?'

The five mice nodded and saluted him, then got down onto all-fours and scurried away.

'What do we do, Mr. Cat?' Ellie asked him.

Salmona looked at the remaining four mice. The one who'd ridden on his back stood with them now. 'We're going to distract the pirates,' the cat replied.

'I be counting down from ten,' the Head Pirate was announcing, over at the mast. 'If you don't be telling me where the treasure is by the time I get down to that number, uh...'

'Psst, Captain,' Lars whispered. He pointed with his eyes to where the mice were busy at work chewing through the ropes.

'Salmona's mice!' the Captain whispered back, astonished.

'Zero,' the Head Pirate said. 'There you go. I be making you walk the plank if you don't tell me before I get to that number there. I be counting down now.... Ten... nine... eight...'

The Captain and Lars felt the ropes loosen as the mice chewed through them.

'. . . seven . . . six . . .' the Head Pirate continued to count, '. . . five . . . 'four . . .'

'Free,' the Captain and Lars said together, quietly.

'Oi, I be doing the counting round here,' the Head Pirate sneered. 'Three, two . . . one and zero.' He stared at the mast, and then at the Captain and Lars, who were springing away from it. 'Oi, where're you both going?'

'There they go, H.P.!' the other pirate called out, pointing to them, running towards the bridge with the rope-chewing mice.

More pirates ran out from the sides to intercept them. The four mice scurried in the way and the pirates stumbled and slipped and tripped and collided with each other, while the Head Pirate and his assistant ran after Lars and the Captain.

Meanwhile, Salmona shot up the mast and clambered onto the flagpole and tugged at the strings holding it in place. He pulled and worked at it with his claws and teeth, and suddenly the flag gave way and came tumbling down over the Head Pirate and the other pirate. He rode it through the air and leaped off, landing next to the Captain and Lars while the remaining four mice grabbed onto him and they all raced across the bridge together.

As soon as they were back on their own ship, the Captain grabbed the bridge and tossed it away, while some of the pirates raced to the edge, only to find the bridge dangling in the water. The Captain grabbed the helm and steered the ship away, out of reach of the pirates.

The pirates didn't like this very much, and they jumped up and down and yelled out in gibberish, as they got further and further away from them, until they were out of sight.

IT WAS FOUR DAYS LATER, and the Captain, Lars, the other sailors, Salmona, and all the mice were on an island they'd found in their directionless escape from the pirates.

The Captain was collecting his thoughts until they were ready to continue on their journey.

'All the others always said that the edge of the earth was a fully understood scientific reality,' the Captain was saying, 'and who was I to look for proof?'

'Well, it seems the pirates are also looking for the edge of the earth,' Lars commented.

'It seems they are,' the Captain agreed. He fell silent.

'Maybe the earth has an edge,' Lars said, 'or maybe it doesn't. Maybe everyone's missing something. I suppose the important thing is to be honest with what we *do* know.'

Salmona and the mice were exploring nearby, but not so far away that the Captain couldn't see them. 'At any rate,' the Captain said, 'I think I'll write a letter home.'

'I think I'll do that too, Captain,' Lars said.

They walked toward the ship.

'What now, Mr. Cat?' Ellie asked Salmona.

'Now,' Salmona replied, 'we begin another adventure.'

Soon they would be sailing to the edge of the earth once more.

WAITING FOR MY TEST RESULTS
Vera Murray

My heart it quickens
And becomes a violent drum.
My stomach turns and sickens,
As I wait my dreaded destiny.

When will this end . . . this suspense?
That suffocates my senses?
Will Doc tell me 'yes' or 'no,'
And thus disperse this load?

My brain and mind compressed.
I think of nothing else,
No matter how I try.
I just keeps asking, 'Me? Why?'

Oh, tired and weary me'
What will the verdict be?
If 'yes', my will I'll sign,
Then end it quick I swear.

If 'no', my life will be forever changed.
I'll drop it all, plus drugs and grog,
I'll even get a job.
I will. I swear to God.

At long last, the Doc I see.
No worries . . . I'm fine, he tells me.
But the rest he spouts I do not heed.
It's not for me. Change I don't need.

MISSING

Ronald Holt

I WAS ONLY METRES from the edge with a monster resembling the Hulk trying to push me to a certain messy death on the bitumen road several floors below. Who would have thought I would go this way?

Funny things come into your mind when your life flashes before your eyes. If I wasn't so stingy, and probably lazy, and had not given up my gym membership, maybe I could handle this gorilla. Too late for that now.

How do I get myself into such situations? I've always tried to do the right thing in my passion for justice. I've had a couple of indiscretions over the years – my two ex-wives would attest to that. My present predicament was caused because I wanted to help the vulnerable. Well partly. I was warned and should have known better than messing with this mob. Maybe I should have said 'no' but I'm a sucker and besides that I needed the money.

A couple of days ago I was sitting in my office playing laptop computer games to fill in time. Business was poor and I was wondering how I was going to pay my bills. The door opened and a couple, he mid-sixties, she some years younger, came in. Their faces creased with deep concern.

'Good morning. Take a seat,' I said extending them a welcome, closing my laptop to hide the computer game. 'My name is Tom Cruz. I'm not the Hollywood actor. He spells his name differently. I am a licensed private investigator with over 30 years police service. How can I help you?'

The man was slimly built with thin greying hair. He was smaller than his wife and had a rather shrivelled appearance. He was wearing a dark suit, probably a past workday relic. He was carrying a black briefcase probably also from that time. The woman was much larger in height and build and wore a floral dress which also gave the appearance of a past era. Her dark hair was obviously dyed as streaks of grey were appearing in her part.

'My name is Harold Watson. This is my wife, Mavis. Our youngest daughter Samantha, has gone missing. She is nineteen and we are concerned for her safety. We believe she may have gotten into some bad company or been abducted,' the man said shakily while comforting his wife with an arm around her shoulders.

'Have you told the police?' I enquired. 'Maybe it is a job for them.'

'We have,' the woman responded. 'They said that often teenagers chose to disappear. They want us to wait a bit longer to see if she calls. One of the detectives gave us your card and suggested we contact you.'

'We believe her best friend, Amanda Whitworth, may know something but she won't tell,' the man added. 'We have tried but she has virtually locked herself away in her room and seldom comes out. Maybe she would talk to you.'

'Has Samantha disappeared like this before?' I asked watching the mother's eyes tear up.

'No, never before. We can't understand it. She has a good home and was a great student at high school. She was attending and really enjoying university. Then she just disappeared,' the man explained.

'Did she leave a note or phone message?'

'Not a word, which in itself is strange. We have to find her. Can you help us?' the man pleaded.

'This is my fee schedule,' I said pushing a piece of paper towards the couple.

Both read it and I was not sure that they would accept as they did not look like wealthy people.

'Yes. We accept, Mr Cruz. And if you bring her home we will double your fees,' the man said firmly.

I am usually not mercenary but this was too good to miss.

'Do you have any bank statements or mobile phone accounts to see if she has been using them?' I asked.

Mr Watson pulled out a folder from his brief case. 'We have put together some of the things we thought you may need. This is her last bank statement showing no withdrawals. She has a credit card but there is nothing on that statement either. And her mobile phone account has no entries. Here are a few photos of Samantha and her friend Amanda.' His thoroughness suggested a very efficient accountant in his working days.

I flicked through the folder and in particular looked closely at the photos.

'A very nice young lady. You must be very proud of her,' I observed. She did look a picture of sweet innocence so I could easily understand their concern. She had blonde hair and blue eyes. Amanda was also an attractive person. She had brown hair and brown eyes. Neither looked the type to cause their parents heartache. 'Nothing on social media, I presume?'

'No. Nothing which is strange as she spends a lot of time on social media. Samantha and Amanda were inseparable. They were in the same class at school. Samantha went to Uni but Amanda wanted a gap year. We spoke to Amanda's parents but they know nothing of Samantha's whereabouts and they are worried about Amanda being so withdrawn. Something terrible is worrying her.'

'Does Samantha have a car?' I asked.

'No. She has a licence and was saving to buy one,' Mrs Watson replied, wiping away her tears with a tissue. 'I do hope you can find her. She means the world to us.'

After the Watsons left I looked through the folder. Amanda obviously knew something but was too scared to tell. I picked up my telephone and called the number in the folder.

John Whitworth, Amanda's father answered and I introduced myself. 'I have been hired by Mr and Mrs Watson to find their daughter, Samantha,' I explained.

'They told me that you may call. My wife and I have known Samantha since she was born. We count the Watsons amongst our best friends. We don't know what is going on but Amanda is very worried and scared. She just won't tell us anything and spends most of her time in her bedroom.'

John was happy for me to see Amanda and expressed hope that I could find out what was causing her so much concern.

'I can't help you,' Amanda replied abruptly after she reluctantly agreed to talk to me well out of earshot of anyone else. She looked confused and her face showed a mixture of fear and concern. Something's going on and I had to know. She needed some encouragement.

'I was told that you have been best friends all your lives and if anyone could help me find her, it would be you. I am sure you would like to help her. If you were in her position, she would do anything to help you.'

'It is too dangerous for both us and our families. I can't take the risk.'

'Have you heard from her? Is she still alive?'

'She called briefly a couple of days ago. She is alive and being treated reasonably well under the circumstances. But if anyone finds out where she is, that person's life will also be in danger. These are pretty scary people. I can't say anymore.'

'Can you tell me anything about how the situation arose? She obviously needs help and you are the only one who can do so.' I had to keep her engaged without making her too uncomfortable.

'I have kept this bottled up inside of me but I need to tell someone.' Her tears began to flow as she went on, 'We went to a nightclub, a place called Benny's, more or less as a dare from some of our friends. We were probably too naïve or stupid. We got talking to some men and they bought us drinks. The next thing I know I passed out. When I came too, Samantha was gone and this very large frightening man said if I told anyone about what happened I would never see Samantha alive again. He also threatened to kill me and my parents and Sami's parents too. I have been too terrified to talk to anybody about it. Please don't tell anyone.'

'Samantha's parents are distraught and your family are worried about you. You should let them know that Samantha is alright and leave the rest to me.'

I had heard of Benny's from my policing days. It was well known for its bad reputation, the usual problems – drugs, prostitution, standover tactics, money laundering etc. A computer search found that the owner of Benny's was Antonio de Silva.

My long time work partner, Detective Sergeant Rob Hartley, was my next call. 'Hi, Rob, it's Tom. How are you and the family going?'

'We are all well but I am sure you did not ring to inquire about our health. What do you want this time? What sort of trouble have you gotten yourself into?'

'Ah, Rob. You know me. I can get myself out of trouble. I just need some assistance with a case I am working on. It appears that it may be a job for police. Involves possible abduction and threats of violence. I need to make sure first. At the same time I don't want to interfere with any police interest or activity in relation to the suspects.'

'You pulled me out of trouble a few times and I owe you but I can't compromise my job here. I am up for promotion to Inspector soon and I won't jeopardise that. What do you want Tom?'

I ran by him the name Antonio de Silva and the nightclub, Benny's.

'Bad news, Tom. De Silva is a member of the local Mafia and should not be messed with. He has a number of well-paid thugs working for him who kill just for fun. They have been suspects in a number of murder cases but they cover their tracks well and leave no witnesses. Police have been after de Silva and his gang for years but he's virtually untouchable. Some say he has political influence. I would be very careful Tom. These are dangerous men.'

I thanked Rob for his advice but the photos of the young girls kept jumping into my mind. I had to do something. But what?

It was not difficult to find de Silva's address. He was well known in social circles – perhaps due to his infamy or wealth or both. Maybe that's how he gained his political influence. Sometimes politicians need dirty jobs done.

Dressed in my best tradie's outfit and in a borrowed electrician's van, I rocked up to the street where de Silva lived. What a mansion! Obviously crime does pay. The massive house was set back from the road with a shrub-lined paved driveway leading to a circular drive near the front door. A water fountain with a god-like figure with water flowing from an upturned vessel was the centre piece. The spectacular white shining building featured four massive columns holding up the covered entry area.

The surveillance equipment available today is really something even for a techno-dinosaur like me. I took the ladder from my van and climbed up the street light pole where I attached a miniature camera and listening device. I then drove away and parked where I could sit in front of the monitor and observe the de Silva house.

The camera resolution was great and the zoom facility allowed me to get right in near the front door. The listening device was not as good but I could pick up some noise coming from the house probably from a TV set.

I was not sure what I was going to achieve but perhaps I may find out if Samantha was still alive. My prospects of getting into the house were remote. There were security cameras all around the property. I was getting a bit sleepy watching the monitor when I had a stroke of luck.

A very large muscular man came out of the front door. He had to be at least 220 cm tall and probably about 150 kg. He was wearing a green shirt and I nicknamed him 'the Hulk'. Certainly not a person you would like to run into on a dark night. The Hulk went around the side of the house and returned in a black Mercedes.

The house door opened again and a slim, young woman appeared. I recognise her from her photos, it was Samantha. She hopped into the front passenger seat and the car moved off towards the gates of the property.

I had to follow that vehicle. Maybe it was my chance to talk to Samantha.

The vehicle stopped at a local shopping centre and the Hulk and Samantha got out. I parked nearby without getting too close to raise suspicions.

They went into a pharmacy and Samantha went to the counter with the Hulk right behind her. I picked up a bottle of perfume off a display shelf and went to the counter.

'Excuse me, Miss,' I said to Samantha. 'I have a daughter about your age and I was wondering if this perfume would be right to give her for a birthday present?'

The Hulk intervened in a deep, threatening tone. 'Get lost, buddy!'

'I'm sorry,' I replied. 'I was seeking advice from this young lady about perfume for my daughter. There is no crime in that is there?'

'Beat it!' he threatened coming up closer with his face only centimetres from mine.

'Okay,' I stammered, moving away from his piercing gaze. 'I am sorry Miss. I did not mean to upset anyone. I was wanting help for 'what's-on' next week. You know how parents are always worried about their children.'

Samantha looked at me with a curious expression on her face. Did she pick up my reference to parental concern and the name similarity 'what's-on'? The Hulk had not, but maintained his threatening stance. I put down the perfume and beat a hasty retreat. Somehow I had to get Samantha away from the Hulk. I had an idea.

I glanced around to make sure no one was looking and drove my knife into the wall of the driver's side front tyre of the Mercedes. It was still making a hissing sound of air escaping when I drove my knife into the back tyre. I moved away quickly waiting for the Hulk and Samantha to return.

The comic book Hulk had a green face but this Hulk's face was red with rage when he saw the flat tyres. He stood there cursing pointing to Samantha to get into the car.

Samantha must have suspected something because I saw her looking around. While the Hulk was on his mobile phone, I drove my van alongside the Mercedes and shouted to Samantha to jump in. She did not hesitate and I drove off in a hurry adding to the Hulk's rage.

I filled Samantha in about myself and her parents' concerns. She was still quite scared and worried about their safety. In the hope that somehow she could escape if she could get away from the de Silva home, she feigned the need for some pharmacy medication and her watchdog fell for it. Apparently de Silva was involved with a gang kidnapping young blonde females to send to foreign countries as sex slaves. I made a phone call.

'Rob, it's Tom. That case I was telling you about. I have rescued Samantha but need back up.

'Her parents may be in danger. I am going to bring Samantha to the Police Station where she can give you a statement what de Silva is up to. She needs a safe haven and protection.'

Rob was a bit astounded but he trusted me and agreed to arrange security. Hopefully what Samantha could tell would be sufficient to get a warrant to search the de Silva home. This may be the break police needed.

Samantha was re-united with her parents who had been brought to the police station in a police car. They were delighted despite their safety fears. Amanda and her parents were also brought in and the two friends hugged. Rob looked after them well and I thought that he deserved his hoped for promotion to Inspector. It felt like old times and how much I missed the job.

We waited for the warrant to be executed on the de Silva home. At last, word came through that the search had been successful in releasing three other girls and de Silva being taken into custody. While it was still not all over, there was a sense of relief.

There was no mention about the Hulk during the search. He may have still been getting his tyres fixed.

I returned home to my small one-bedroom flat, all I could afford after having to pay two lots of alimony. I grabbed a stubby from the fridge and sat back reviewing in my mind the events of the day. The Watsons were so happy and were more than pleased to pay double fees into my bank account. I slept well that night.

The next day I was back in my office missing the previous day's excitement. It was going on five that afternoon when the office door flew open. Standing there was the Hulk, his face even redder than the last time I saw him. This was not good.

He produced his Glock G45 auto pistol and shoved it in my face.

'Think you're smart don't you,' he roared. 'Letting down my tyres. My boss just got out on bail and we have unfinished business with you. No one messes with us and lives to tell the tale.'

'How did you find me?'

'We have eyes and ears everywhere, including police. You're not hard to find.'

He instructed me to write what was effectively a suicide note. My mind raced as I sought a way out of this situation. There was no one left in the building at this time of day so I could hardly expect anyone to come to my aid. I had the option of better premises with some security but this was all I could afford.

'Get up,' he yelled waving the gun around. 'We are going to see if you like heights.'

This building was only about 6 stories but enough to do a lot of damage if one were to fall. I got the impression that was what he had in mind.

As he was about to go through the door to the roof top, I saw my chance and slammed the door hard on his gun hand. The gun fell to the floor and rolled back down the stairs.

If you ever wondered what a charging wounded animal looked like, this was it. He came at me with his bright red face, physical size and strength and the impression of steam coming from his ears.

We wrestled on the floor as he pushed me slowly but surely towards the edge of the building.

It was then that I heard a loud thump from the back of the Hulk's head and his body went limp.

'That's one you owe me, Tom,' said a smiling Rob Hartley, holding in his hand a piece of iron pipe.

I was ever so grateful to see Rob and watched him handcuff the groggy Hulk. A couple of uniform officers arrived and pulled him to his feet. He was not in a fit state to be any trouble now.

'How did you come to be here?' I asked still shaking.

'Well, we knew that you would be a target so I had a tail put on you. When I heard that this fellow came into your building, I got here as fast as I could. Lucky I did.'

'You know me Rob, I was just getting started. I had it all in hand.'

'It did not look like it to me. We'll charge him with attempted murder. He has probably carried out a number of past murders and hopefully we can get evidence for some of those as well.'

'He said de Silva was out on bail.'

'True unfortunately. Probably his political influence. Now he has left the country by private jet. We have alerted Interpol and maybe we can still catch him. He has been running this sex slave racket for some time. With the records we found at his home maybe authorities in those countries can rescue some of these young women. His wealthy slimy clients wanted blue-eyed, blondes and this was why Samantha was chosen. Her friend Amanda has brown hair and eyes.

'The top brass were very impressed with what's happened and my promotion is looking very good. I was going to recommend that we engage your services as a consultant to make use of all your knowledge and skills in the job. We won't pay as much as the Watsons but it could work to the advantage of everyone. At least then I won't have to be compromised by your requests.'

Just a few minutes ago I looked like going over the edge to certain death but now I was looking forward to a new life or should I say, a return to the old job.

RETROSPECTIVE: From the 2011 anthology:
Can you believe it . . .

BEST MATES

Anne Olsson

THE KELPIE WAS SEVERELY INJURED and heavily in pup when found by the roadside. Old Nancy McConnel agreed to nurse her. Nancy was a solitary soul with a great love of animals and a scorn for human company. Whether this dog had been beaten, or had been hit by a car, she was unsure, but her injuries were serious. Nancy called in a vet who was not optimistic.

'She won't live long, Nancy,' he murmured. 'It'd be kinder to put her down. Her pups won't survive and she's obviously in pain.'

Nancy looked up at him with irritation. 'No,' she muttered, 'I'm not giving up on her.'

Nancy cared for her lovingly. The kelpie responded with gratitude and affection. When Nancy stroked her, her tail thumped against the floor. Her good breeding and intelligence were obvious. Who owned her and what had led her to a patch of gravel beside a lonely country road, Nancy never discovered.

Three days after she was found, the kelpie gave birth to six pups prematurely. Only two were alive. Having buried the dead pups, Nancy lifted the feeble survivors to their mother to drink. The mother showed increasing signs of weakness. Despite this, she seemed contented. Nancy supplemented the pups' food. Weak as they were, she could see that they were growing stronger.

The kelpie lived four more days. Her milk had been drying up, but with four-hourly feeds from Nancy, the two pups continued to live. When their mother looked up into Nancy's wrinkled face for the last time, trust and acceptance shone from her warm brown eyes. Nancy asked a neighbour to help her bury the dog. She wept unashamedly over the grave, for she felt that this dog deserved a better ending.

Though the kelpie's life had ended, her pups survived. Under Nancy's care, they grew and flourished. Nancy decided to keep the female, but she gave the male, when three months old, to her old friend Tom Harkness who had recently lost his own dog.

Tom loved the playful pup. He was a distinctive dog. He had one blue eye and one brown, and an unusual patch of white hair on his left hind leg.

Tom began to train him but something happened that Nancy had not anticipated. Tom had the dog only two months when he suffered a serious heart attack. He died several hours later. Nancy tried to retrieve the pup, but Tom's son sold him on to a stockman. Nancy lost all hope of finding the dog again.

JACK NANCARROW WAS A STRIPLING OF 18 when he began working on Barooka Downs. He spent long days mustering and branding and drenching the livestock. The station carried 200 head of cattle and several thousand head of sheep. Jack soon learnt the value of a good working dog. A well-trained dog could do the mustering work of several men.

One hot autumn day Jack was out on horseback checking the boundary fences. The country was too rugged to permit the passage of a vehicle, so Jack carried all he needed with him. He was riding along the western boundary when his horse whinnied uneasily. In the distance behind him he thought he saw a dingo. He whispered reassuring words to the mare. He rode forward 100 metres before looking behind him again. He was being followed but not by a dingo. It was a young male kelpie, in very poor condition. It was thin and its coat was matted with dust and burrs. Jack called to it, but the dog hung back.

Jack rode on, continuing to check the fence line. He cast an occasional glance behind. He lost sight of the dog for a time but, when he dismounted to repair a broken wire, there it was, standing 20 metres away.

Jack decided to stop for lunch. He tossed a sandwich towards the kelpie and watched to see what would happen. The dog looked at the food and then up at Jack uncertainly. Moving rapidly, it snatched up the bread, and rushed away to a safe distance.

'Where've you come from, you poor bugger?' Jack murmured. 'Come here . . . I won't hurt you.' The dog looked at him askance, its head cocked. 'Come on, fella. Come here.' The dog hung back anxiously, a bewildered look of longing in its eyes. When Jack continued on his way, the kelpie became his shadow. If he tried to coax the dog towards him, it would back off. So Jack ignored it and went on with his tasks.

Jack camped out for the night in a dry riverbed. He tethered his horse and lay out his swag beside a fire. He poured water into an enamel dish and placed it some distance away. He watched as the kelpie lapped it up. He had plenty of food and tossed the dog some salted meat which disappeared quickly. The dog was watching his every movement. Jack threw some meat to within two metres of the fire. The dog was wary of Jack but finally crept towards it on his belly. This time it did not move away.

He was an unusual dog, a black and tan kelpie with one blue eye and one brown. Despite his poor condition, he seemed intelligent and well-bred. Whenever Jack awoke during the night, he looked across to where the dog lay. He smiled to himself. It would be good to have a dog for company.

When he awoke next morning, there was no sign of the kelpie. No hungry eyes watched him eat his breakfast. He packed his gear onto his saddle disconsolately. As he rode on, he kept an eye out for the dog.

It was almost noon when Jack saw him again. The dog fell in behind the horse, about three metres away. 'Where have you been, fella?' called Jack. 'I've missed your company.' The kelpie looked up at him, a questioning expression in his eyes.

Jack camped out again that night. The kelpie seemed more at ease. When Jack tossed him meat, his tail wagged for the first time. Holding meat in his hand, Jack coaxed the dog towards him. The kelpie approached cautiously and snatched the meat from his hand but did not move away. Slowly Jack raised his hand and gently stroked the kelpie's head. The dog tensed under Jack's touch but stayed. The battle to win his trust was over.

Jack returned to the homestead the next afternoon. The kelpie followed him faithfully. It was dark when they drew near the outbuildings. The kelpie seemed anxious. The boss's dogs barked warnings, but they had been tied up for the night.

When Jack settled down to sleep in the bunkhouse, the kelpie was already asleep on the floor beside him.

The next morning, the kelpie was introduced to the station dogs and was grudgingly accepted into the pack. Jack began his education. He named him Trigger, because of his habit of bursting abruptly into a run from a standing position. He taught him basic commands but the dog needed little teaching. His natural herding instinct shone when he shepherded a bunch of sheep through a gate into the home paddock. Jack watched the dog, half-crouching as he circled the mob, his eyes bright with concentration and excitement. He anticipated the slightest movement of the sheep, keeping them under strict control.

The boss watched him with interest. 'You've got a good dog there, Jack. Treat him right and he'll work his heart out for you.'

In the months that followed, Jack came to appreciate the dog's zeal and stamina. He would work tirelessly for Jack, but would rarely respond to the commands of other men. He filled out and grew stronger. He seemed to know exactly what needed to be done without being told. He could quickly retrieve a recalcitrant ewe hiding in thick scrub, or separate a fly-blown sheep from the mob. The men began to speak of him with respect.

Jack began to see Trigger's potential fulfilled. When two steers broke through a fence and joined the Brahman cattle on a neighbouring property, Jack sent Trigger out alone to bring them in. The dog singled out the steers and shepherded them back through the gate adjoining the properties.

There was a time when Jack was asked to bring in a mob of sheep for drenching. He was suffering from gastroenteritis and felt too weak to ride. The sheep were spread out in a paddock notorious for its thick scrub. Trigger was sent out to bring them in. Two hours later the kelpie had the sheep corralled in the holding yards. Not one was missing.

JACK RECEIVED A PHONECALL from his mother. 'Jack,' she said, 'Tom has leukaemia.' Jack was disbelieving. His little brother ill? 'We've just heard from the doctor. The initial diagnosis is confirmed . . . Jack, come home. I need you here . . . Please, Jack.'

He could hear the fear in her voice. 'Of course . . . The shearing is due to start soon . . . I'll talk to the boss.'

With Trigger beside him, Jack arrived in Stanthorpe two days later. He saw the gratitude in his mother's tired face. Tom was lying on the sofa in the living room. He looked pale, but he welcomed Jack heartily. Trigger was introduced to the family. He made himself at home immediately. Jack walked him every afternoon. Trigger greeted Tom with a lick on their return and settled down beside him. It always brought a smile to Tom's face.

Jack decided to return to the station alone for the shearing. He ordered Trigger to 'stay' and set out without him. Trigger was uneasy but he remained beside Tom loyally.

When Tom was driven to the hospital for treatment the following Monday, Trigger was left alone in the backyard. Jack's parents arrived home later that day, and there was no sign of Trigger anywhere. They searched the neighbourhood, but they could not find him.

Jack heard the news. He wanted to return to Stanthorpe immediately. The boss dissuaded him. 'They need you there, Jack. Trigger will turn up eventually.'

Jack was kept busy, but felt restless and uneasy. He worried about his dog. What had happened to him? Had he been injured? The uncertainty plagued him. He came to appreciate how deeply he loved this dog.

Jack awoke one morning and heard a familiar bark in the distance. He sat up and listened intently. There it was again. He rushed to open the door. There, across the paddocks, running eagerly towards him, was Trigger. When the dog arrived at his feet, he jumped up excitedly and licked Jack's hand frantically. He was tired and footsore and very hungry, but he was happy and unhurt. Jack exuberantly lifted him in his arms and spun in a circle.

'Oh, you crazy dog, I'm so happy to see you!'

The kelpie had travelled 150 miles to the station, across busy roads and through wild stretches of countryside.

'Can you believe it!' Jack yelled excitedly to the other men. 'He's come all the way from Stanthorpe.'

When he told the boss, his employer was unperturbed. 'I told you he'd turn up. Trigger wouldn't walk out on his best mate.'

Jack stayed on at the station but he and Trigger had regular trips back to Stanthorpe.

Initially Tom responded well to the treatment he received, but the wan look returned to his face.

When the family gathered around Tom's grave to say the final farewell, Trigger was at Jack's side. The man struggled to accept his brother's death but wounds heal with the passage of time.

Jack sought change and became manager of a property near Inglewood.

As he watched his dog running before him, piloting a group of lambs through the gateway ahead, Jack felt happy again.

Trigger was happy too. A look of eager excitement returned to his eyes.

The years the two spent together here were rich and fulfilling. It was trap-rock country, but sheep did well. Jack bought a saw-mill, and made extra money milling timber from old ring-barked trees. He was saving assiduously to buy a property of his own.

It was at a clearing sale near Texas that he met Nancy McConnel. He was wandering about, with the kelpie at his side, when the old woman approached him.

'Is that your dog?' she challenged him, looking at Trigger with great interest.

'Yes,' said Jack, 'and he is the best dog in the world.' He fondled Trigger behind the ears.

'Well,' she said smiling, 'I'm glad he's found a good home.'

Jack looked at her in surprise.

'Oh, yes, I know this dog. I know him very well . . . those strange eyes . . . that odd patch on his back leg.' She stroked Trigger's head affectionately. 'Let's go and get ourselves a cup of that tea that's on offer. I'll tell you about his birth.'

So Jack heard the tale of Trigger's early months. He never found out what happened to his dog in the weeks that followed.

Jack eventually bought 400 hectares from one of his neighbours. There was some good pasture on the block, and a spring and a dam provided water. He built himself a house.

When he moved to the block permanently, he was quite content. Trigger was no longer a young dog, but he still had that passionate will to work. He moved more slowly, but the old eagerness still shone in his eyes when he trailed a flock of sheep. He grew tired more easily but his loyalty and intelligence never wavered.

Late one afternoon, Jack was checking a densely timbered gully for stray sheep. Trigger was unseen down in the gully when Jack's horse started at a kangaroo that bounded up the slope. 'As the horse reared, Jack was caught off guard and fell. His head struck a rock and he lost consciousness. Later he tried to piece together what had happened afterwards. The kelpie must have returned and found him on the ground.

Jack's immediate neighbour was away from home. Did Trigger go to his farm first, or did he go directly to the Penshorn homestead? The night was dark when Trigger reached the house, but the kitchen light shone out over the garden beds. He scratched at the door and barked frantically.

When Dick Penshorn opened the door and saw a dog out there, he kicked him away. 'Get out of here,' he yelled.

As the dog continued his frenzied barking, Dick recognised him. Surely that was Jack's kelpie? He was perplexed. When Trigger grabbed a fold in the sleeve of his jumper and began pulling him away from the house, Dick knew something was amiss.

'Honey,' he called out, 'I'm going over to Jack's place. Something's wrong. Get Peter out here. He can come with me.'

He and his son set off in his old ute with Trigger riding in the back. When they arrived at Jack's place, Trigger jumped out and ran ahead barking. As they drove off the track across the paddocks, Dick struggled to keep Trigger in the range of the headlights. Eventually they had to stop. Thick scrub blocked the passage of their vehicle.

The night was growing colder. They trudged cautiously over the rough ground, following the dog. They found Jack unconscious at the head of the gully. His body felt very cold.

'Run back to the ute and get that old blanket,' Dick called. When they had carefully wrapped him in the blanket, they carried him back to the ute and lay him in the back.

'Get in with him, Peter. Cushion his head. He'll have a rough ride home.'

The time passed slowly before the ambulance arrived. Peter found Jack's horse outside the yards. He removed the saddle and bridle and set it free in the front paddock. Dick tried to keep Jack warm and comfortable. He did not regain consciousness. As Jack was finally driven away to the hospital, Trigger looked after the receding vehicle anxiously.

'Don't worry, fella. He'll be all right. You'd better come home with us for now.'

They tried to persuade Trigger to jump back into the ute but he backed off. They attempted to lift him in but he struggled free and ran away from them. So they ensured that he had plenty of food and water and left him behind. Trigger sat and waited for Jack's return.

Jack was driven home two weeks later. Trigger was overjoyed to see him. He pranced around him, barking with excitement.

'How's my old mate?' laughed Jack, as he ruffled the dog's coat.

He returned to work the next day. Watching his dog, Jack grew concerned. Trigger was lagging behind him, breathing heavily. His eyes looked dull.

One night, after a day out in the paddocks, Trigger arrived home limping. He lay down on his bed on the veranda, and did not look up when Jack brought him his dinner. Jack cradled the kelpie's head in his hands and looked into his eyes.

'Did I work you too hard today, old fella?' He brought him a bowl of water. Trigger made a half-hearted attempt to drink. 'Jack stroked his head but there was no corresponding wag of his tail. 'Rest up, old boy. You'll be right in the morning.' Even as he said the words, Jack did not believe them. Next morning, he found Trigger still lying in the position in which he had left him. When he touched his flank, his body felt cold and lifeless.

His dog was gone ... His dog was dead. Numb with grief, he buried Trigger amidst a grove of casuarinas near the dam. It was a peaceful place, a quiet resting place for his beloved friend ... the best friend he would ever have.

RETROSPECTIVE: From the 2017 anthology:
Redemption

FIVE WORDS ECHO THROUGH TIME
Pauline Davies

THIS IS A TRUE STORY, whatever that means. Real truth is elusive, if it exists at all, but this is my truth, recounted as clearly as I can remember it; as a series of colourful snapshots that have played out in my mind in the same way for the last forty or so years. You know what early memories are like – they're fragmented, random, and mostly insignificant. We never know why some remain after most have faded. I remember falling through a glass door in England when I was three and the frantic rush to the hospital in a neighbour's car, and I remember a packet of crayons that melted in the Australian sun when I was six. But these are just moments, barely perceptible glimpses of a time lost forever. The memory I'm about to describe is as clear to me today as it ever was. The brief scene that took place on a warm afternoon when I was around eight years old always comes back to me in the same familiar way, and yet I'm no closer to solving its mystery.

I know how old I was because from 1972 to 1974 my family lived in an old green weatherboard house on the edge of a small town in rural Queensland. Murgon was home to a few thousand people and depended on meat, dairy and peanut farming for its survival. We had followed relatives there from a northern English industrial town whose noisy, narrow streets and bitterly cold winters were a stark contrast to the wide open spaces, dry heat and sudden storms of our new home.

The relocation from one side of the world to the other is a major disturbance in a child's life. Everything familiar is destabilised and has to be learned again: new faces, places, accents, routines. That wrench serves to divide childhood memories into either before or after, and the strangeness of the new environment crystallizes experiences into vivid memories. I remember the ancient wood stove that my mother fed every day, and its long chamber with the tap on the front that we used to heat water for baths and dirty dishes. Perhaps the contrast with the instant heat of our gas stove and hot water taps in England caused those memories to remain? I remember my father learning to drive so he could go to his new job at the abattoir; in England he had ridden a bicycle to work and we travelled everywhere by bus. There was no public transport in Murgon; instead everyone drove cars – to me they were strange, cavernous creatures with hard vinyl seats that scorched bare legs in summer. We were a long way from everywhere. I remember a recurring dream: running wildly down a familiar street lined with semi-detached houses and stopping, breathless, outside number seventy-three. I remember the overwhelming rush of exhilaration as I realised I had found my way home, and the agonising disappointment on waking.

I already told you that my memory of the mysterious incident is clear, but what is perplexing is that I can't remember what I was doing before or after it. That's the beguiling thing about memory – it is selective. The event took only a minute or two in real time, and yet it plays over and over in my mind like a short film on a loop; the images colourful and the sound audible. I remember a tree in our garden with smooth silver branches and bright pink blossoms that fell on parched brown grass. Nearby was a curved corrugated iron tank that supplied water to the house. The tank stood on an ancient timber stand that was tall enough for me to step under without bending. I remember playing with my cousin in the garden between the pink blossom tree, the house and the water tank. An unruly seven year old with sandy hair and freckles, Peter's arrival in Australia a year before us entitled him to an air of defiant cockiness.

This is the strange part.

I remember a voice. I heard it as we were playing. The memory commences with the sound of that voice. The images of the garden and Peter's presence only appear in my mind with the arrival of the voice. It sounded like my own voice, but didn't feel like me because I wasn't controlling it. It came from inside my head. It was loud and clear.

Authoritative. Uninvited. Intrusive.

'Get under the tank stand.'

Perplexed, but not alarmed, I heard my own internal voice ask why.

'Get under the tank stand,' the voice responded.

It didn't make sense. There was no reason to. My cousin would think I was strange. I proceeded to have an internal argument, resisting the order to move.

'Get under the tank stand!' the voice insisted, even louder than before.

Urgent. Hard to ignore.

Feeling foolish, I pointed to Boat Mountain; perched on the horizon, flat-topped and blue in the distance, nothing but paddocks and scrub between us and it.

'Hey! Look at those clouds over Boat Mountain. There's going to be a storm soon.'

There was barely a speckle of rain in our yard, and there was more blue sky than cloud above us.

'Let's get under the tank stand before it rains,' I said with forced enthusiasm.

I knew it was lame, but to my surprise, Peter obeyed and took one step backwards with me, to the shelter of the tank stand. My eyes were still facing forwards, focused on the space I had just occupied. In that instant I caught sight of a thin, vertical, white line, barely an arm's length away, at about my chest height.

In the exact spot where I had been standing.

Silent. Harmless.

'Hey! Did you see that?' I shouted in surprise.

'See what?' He was still looking at the mountain.

'Lightning!'

It was gone in a moment, but had been about the length of a school ruler and hadn't touched the ground. Hadn't connected with anything. I laughed out loud in surprise, but felt sorry my cousin had missed it.

In the months that followed, I remembered the events of that afternoon simply because of the novelty of seeing lightning up close. It was a minor oddity, an unimportant incident that would have slipped into the abyss of forgetfulness had I not learned soon after that lightning is dangerous.

Deadly.

I remember the feeling of shock as I absorbed the revelation. I replayed the garden incident in my mind, trying to reconcile the memory of a small and silent lightning bolt that had seemed so harmless with the notion that it had been dangerous. As the scene played over and over, so did the sound of the voice and the words that had saved me from either death or significant injury.

I had almost ignored that voice!

That's what was most shocking to me. What if I had defied that instruction? What would my life have been like? Would it have been snuffed out in that instant? I could not explain that intrusion in my mind, but I never doubted that it had happened exactly as I remembered. The significance of the near miss, and the repetition of revisiting the scene, ensured that the incident became lodged in my long term memory.

I am reluctant to embrace the idea of the supernatural. Even as a child I found it hard to believe that a busy god would have bothered to save me from danger. What was it then; that voice?

Angel? Ancestor? Intuition?

Exploring any of these options opens so many areas of uncertainty and conjecture that it seems pointless to bother. Instead, I accept that I will never know and feel grateful that I listened to that inner voice.

I don't expect you to believe me.

I have shared my story with a number of people over the years, but it always seems to lose something in the telling. Perhaps the listeners have been too polite to be openly sceptical? I have the advantage of personal experience, but you must decide if my memory is accurate, or if time has caused me to become whimsically creative.

We all have occasional brushes with death. They remind us to appreciate how precious life is and to value our time here. Without the memory of the experience in the garden I think I would be a person who dismisses everything in life that cannot be seen, touched or proven. I feel extraordinarily fortunate; not just because I missed being struck by lightning, but because that mysterious incident has allowed a window in my mind to stay open.

Just a tiny crack.

But enough for me to be occasionally receptive to the unknown possibilities of the Universe.

THE MAY FIRES
Virginia Miranda

Oh, do not tell the priest our plight,
Or he would call it a sin;
But...we have been out in the woods all night,
A-conjuring summer in!
And we bring you good news by word of mouth...
Good news for cattle and corn...
Now as the Sun comes up from the south,
With Oak, and Ash and Thorn!
Rudyard Kipling

THE MAY EVE FIRES BURNED on the hills surrounding Grace's village. She watched them flicker and dance from her bedroom window, the pre-dawn sun a faint glow of pinks and purples on the horizon.

Last evening Grace's Pa, along with the villagers, extinguished their hearth fires for the first time in a year. Beltane, halfway between spring equinox and summer solstice marked the beginning of the pastoral summer season.

The villagers walked with their unlit torches up the hills. As was Beltane Eve tradition, after the ceremonies they would reignite their torches from the flames and return home to relight the hearth fires.

On the hills they danced around the bonfires singing songs of protection and purification. They herded their cattle and sheep between the fires in a bid to protect them from unseen forces. For tonight the veil between the fairies' world and that of humans was at its thinnest.

Later in the evening, Grace's parents and her younger siblings returned home with their lighted torch, leaving Grace with her friends.

Stories were told of blossoms bursting forth with a profusion of colour and scents that stirred the senses and aroused the bodies of the uninitiated. The newlywed and those seeking pregnancy performed fertility dances around the bonfires. Grace and her friends giggled as they watched couples disappear into the fields.

Soon only the young unmarried ones remained. The young men huddled together on an old log, across the fire from the girls.

'Cathal hasn't taken his eyes of you all evening,' Bridgette whispered.

Grace said nothing. She knew Bridgette was right.

Grace watched Cathal stand and bid goodnight to his friends. In the reflected glow of the fire she saw him leave. Her heart sank. Seconds later he was standing beside her, his hand outstretched. She took it, nodded goodnight to her friends and let him lead her away from the firelight into the moon's glow.

Here, amongst the ancient standing stones, they danced the dance of lovers, yielding to each other . . . waking to life, to possibilities, to a future, after the dormancy of winter and early spring.

Now, as the sun crept towards a new day Grace left her home. She ran towards the forest in search of the morn's first dew, another Beltane custom. Dew from the Oak or Ash trees would enhance her beauty and ensure her health for the next year.

Forgetting all warnings, she stepped from the edge of the path, a solitary mortal wandering the secluded depths of the forest. The sound of harp music slipped into her conscience unannounced. The music played her emotions; she was one with the forest...any fear she may have felt wandering alone, was banished by the heavenly sounds.

Brianna, a Solitary Fairy, played louder, coaxing the mortal to step closer. She, who dared lie with the fairy King Cathal, must be punished.

Grace lay down at the foot of an old oak tree and closed her eyes, succumbing to the soft melodious sounds of the harp.

Sometime later she woke, letting her eyes survey her surroundings while her mind sifted through her memories. She recalled leaving home at sunrise in search of the first morning's dew. She put her hands to her face and sat up.

No longer was she beside the old oak tree. In its stead, she sat in a bed of straw . . . a quilt of silver, green and red across her feet. Sparkling crystal walls disappeared into the heavens. A golden stone floor spread before her. Large silver columns soared above, disappearing into the shimmering distance. She searched the heights for some sign of a ceiling, but nothing was definable.

Scattered across the floor were the finest of silk carpets. Grace frowned.

'She wakes.' The female voice was menacing.

Grace swivelled, in search of the speaker. What she saw snatched her breath, leaving it caught in her throat. She coughed, spluttered, choked. In the next instant the monstrous old hag screeched and covered her grotesque face.

With a flick of her fingers, where once stood an old hag, was now a beauty – her blonde hair hung below her waist. Diamonds and pearls adorned her hair and neck. She wore a long silk red dress and a shawl of emerald green.

'Where am I? Who are you?' Grace's voice came out as a whisper.

'You are in the King's palace and I am his Queen.'

'You, you are old. I saw you. You used 'the glamor' to change. You are a wicked old witch, an ugly wicked old witch.'

'What do you know of 'the glamor'?'

'Enough,' Grace answered. 'We have a seanchai in our village.'

'A storyteller – a chieftain's servant, their storytelling is dangerous.'

'Why am I here?'

'You dare lay with the King of the Fairies. Now you are with babe. We will return you to your family when the babe is born. But – the boy will stay here.'

Grace held her stomach. 'How do you know?'

The Queen clapped her hands and a young girl appeared. 'Get some food for our guest.'

'What do you mean; I dare lay with the King of the Fairies? I lay with Cathal, no one else.'

'No, No, No!' The Queen screamed, 'You will call him King.'

'Cathal, King of the Fairies?' Grace looked to the Queen for a reply, but she was gone. In her place was a silver platter covered in all manner of delicacies.

Grace was famished. Tantalizing aromas filled the space. She selected grapes, cheese and slices of meat. Hesitating, she remembered the words of the seanchai – a story told of mortals lost to the fairy world, mortals who ate fairy food, never to return to their world.

Music came soft and melodic across the room, a fairy harp. Grace looked at the food and could not recall why she hesitated. Soon the food was gone, the silver goblet empty. Grace curled up on her straw bed and slept.

Sometime later she woke. She was alone. Daylight seeped through the crystal walls. High hedges blocked the exits or perhaps they blocked the entrances. Grace could see escaping from, or entering this crystal palace, would be difficult.

In the quietness of her surroundings she felt gentle vibrations. They were musical, but not harp music.

She searched for the source. High up in the corner of the wall a spider plucked the threads of its web, enticing its prey with a silken tune.

She watched fascinated, forgetting for a moment her incarceration at the hands of the wicked Fairy Queen.

The spider swung low spinning a new path making a new tune. Grace climbed from her straw bed. The spider deftly wove its web above a hedge of foxglove . . . purple bell-shaped flowers. Grace knew these. She crouched before the plant examining its tiny bells. She recalled a children's game . . . hold one end of the flower bell and strike the other on your hand. You will hear the clap of fairy thunder. Foxglove was said to be the home of fairies. The flower bells began to move.

'Excuse me!' a voice said, 'this is our home.'

Grace stared in astonishment, as from each bell, flew tiny winged creatures. They wore clothes of many colours, violet, indigo, blue, green, yellow, orange and red.

'Who are you?' one asked.

'My name is Grace. Your wicked Queen lured me here with her harp music. Now she won't let me go.'

'What did you do?'

Grace thought for a moment, tell the truth or not. The seanchai in her village said fairies knew when you were lying.

'In my world, on Beltane Eve, I lay with my love, Cathal.'

'Oh my.'

'Oh no.'

'How could you?'

'What do you mean, how could I? Because Cathal . . .'

The fairies covered their ears, 'King Cathal.' They whispered together.

'In my world, Cathal is a boy from County Kerry. He is not King of the Fairies.' Grace whispered, for she did not wish to frighten the tiny beings.

The fairies looked from one to another. 'She tells the truth,' they said.

'And now your Queen tells me I am with babe and must stay here until he is born. Then she plans to steal him and send me home.'

Sounds like butterflies flapping their wings in fear, came from within the foxglove bells.

'I must find a way back to Cathal.'

'We can help you,' one said. 'We will make you tea from the foxglove leaves. The tea will release you from the Queen's charm.'

'Then you will be able to find your way home,' said another.

'Have you eaten here?' A third asked.

'Yes.'

'Oh, we will have to make the tea stronger.'

The spider's music became louder. The fairies stopped their chatter.

'We must go.'

'Will you return?'

'Yes, soon.'

The spider hastened its journey back up the crystal walls while the fairies disappeared inside the flower bells.

'You are awake.' The Queen came towards Grace, a platter of food in her hand. Harp music began to play. Grace took the food and ate.

Oh! Thou who hear my cry of fear,
To my family's home, these tidings bear.
Bid them bring a tea of foxglove leaves,
At whose sip this charm will fade

Grace stirred; a soft wind caressed her face. She opened her eyes . . . tiny colourful figures danced before her.

'You must learn to resist,' the red one said.

'Or we will not be able to remove the Queen's charm,' added a blue one.

She sat up, her face a picture of puzzlement.

'The queen, the queen fed you again. Each time you eat, we must make the foxglove tea stronger. Too strong and it can kill.'

She remembered . . . the Fairy Queen, Cathal, the purple foxglove flowers . . . the fairies.

'When will you make the tea? I must get back to Cathal . . . King Cathal.' She bowed to the tiny beings before her.

'The tea is made.'

'Where is your Queen?'

'She prepares to leave. Tonight, is Samhain Eve, a time when we can cross into your world.'

'Samhain? Impossible!'

'Time is different in our world.'

'What will she do in my world?'

'She goes to steal more humans.'

'Why?'

'Because she desires them for her slaves.'

'What if like me, they don't want to stay?'

'She takes who she wants, their wishes are no concern of hers. The more food she gives them the more they forget their other life.'

A strange sound came from across the hedge, past the purple foxgloves. Grace crouched and made her way to the edge. Her tiny friends hid within the swaying bells.

Chestnut coloured horses kicked up whirls of dust. They cantered in straight lines, two by two, strong steeds, red eyes smouldering with strange beings atop. Grace stared; she held her breath as they passed.

'Be still,' she heard from within the purple flowers, 'the Queen comes.'

A white steed came into view, sitting upon a glittering bejewelled saddle . . . a woman. Her porcelain face, doll like, her beauty unnatural. She wore a dress of shimmering silver. Diamonds and pearls adorned her long blonde hair. Grace stared . . . it was the Queen using the glamor.

'Your tea is ready. Drink it. We will follow behind the Queen at a safe distance.'

Grace drank the tea. She stumbled. It was strong and tasted metallic. She gagged.

'Drink it all,' a small voice commanded.

She finished the cup and looked around. A path through the hedge came into view. A path she had not seen earlier.

'Come quickly.'

Grace followed her tiny friends. The sky was black, moonless.

They reached the edge of the forest. She recognized the hills. They were near her home. She turned to thank them, but they were gone.

On the hills around her village Samhain fires were burning.

She looked down at her clothes. For the first time she noticed her rounded belly. Her thoughts scattered on the breeze. Would Cathal believe her? Would her parents disown her? If Cathal was King of the Fairies, why didn't he come for her?

She reached the edge of the circle, unnoticed. She saw her sister; her friends . . . an anguished cry brought the attention of all, upon her. Her sister ran to where she stood. Cathal, who had been chatting to friends, turned towards the commotion, alert for danger. He stared in disbelief. His eyes coveting her body.

Tread softly because you tread on my dreams.

Grace was frozen, unable to move. She watched Cathal, but the glowing fire obscured his face. Would her dreams shatter into a million pieces or would he give her the chance to explain?

Three strides across the circle . . . he stood before her. She felt his confusion mixed with a barely controlled intensity exuding from his body. His eyes questioned her. She took strength from his intenseness and smiled.

'You look beautiful,' he whispered.

'Grace, Grace we thought you were dead.' It was Niamh, Grace's sister. 'Where have you been? And . . .?' She pointed at Grace's bump. 'Father will be . . . '

'Niamh please say nothing to your parents. Grace and I need to talk. I will bring her home later this evening.'

Cathal lead Grace away from the fire into the dark night. They walked in silence, making their way down the hill into the Churchyard. An ancient stone round tower stood on the edge of the graveyard, a sentinel guarding the resting place of warriors and ancestors past.

Grace sat on a stone ledge on the eastern side of the tower; its iron-rich red sandstone walls glowed in the starlight.

'Tell me what happened. I took you home. I thought you were safe.'

Grace hesitated then began, 'I woke early. It was Beltane morning. I wanted to make myself beautiful for you. I ran into the forest to find the first morning's dew.'

'We found no trace of you. I searched. Your father searched. The village searched. You disappeared.'

'I heard music. It came from behind a blackberry bush. I followed the sound. When I woke, I was inside a crystal palace.'

Cathal paced. 'Go on.'

'I was the Queen's prisoner. Although I saw her as she truly was, an old witch. She told me you were King of the Fairies . . . and . . . I was with babe.'

Cathal sat down. He took Grace's hand in his. 'I'm sorry Grace.'

'She said I must stay until the babe was born. Then I could go home, without my babe, your baby. Are you their King?'

'I would be if I went back. The Queen is my mother.'

'Why did you leave?'

'My father brought me out as a child. He was a mortal. We moved away, lived on Inishnabro across the sea.'

'Why?'

'The Queen wanted an heir, someone to lead her forces, to help her fight a war against mortals.'

'Why come back here?'

'My father died. I hoped my mother had changed. How did you escape?'

'Fairies helped me. They brought me to the edge of the forest.'

'We must leave Grace. Go far away . . . before the babe is born.'

'My family?'

'No one can know where we are. If she finds us, she will take our son.'

In the dark Samhein evening, Grace and Cathal began their journey over the green hills to the sea, back to the safety of Inishnabro.

AN AWAKENING

Ann Lewis

As I stand upon the precipice,
Wondering if I'll fly or fall,
I take this opportunity,
To survey and reflect on it all.

Choices, fears and questions,
Like wind – swirl around me now,
I try but I can't ignore them,
Louder and louder they start to howl.

In my search for truth and meaning,
And a purpose to see me through,
Learning to love myself again,
Presented as a challenge, not a clue.

I went looking for an answer,
Not knowing what I'd find,
Hoping that the truth was somewhere,
Hidden deep inside my mind.

Somehow I found her waiting,
Like she knew this day would come,
The person I was meant to be,
No longer lost, scared or numb.

Now with eyes opened widely,
And toes straddled over the ledge,
I still my beating heart – and breathe,
Unafraid of what lies beyond the edge.

THE OUTLIER
Bernie Dowling

In memory of more than 2000 people who suicided, after receiving computer-generated 'robo debt' demands – many erroneous – from the Federal Government Centrelink social security organisation.

South-east Queensland, September, 1998

IT WAS BARBIE THE BARITONE who recommended me.

'Barbie the baritone suggested you might talk to him, Steele,' the Gooroo said.

We were sharing tea and scones on a bright spring morning in Con's Tweed Heads unit. The Gooroo had just turned 68 and he had decided to retire from his somewhat illegal SP bookmaking business. It was fun while it lasted but legal corporate bookmakers had begun to compete with the previous trilogy of government totalisators, on-course bookies, and the dwindling numbers of illegal SPs like the Gooroo.

I had given my best mate, Con Vitalis, 35 years my senior, the nickname the Gooroo after the Local Aboriginal word for deep place or something like that.

'I've created a spreadsheet to map all the punters who owe me money,' the Gooroo said. 'I've worked out probabilities of people paying me back and also the percentage they are likely to pay if they refuse to fork out the full amount.' He smiled. 'I was pleasantly surprised at the results and I have only one outlier.'

I took a sip of tea before I inquired if the Gooroo was talking to me. 'Are you talking to me or to yourself? Because I don't know what a spreadsheet is and I don't know what an outlier is. I pretty much understand the stuff in the middle and it's good that it looks like you've got a pleasing result coming your way.'

'You know what a spreadsheet is, Steele. It's got information and maths calculations on it. A bookmaker's ledger is a spreadsheet. You've been working with spreadsheets for 10 years. Just not as sophisticated as the modern computer ones. An outlier is a result far different to the average.'

'Like an outsider in a horse race,' I said.

'Yair, something like that and Charlie Barra has come up as an outlier with me having next to no hope of collecting what he owes me.'

'How much does this Charlie Barra owe?'

'Three grand.'

'Write it off,' I advised.

'This may surprise you, Steele, but writing off bad debts without trying earnestly to collect is frowned upon in the business world.'

'Then talk to him,' I said

'I was going to, but Barbie the Baritone was concerned he was emotionally fragile.'

I saw what the problem was. 'Charlie's dropped three grand betting on the ponies. Of course he is emotionally fragile. Once he's wiped the slate clean, he will feel much better.'

The Gooroo was not convinced. 'I don't know so much. Barbie is concerned.'

'Did Barbie offer to clear his slate?'

'She isn't that concerned. She suggested you talk to Charlie Barra.'

I might be 6-foot tall but I wasn't coming at this. 'I'm not heavying a bloke about a gambling debt. No way.'

The Gooroo was offended. 'Who said anything about heavying anyone? I'm just asking you to talk to him so I know what the score is. I'll give you a couple of hundred even if we have to write off the whole 3-gees.'

I was embarrassed after being reprimanded for my dark thoughts. 'Awlright, I'll give it a go but I don't need any money for it. I've had a good week on the punt. Maybe Charlie Barra has too. Where does he live?'

'Dunno,' the Gooroo said, reaching into his wallet for $40, what he called 'petrol money'. 'We did business on the telephone and settled debts in cafes.'

'I thought it was frowned upon in business not to know the address of customers.'

Barbie's mum called her Barbara and I called her Barbie the Baritone because it always made me laugh or, at the very least, smile to hear the moniker. She was the lead singer of an all-girl pub band which moved up financially to do cabaret and play corporate gigs for the big money. As a novelty, the blue-eyed blonde sang a set of songs usually performed by baritone or bass vocalists. She would do *The Superman Song* by Crash Test Dummies, *Better Get a Lawyer* by the Cruel Sea, the Red Hot Chili Peppers' *Fight Like a Brave*, *It's Midnight* by Elvis, *Light My Fire* by The Doors, *16 Tons* by almost everybody, and even way back to *Old Man River* by Paul Robeson.

The punters loved Barbie's baritone/ bass set and why wouldn't they? It was way cool.

She opened the door to her unit beside the Brisbane River and I admired the views outside, through the patio window, and in. 'So, this is your new place. Wow, you done all right for a girl.'

Barbie drummed her fingers on the back of the open door to an old Melanie tune, and invited me in. 'You know you're not supposed to quote song lyrics without permission,' she said. 'How's Natalie?'

'We're kind of taking a break at the moment,' I said.

'Why does that not surprise me? You know, Steele, you'd be a good catch for any woman. If you were not such a hopeless arsehole.' On cue, Barbie's CD player gave us the satirical *Pretty Fly (For a White Guy)* from pop-punkers the Offspring's new album *Americana*. 'And what brings you to my humble abode?'

I scoffed. 'Humble abode, that new group of yours, Barbie and the Beetroots, must be going sensationally.'

'It's Kirsty and the Kalettes. We were going to call ourselves the Scalettes but that was taken. So, we went with the vegetable.'

'Like in that prickly stalky cabbage stuff. That tastes yuk. That kale will never take off. Kirsty and the Kalettes is cool for a band name, but.'

'Way cooler than what you called us. As a name, Barbie and the Beetroots wouldn't work, not even in those pub dives you frequent.'

'You mean those pub dives where you learned your trade, Barbie.'

'Fair point but I've told you not to call me Barbie.'

'I always call you Barbie.'

'And I always tell you not to.'

We bantered about this for a minute and it led to good band names and great song titles and killer lyrics. We had to stop so the whole morning was not done before we talked about a more serious matter.

Barbie was still playing the pubs for peanuts when she first noticed Charlie Barra at one gig. He was at others and he always sat in the same spot to her right, three tables back. He never tapped his knee in time with a song or mouthed the words. At the end of a number he would only clap politely. It was quite disconcerting.'

I nodded. 'I bet it was. For Charlie. Sounds like you were stalking him.'

'That's not funny, Steele. You can get some creepy guys at gigs. That's how I met you, remember.'

She got me there. I raised my hands in surrender, and sat mute as she continued her tale.

'He surprised me one night when he came over during the break between sets to buy one of our EPs. He said he really liked the sad song I had just done.'

Barbie appreciated the compliment because the song was an original she had performed in public for the first time. It normally takes quite a few listens before a punter catches onto a song and decides they really like it.

Charlie seemed safe enough and Barbie talked to him at gigs and occasionally they met over a coffee. Small world and all that, it turns out Charlie bets on horse races with Con Vitalis who is Barbara's grandmother's second cousin.

When I ask, Barbie does not know what Charlie does for a living. She suspects he may be on a pension as his complexion is pale and he is prone to bouts of coughing. She does not pry into any medical issues. At one time, he mentioned working in an air-force base, maybe as a civilian, Barbie thought.

'Do you have his address?' I ask.

She sat silent for a while. 'What do you want with him?'

'I thought you said to the Gooroo I should talk to Charlie.'

'No, that's not what I said. What I said was you and Charlie probably spoke the same language.'

I had some idea what Barbie was driving at and was not really offended but it was only fair to embarrass the successful performer. 'What's that supposed to mean?'

Barbie's face tinged reddish but she was saved from attempting an awkward response. Dexter Holland, vocalist of the Offspring, burst into the song *Why Don't You Get a Job?* Barbie laughed.

I laughed. 'Don't like that song much,' I said. 'I suppose it's about the band inheriting a bunch of hangers-on since their success. It just comes across as judgemental. Nice tune, but.'

'It's a hit with a lot of people,' Barbie said.

She got up and walked towards a coffee table with one CD and a sheet of note paper on it.

'Sure is,' I said to her back.

Barbie handed me the CD and the paper with an address on it. The CD was *Dream's Up*, Kirsty and the Kalettes' new album. 'I was supposed to post this to Charlie. You can take it to him if you like. I've got a copy for you, too. Just promise me you won't ask Charlie for money until you come back to see me. Maybe we can work something out. I've a bit of cash at the moment but you know what the music biz is like, Steele. One day you're a bird of paradise, the next day you're compost.'

Brendale is an industrial suburb north of Brisbane in the shire known as Pine Rivers named after the north and south Pine Rivers. The north and south branches merge into just the plain old Pine River before it empties into the sea. Everything's pine, up that way.

Brendale has lots of industrial buildings, mostly small. But also modest houses and flats for some of its thousands of workers to live in. I was visiting an octet of brick flats, one of which might contain Charlie Barra. The flats looked like they were built on the cheap with bricks of varied colour. Some bricks were cracked and a few jutted at dangerous angles to the horizontal. Moss stained the base of the two-storey building. Some brick buildings lasted hundreds of years. This one would be lucky to see fifty.

I knocked on the thin wooden door of ground floor flat no. 4 and a tall man, maybe 6 foot 3, stooped over me, and I was looking at his forehead and the receding grey hair above it.

'Hi,' I said. 'I'm Steele Hill and I was driving out this way so Barbie asked me to deliver this CD.'

The man straightened his head but his shoulders still appeared hunched. 'Who's Barbie?' he asked warily.

'I mean Barbara,' I corrected. 'Barbara Truscott, Kirsty.'

'But I already paid for the CD.'

'I know, Charlie. I'm a friend of Barbara's and I'm delivering it for her. There's no charge.'

He was trusting enough to invite me in. It was a one-bedroom flat which despite its small size looked larger because of the lack of furniture. A television set and a CD player sat on a round cane table. One lounge chair faced the entertainment devices. Another cane table had two cane chairs underneath. In the kitchen was a thin stove, a noisy old refrigerator, a single wash basin, and a bench running along one wall with a set of three drawers underneath. On the bench were an electric jug and a toaster.

'Would you like a cup of tea, Mr Hill? I only got tea. Coffee is very expensive except for the cheap stuff which doesn't taste nice and I would rather go without.'

'Tea's fine, thanks. No milk, no sugar.'

He indicated one of the cane chairs for me to sit in and retrieved tea bags and cups from one of the drawers beneath the kitchen bench.

As we sat drinking bland tea and munching plain biscuits, I realised I would need to lead the conversation as the man had exhausted his dialogue with his observations on cheap coffee. Looking at him, I would say he was about 50, which made him 15 or so years my senior.

I decided not to mention the Gooroo. 'You go to a lot of Barbara's shows?' I asked.

'A few. What about you, Steele? Did you ever go to the Storey Bridge Hotel when Barbara was in her other band? You look familiar to me.'

'In '94, '95?'

He nodded.

'Probably. Yair, for sure,' I said.

He seemed satisfied at his memory. 'At first I thought you were from the Air Force. Under cover. But you don't look like you're Air Force.'

'No I'm not in the Air Force. Are you in the Air Force Charlie?'

'No. I'm in dispute with them.'

'Over what?'

'I used to work for them. As a civvy in the F-111 Deseal/Reseal section.'

'Sounds heavy,' I said. 'What's that?'

'Cleaning and patching up the fighter jets' fuel tanks. That's what I did for 12 years, the 12 years from 1981 to 1993. For 12 years.

'I've always been a big bloke but I would crawl into those F-111 jet fuel tanks. I would scrape off all sorts of toxic shit and patch up holes with other sorts of toxic shit and seal the whole thing with different toxic shit.'

Charlie sounded more regretful than angry. 'Do you ever get depressed, Mr Hill.'

'Call me, Steele. I guess we all do sometimes.'

A wave of sadness crossed Charlie's face. 'People who say that, who say everyone gets depressed at some time, are usually the lucky ones. They don't get real depression. They don't get so anxious they can't open the door to collect the mail. How old do you think I am, Steele?'

I replied truthfully I was no good at ages but he insisted. I decided to be kind and shave a couple of years off what I thought his age was. '47-48,' I said.

It turned out he was 38-years-old. 'I have grey hair. I have emphysema and I've never smoked in my life. I have depression, migraines, and anxiety attacks. I take seven types of medications every day. Some of my medicines are not subsidised on the pharmaceutical benefits scheme. After I started to get depressed, Amy took the kids and left.'

This was not going well. I could not see any lead-in to questions about Charlie's debt to the Gooroo. 'Doesn't the Air Force pay for your medication?'

'I've been battling them for compensation for three years. They keep saying it is under assessment but my condition could have been caused by something else. I never had a day's sickness in my life before this. I thought that would work in my favour but they say they haven't got my medical records to eliminate other possibilities.

'They have their own medical records on me. The Air Force won't give them to a journalist following my story. They say they're protecting my privacy. Even my specialists are having trouble getting information from the Air Force. I'm just about at the end of my tether. If I can put enough money together, I'm going to Vietnam. It's cheaper to live over there and I'm hoping I get to keep my invalid pension. I don't think I've got that long anyway.'

Not knowing what to say, I sat silent for a while. 'I probably can't do much, Charlie. But if there's anything, here's my phone number. There is one thing, though.'

'Yes.'

'If I leave you 20 bucks, will you promise to buy yourself two giant jars of expensive coffee?'

He smiled ruefully and the deal was done.

I knew the Gooroo would anonymously send Charlie the money for the airfare to Vietnam and some more to set himself up there. Who knew what tall tale Con concocted to explain why Charlie was receiving the windfall?

I did drop back into Barbara's place. I stopped calling her Barbie because she probably didn't like it. I told her the Gooroo had written off Charlie's debt and she was pleased.

Charlie and I corresponded for a while – neither of us owned a computer for those new emails thingos – and I was most pleased when he wrote he was seeing a young woman.

His last letter to me told how he had lost his latest review for compensation and he was not sure if there were any more appeal avenues to travel down.

My last letter to Charlie was returned to me along with a note from the Vietnamese police. Charlie Barra had hung himself.

VISIT TO A NEW WRITERS' MEETING
Vera Murray

I WENT TO A NEW and distant writers group, hoping to get help to polish up my poetry, and head with speed, through the door marked *Success*. The co-ordinator said, 'This group is like family,' and I guess it's true, 'cause the room was full of characters I could write about for years.

All were female members, except for one lone male. He brought 'beaut' biscuits; made by his own hand. They were at once commandeered by the largest lady present.

A late-comer arrived. Her dog was on a leash. She let it loose, to squeeze 'tween our legs to search for bits of bickies dropped, then gobbled up real quick – unseen by most.

Nearly all the readings were quite interesting. But some were too revealing – mainly of emotions that ran higher and higher as the writer reads them.

One lady, with red-ringed eyes, outlined the confrontation within her family group . . . part of a family altercation. It seemed it had gone on for years. 'So sad,' I thought.

Another lady past her prime read a poem of lost love, but obviously not forgotten but I missed a lot, 'cos somewhere in the midst of it, I dozed off 'til the clapping.

Yet another shed some tears, while reading the life history of a long departed family member, or so I think he was, who died bravely in some war . . . out there somewhere . . . seems he won the war on his own.

One large lady with an accent too thick to be recognised as English, bored us all into a state of semi-consciousness, as she travelled through what seemed reams of written words galore.

She did receive a reprimand from the 'boss cockie' himself, who said in soft tones, 'What excellent work, but it could've been . . . umm . . . , a wee bit . . . a lot . . . ..umm . . . shorter.'

I agreed with him.

She tossed her head and gave a sour grin before she flopped down heavily back into her chair, almost making it collapse.

All finished. Good! What!! All eyes are now on me, with nods, and grins on faces. After I watched many nods and finger-pointing, I coughed several times before stretching my body as I stood and faced them all, to tell the best story of the day.

First, a lengthy description of my pet mouse who snuck onto a space ship and then got off and got lost on Mars. I heard his cries for help through his 'telesender' and so I sent my cat via long range catapult to go and find him.

I landed her on a U.S space ship, passing over slowly, with orders to hide. Once on Mars she soon found him and they crept back and hid on the space ship.

'As the return ship passed over my house the two parachuted down to me.'

'Where are they now?' you ask. 'The mouse is happily living behind the kitchen fridge. The cat? Oh yes. She, with her nine kittens – not hard to guess who their father is – have pride of place under the kitchen sink, where I placed a mini moon which glows above a miniature space ship for them to get used to for their next trip.'

I was clapped madly.

About to leave, one lady collared me, intending to chat. Apparently she dreamed of being an actress, but had to give that up 'cause being half deaf, she couldn't hear the prompts, or, if any, clapping.

If they did clap instead of probably falling asleep, I thought. She gave a 'demo' to prove what she had told me twice already. Don't know what it was exactly, and still don't. I nodded, smiled, and almost ran away.

They want me back. I don't think I will go back, but then I must . . . to find out how some stories end. Like if Jo's 2nd moon returns, or is it hiding, or lost forever? And, I want to know if Bill's elephant is rescued after that angry ant who hid in his trunk thinking it was a tree is finally lured out and sent off home.

TRANSITIONS
Pauline Davies

'PETRIE STATION, platform on the right-hand side.' I glanced up from my book as a punk kid wearing a back-to-front baseball cap charged too late towards the closing doors. He slammed his fists against them and let out a roar of frustration and rage. As he swung round his wild eyes darted around the carriage and saw the afternoon commuters watching with interest. Suddenly embarrassed he plonked into a seat, hunched over his phone and prodded the screen with urgent fingers. The voice of my upbringing said, *stupid sod, missed his stop, should have been paying attention.*

He told someone on the other end of the phone that he'd try to catch a bus from the next stop. *He'll be lucky*, I thought. The next stop was mine and I knew Dakabin Station had no services; only a shelter and an automated ticket machine.

He was wearing the uniform of his generation: hoody, backpack, trainers, long shorts and t-shirt. His pale skin hinted at long hours in front of a gaming console, and the pimples on his face suggested he was around seventeen or eighteen. His phone call over, he leaned back in his seat, his face impassive as he gazed out of the window – his jiggling right leg the only indicator of his agitation. At least he had a way of communicating. When I was his age it was a lot easier to get lost or stranded when arrangements didn't work out. That was back in the early eighties, before everyone carried mobile phones and ATM cards.

Thirty-five years have flashed past since I was his age, yet pockets of memories remain fresh and clear, especially those that hold some significance. As I sat back in the rattling carriage, I reflected that eighteen is an age when we're on the brink of adulthood and the million little moments we collect at that time can have a profound effect on shaping the person we become.

I was only eighteen when I met the man who was to become my husband, and was welcomed into his family by his mother.

When I first knew her, Norma was in her fifties, with small, lively brown eyes, a mass of black curls and fine olive skin. Brett was tall like his father had been, with the strong nose and high cheekbones of his mother – and he was very handsome. He was also a quiet non-drinker who had apparently given his mother less trouble than any of his brothers.

Norma enjoyed a chat as much as I did, and over the years I spent many long afternoons stretched out in an ancient sling back chair on her front porch listening to the stories of her life. Post-war Brisbane in the mid-forties sounded like an exciting place to live for a young woman with a nursing career. When Norma talked of those times she smiled and described hats and gloves worn with dresses that cost a week's wages; going out to dances with her friends in the evenings; and taking the tram to Fortitude Valley for shopping trips on days off.

Her face grew sad though when she shared stories from her childhood. She described the times she and her younger brother were left at home while their mother was on a three-day bender. Too young to be in school, nobody noticed they'd been left to fend for themselves, surviving on tap water and biscuits by day and clinging together in fear at night.

When their mother left for good, the Nudgee Orphanage provided dubious shelter for a few years until Norma was released into domestic service at the age of fourteen; swapping life under the rule of tyrannical nuns to one of dodging the wandering hands of the head of the family. The turning point in Norma's life came at the age of eighteen when her nursing training led to good wages and independence.

She soon traded that freedom for marriage to a merchant seaman after a short and passionate romance, and though he turned into a volatile alcoholic, she acknowledged that in buying the solid timber house in the inner northern suburb of Brisbane, her husband had given her the only home she'd ever known.

'They were the best times,' she'd say, with her faraway look. 'When the kids were little and their dad was away at sea.'

But when the older boys were teenagers, clashes with their father often brought lights and sirens to the house, and the twitching of curtains in the street. Norma used to say that's when Brett would retreat to the back steps where he'd sit with his arm around the dog, waiting for the trouble to be over.

Brett and I found our own place shortly after we met, but we were frequent visitors to his old family home. We used to take Norma out for a meal on Friday nights and she always made an occasion of it by dressing up in style with bold colours and fashionable shoes, even though we only ever went to the local services club.

Even after all these years I can remember one of those evenings clearly because of an incident that occurred as we were driving Norma home. As we turned into her dimly lit street, I saw a man hunched over on the ground with his head bowed down over his knees.

'Look at that drunken bum over there,' I said, hoping my tone conveyed an element of pious condemnation.

Norma leaned forward from the back seat and spoke to Brett. 'Pull over a minute, would you, Love?'

'What?' I shrieked in surprise.

When he slowed the car, I shouted at him. 'Keep driving!'

'Just stop here for me, Brett.' Her voice was soft but commanding.

As Brett pulled up against the kerb, panic made my heart pound as I foresaw my boyfriend's mother being attacked by a drunken stranger.

'What do you think you're doing, Norma? Get back in the car!' But she was already heaving herself out of the back seat.

Brett glanced at his Mum as she hobbled over the grass in her high heels, handbag clutched under her arm. She reached the man and bent over him for a few moments then motioned for us to move on. To my horror, Brett eased the car away from the kerb and drove the fifty or so metres to his mother's house.

'What are you doing? You can't leave her out there!'

I had always liked that Brett was a man of few words, but at that moment I found his silence infuriating. He walked up the path of his family home, unlocked the front door and went through the empty house to the kitchen. I trailed behind, still berating him. I'm not sure whether I was angrier at her disregard for her own safety or his passive obedience. I didn't stop ranting until I heard the solid clink of the front grilled security door and Norma's crackly high-pitched voice.

A man's low, muffled voice responded to hers, causing me to feel a spike of alarm.

Norma's tone was warm assurance. 'It's all right, Love. Just go on through to the kitchen. I won't be a minute.'

A startled young man appeared in the doorway and lingered there, his eyes blinking as they adjusted to the light. He wore jeans and a collared shirt that looked like it might have been ironed before he went out that evening, but now it was partly untucked, and his hair was dishevelled. Neither of us greeted him, nor invited him to come into the room, so he hovered in the doorway, taking in the hostile atmosphere. To his credit he managed a few words.

'Your Mum's an amazing woman.' His voice was husky and tentative.

I felt obliged to be the spokesperson since my boyfriend had apparently taken a vow of silence. My response was cold and begrudging.

'Yeah, well, she's raised five boys.'

Norma called him back and I realised later she had steered him into the kitchen so she could go to her bedroom where she hid her cash. He turned towards her voice and I heard her asking his address as she dialled a number on the living room telephone.

The taxi took ten minutes to arrive and while she and the man sat on the front porch waiting, Brett and I sat in silence in the kitchen. By the time she came back to the kitchen my anger had subsided – I was just glad she was safe, and the stranger was out of the house.

I tried to question her, but she brushed away my concerns. 'He was all right. Just had a few too many drinks, that's all.'

As I watched her put the kettle on the gas stove and set out cups, I realised this incident wasn't significant for them, but for me: It was the first time I had witnessed a selfless act of kindness towards a stranger. I remembered my parents stopping to help a guy who had hit a kangaroo on a country road and come off his bike, but for the most part we minded our own business. Looked after our own. And if someone found themselves in strife because they were worse for wear from drink, it damn well served them right. Until that moment I hadn't considered there was any other way to live.

The last time I saw my mother-in-law she was in her eighties and teetering on the edge of life; her shallow breaths forcing oxygen into a heart and body that had long since given up the will to live. It was hard to know how much remained of the vibrant and compassionate woman I had known, but I sensed that what was left longed for the beckoning embrace of the darkness.

* * * * *

'Dakabin Station, platform on the left-hand side.'

Baseball cap boy was first off the train and I saw him charging around the platform asking people if there were any buses to the shopping centre. Someone told him no, he'd have to take the next train in the opposite direction to the buses at Petrie Station. Should be one along in half an hour.

The kid's face went back to the wild-eyed panic of a few minutes earlier. I started to walk away. Not my problem.

Go on Love, it's only ten minutes out of your way. Norma's crackling voice was warm and familiar inside my head.

I can't say I gave him a lift gladly, but I found myself unable to leave him stranded there.

My beautiful mother-in-law had a long and difficult life, and it would be easy to believe her only tangible legacy in this world is in the genes of the children and grandchildren who remain, but I believe there's more to humanity than that. The ripples of our actions continue long after we're gone. Norma gave me the unconditional love of a mother, which I passed on to my own children. She also showed me that we can care for people beyond our tribe. So, if I help a stranger, I don't do it for any sense of satisfaction or expectation of gratitude, I do it to honour her.

A TURNING WHEEL CONNECTS
Caryn Jacobs

IF HE'D HAD A SHOTGUN he would have walked out with it for dramatic effect. Instead, Stan burst onto the front landing of his neat Queenslander home and yelled,

'I told you, Boy, to stay off my property!'

Outside the front gate below, stopping in his tracks with one hand on the gate latch, the boy's cherub-round face whipped up towards Stan without making eye contact. Releasing the gate latch quickly, the boy's fingers pushed his glasses up his sweaty nose, then interlaced with the other hand. Stan noticed him swallow and take a step back.

'Sir . . . I didn't . . . I didn't step inside the gate, I promise.'

Stan let the silence hang. The boy was right, he was not actually on his property yet.

'I'm sorry sir . . . about yesterday,' he stammered on, 'I didn't mean to break your gate. I needed to hide.'

The boy's hands flapped briefly at his sides then linked up again, squeezing together. Stan thought he could hear a low, monotone hum. The boy was staring intently at the gate post.

'Well then? What do you want?' Stan growled, even though the answer was obvious.

'Sir, can I please get my bike back?' The boy rocked from one leg to the other.

The boy's nervousness disarmed Stan. He had sworn he would never be the cause of white-faced fear in another again, yet the rut of ingrained patterns enjoyed their well-worn paths. Evie had helped him change tack. But she was gone, and old ways were so quick to return. He could stop this script. He needed to stop this script.

Stan sighed. His stance deflated and he descended the porch steps. He looked over at the boy who was still staring intently at the gate post.

'Come on then. It's over here.'

The boy opened the broken gate tentatively and trotted after him.

The bike's muddy tyre tracks had wounded Stan's otherwise immaculate lawn, and he looked pointedly at it when he turned around to check that the boy was following.

The large crack down the length of a terracotta pot fuelled his irritation further. He had used twine to hold it together in the interim, and he hoped the roots of his flowering lemon tree had not been damaged.

The shed was around the back. A footpath ran along the outside of the fence. Trapped heat from the humid summer day escaped as Stan went inside and turned on the light.

'Whoooaaa!' exclaimed the boy. His face lit up as he caught sight of row upon row of neatly arranged spanners, screwdrivers and allen keys. Workbenches filled with cogs, oil cans and spray paint awaited hands that would find the perfect use for them.

'So many wheels!' The boy was drinking in the view of all kinds of wheels, hanging in size order on one wall.

Taken aback, Stan tried to see his old shed through the boy's eyes. It had been years since anyone had intruded this far into his personal space and everything in him needed to divert the situation. Grabbing the bicycle handles he wheeled the bike outside and closed the shed door, snapping the boy out of his reverie. The boy closed his mouth and pushed his glasses up his nose as he looked at his ruined bike. He started to hum and shift his weight side to side. The front wheel was bent, with spokes spearing out offensively into the air. The handlebars and seat were askew. The paint was scratched.

Stan watched the boy reach haltingly for the bicycle, revealing a grazed elbow stained faintly grass-green. He had seen brazen rebellion and he had seen rude indifference. He saw none of that in the boy standing before him now, fighting an inward collapse and not giving in. Something inside him shifted – the first drop of a thawing ice block. He heard Evie's voice, 'Stan, Honey, he's just a boy.'

'So who were you hiding from?' asked Stan.

'Cameron Maclean, sir. If they catch me they grab my bag, dump my books, steal my lunch.' Instinctively, he looked down and continued guiding his broken treasure out of the front gate.

'Hmmm.' Stan knew what it was like to be chased.

That evening Stanley James Woodford sat in his old maroon armchair as he did every evening. He had cooked his meal and washed up as he did every evening. He had turned on the news as he did every evening, but this evening he was not listening to headlines. The afternoon's visit looped over in his mind as his fingers absently traced Evie's embroidery on the armrest covers. The bullying. That wrecked bicycle. The transformation in the boy's face. Stan knew exactly what to do with that bike. His hands were itching again. It had been so long since they had given life to something. So long since the smell of grease had lingered in his fingernails. So long since feeling the satisfaction of slotting in a wheel, tightening a bolt, and testing the spin. But just as quickly his old enemy, memory, ambushed the picture forming in his head. Before he could stop himself his mind warped the bicycle wheel into the wheelchair wheel. His thoughts went back to when he would sit in the shed, spanner tightening, wheel turning, and safe solitude permitting tears to wet his cheeks. Evie would sit vacantly on the porch, there only in body. The guilt engulfed him once again. Shame birthed a new thought – he hadn't even asked the boy's name.

He was weeding the geranium bed edging the front path when the unannounced visitor arrived the following day, just as the evening scent of jasmine was beginning to sing. He had seen her a few times before in the grocery store. She smiled as he stood up, limbs creaking.

'Good evening, Mr Woodford. My name is Kelly. I live five houses down.' Her voice was calm, so calm, yet she wiped her palms down the front of her plain dress, and he saw her take a slow breath.

'Good evening.' He was content to be polite.

'Mr Woodford, I apologise for my son's . . . intrusion . . . on your home. I came to see if there's any way we could make things right.' She gestured towards the splintered gate post. Stan had started to repair it, but it needed a good sanding and varnish.

'He told me he had broken a plant pot too.'

She had the same softness in her eyes as Evie once had, and he couldn't muster his usual gruffness. He sighed and waved his hand.

'Oh, you're alright. There's nothing that can't be easily replaced.' Then before she could reply, 'It sounded like he was having a hard enough time already.'

She smiled and her eyes flitted away briefly.

'Thank you, Mr Woodford, you're very kind. Yes, Trevor's life at school is not easy because he's . . . a little different, but I think he was a little harsh on you – it was probably just fear.' She laughed lightly, but Stan simply turned the trowel around in his hand. So the boy's name was Trevor.

'Well, er, yes,' he muttered in a gravelly voice.

Realising the possible insult, Kelly quickly corrected herself. 'Oh, I didn't mean,' she said . . . um, it wasn't *fear* . . . oh, dear.'

'I know there's talk about me in this neighbourhood, Mrs Kelly,' Stan growled, guard up. 'They get all offended at me. They think I'm unfriendly, but all I want is to be left in peace.' He turned his back on her and began packing up his tools.

'Sorry about that, Mr Woodford. I think I know . . . er . . . I'm sensing that they might be wrong about you.'

Stan looked up at her.

'I've experienced loss too, Mr Woodford. My husband, Trevor's dad, died of cancer. It's not something that is easy for others to understand, being the one left behind.' His motionless silence urged her on. He was listening.

'Mr Woodford, there's a reason I came here without Trevor. Ever since he saw your shed, he has not stopped talking about it. The thing about Trevor is that he can become . . . obsessed with things, to the point where nothing else will distract him. He has always loved anything with wheels, since he was a baby. It's a love that he and his father shared.' Crepuscular light threw her face in and out of shadow, but he could tell the lines there were kind ones, so he did not stop her stumbling on.

'My husband worked in the Holden factory, you see, assembling cars. Building toy cars together was the way he and Trevor seemed to connect best.'

Stan's body turned to ice, and his head whirled. All he could see was the blue Holden Commodore rammed up against a pole, windscreen shattered.

Kelly hurtled on. 'Well, I was wondering, Mr Woodford . . . that is, is there any chance you would consider . . . um . . . helping him repair his bicycle? I'm afraid I wouldn't know where to start on it, and we can't afford to buy another one right now.'

Stan could hear Kelly, but his body was taking him elsewhere. Evie's beautiful head on the dashboard, blood flow creeping over her face as he watched in horror. She looked asleep. If only she were just asleep. The thick blanket of darkness descended once again, threatening to smother him.

'Mr Woodford? Mr Woodford? You've gone very pale.' Kelly's hand on his shoulder pulled him out of the flashback. Human touch for the first time in . . . had it been five years of living like this? He hadn't been aware of her coming through the gate.

Trying to regain composure, he started to speak, but what croaked out of his mouth was simply, 'My wife . . . um . . .' He cleared his throat. 'My wife . . . Evie. She died in a Hold . . . she died nine months after a car accident.' In which I was driving, was what he didn't say.

As if remembering to breathe, he took a deep breath and glanced at Kelly. Tears had filled her eyes, and she could not speak. She didn't need to. She understood. When last had he been understood?

'I need to sit down.' And then, before he could stop the words, 'Yes, I can help your boy.' Leaving her and walking like a limping soldier using his last ounce of energy, he ascended the house steps and melted into his house.

Trevor's free hand flicked and flapped as he bounded into Stan's front yard with his bicycle the following day. As though by an unspoken agreement, neither one needed to say anything to explain, but Trevor knew the protocol.

'Good day, Mr Woodford.'

'You can call me Stan, Son. And your name is Trevor, I hear.'

'Yes, sir, Mr Stan.'

They looked at each other, uncertain of the next step.

'Trevor, do you know what the name Cameron means?'

'No, Mr Stan.'

'It means crooked nose.'

Trevor stared blankly at his feet, and rocked once. Then he snickered.

'Crooked nose,' he repeated. 'That's funny.'

They chortled together.

'Now, Son, let's have a look at that bicycle of yours. That wheel is done for.'

Seizing the invitation to talk about the mechanical workings of the bicycle, Trevor added without pause, 'And the chain's broken, and the gears don't work and the frame is bent.'

'Yeah. That will all need some work. I think I have a good wheel replacement to start, though.' As the shed door opened this time, Stan found himself anticipating the gleam in Trevor's eye and he was not disappointed. Trevor walked directly to the arrangement of wheels along one wall and ran his hands over the tyre treads, trickling his fingers between the spokes. 'This one!' Trevor exclaimed. Stan found himself smiling.

In cool shade outside the shed, Stan laid out a tarpaulin on the lawn and they began to dissemble the injured bicycle. Trevor's impulsiveness meant he needed to be cautioned to slow down a few times, but the boy knew how to handle the parts and the tools for them. He chattered in a lilting monologue about each part and the tool that he was using and how he was using it. 'My Dad told me to keep the nuts and bolt tight but never too tight,' and, 'My Dad showed me how to shift the gears so you can get the chain on more easily.' Stan's heart was warmed by the forgiveness and trust of this boy towards this abrasive old man who had scared him half to death just yesterday.

'Your Dad sure was a clever man to teach you as much as you know now.'

'Yes, he was. Yes, he was,' Trevor said in a sing-song way. 'He died of chronic myeloid leukaemia. He died when I was eight, on 22 January 1980.' Then he began to hum.

Stan recognised the monotone hum. He had heard it at the gate when they first met, and when Trevor first saw his ruined bike. It was a signal that all was not well inside Trevor. The boy seemed matter-of-fact but Stan was familiar with the inside darkness of grief. Stan's signal was isolation.

'I can tell you miss him, Son.' Stan's voice was thin, and he cleared his throat to loosen its constriction.

'Yes, I do. Yes, I do.' The hum continued.

'He told me I should never stop building things with wheels. He told me I was good at that.' A reflective pause.

'Like you, Mr Stan.' Stan looked at him and had no response to this unexpected assumption.

'Aaah,' he offered.

'What are you going to build with all your wheels, Mr Stan?' Trevor's grease-covered fingers left the cogs he was manoeuvring, to push up his glasses, leaving a black stripe along his nose.

Memories of Evie's wheelchairs assaulted Stan. None were good enough. The one she got from the hospital was rudimentary and nowhere near his standards for her. The first wheelchair he fabricated couldn't navigate her favourite bush walk because the wheels were too small. The second one didn't recline enough when she was in pain. The third one . . . well he couldn't get the smell out of it. The fourth one . . . and the fifth . . . he could remember each one of them and each fastidious adjustment to make Evie that bit more comfortable. He was sorry, so, so sorry.

He would give his life to go back in time to that disastrous moment, to do it differently and save her. This unfulfillable wish plagued his dreams. She was the softness strong enough to accommodate his sharpness. She was calm when his mind was filled with fear and panic. Her eyes were the ones that could see the goodness in his soul. Her heart was the one that brought him healing. And then all those parts of her were gone, with just her body left functioning. Nine months later her body gave up and all he had left was her fragrance on the scarf in her bedside drawer.

'I don't know, Son,' he replied in honesty. 'What would *you* build with all these wheels?'

Another turn of the lock ring and the gear cassette in Trevor's hands came free. 'Yaaaah!' he exclaimed as he held the bent cogs high above his head in triumph and looked at Stan with shining eyes. 'Go carts!' He counted silently on his fingers. 'You could make four of them. And race! My Dad showed me how to make a go cart. I can show you.' He squeezed his hands together.

Stan leaned back in his chair and looked through his shed door as Trevor might have. Instead of seeing a wheelchair graveyard, he saw endless possibilities for a ten-year-old boy obsessed with wheels. The boy gave this old shed another chance at life.

Autumn is not distinctive in Brisbane, but the occasional tell-tale sign of bare branches was evident when Stan ventured to the new bike park at Trevor's request. Trevor had discovered a friend who loved wheels almost as much as he did, and it was time to put their self-made go carts through their paces.

A quiet section on the low wall surrounding the bike park was shaded by a flowering silky oak. Stan perched on the section where a sheen of the setting sun rested on him. The voices peppered around him in various volumes of conversation were strangely comforting amidst the familiar chatter of lorikeets coming in to roost overhead.

On the other side of the park Stan spotted Kelly talking to another mother. As Kelly's visual scan patrolled the tracks for her son's whereabouts, she caught sight of Stan, waved at him and smiled. The mother of Trevor's new friend followed Kelly's line of vision and waved too. Stan nodded in polite acknowledgement and waved back.

Four sets of wheels skidded past him in a blur of seats, metalwork, pedals and boys in intense pursuit.

'Mr Staaa . . . n!'

'Go Trevor! Go, David!' he yelled back as loudly as his vocal cords would permit, but the boys were already out of earshot.

He watched a detached flower float a gentle descent from the tree above. He thought of his empty maroon armchair at home. He had just missed the news. He imagined the disbelief on his own face if his present self could describe to his four-month-ago self how he would be cheering on two boys in go carts he had helped them make, and waving and smiling to others in the park.

The flower reached the ground and fused into the carpet of colours already there. He mused over the unexpected story held in the scarred fibres of his repaired gate post and the glue of a repaired terracotta plant pot. For the first time since Evie's accident he was consciously aware of the soft luminescence of human connection that glowed within him.

A CLOUDED MIND

Bakthi Ross

Fear overpowered her emotions,
She cannot see reality like a suicidal person.
She could kill herself without feeling any pain.

Standing alone and a gun on Martha's back,
Pressing against her but she did not tremble.
She faced death many times,
Martha knew it was coming.

The man with a gun pushing against her,
For no good reason had a heart attack.
Rather than Martha having a heart attack,
The man fell backwards and died.

No wallet. No identity,
Nothing to find out why he wants to kill Martha,
Martha relieved, but stood there staring at the dead man.
She took his gun and took some photos of him.

He was wearing winter clothes in a hot climate,
His coat had a tag said 'Soft Wool',
Made in some European country.
With the worn tag she could not clearly see,
Where he could have come from.

His face was the only clue she had,
By the time she gets help to find out who he was,
His body would have decomposed.

She could not get rid of the image of his face and the stare,
The fear should have gone off her after his death but it did not,
Because she did not know who he was.

From the edge of the cliff she added another fear,
That kept pushing her to the edge,
The overhanging fear really taken over Martha's mind.

Someone going to kill her one day!
It is because of her past,
She could not get rid of them wherever she went.
It haunted her everywhere.

She was at the end of her tether with fear.

THE CURIOUS TALE OF STOLEN BLACK ART
David MacLaughlin

JIMMY WAS THINKING about his previous trips overseas. He had retired and lived by himself in a city unit complex. Now he was on the Nambour Express, meandering its way past the green undulating farming country on his way for a short break holiday. Jimmy used the rail system frequently and now he was enjoying the rhythm of the train as he reflected on some edgy adventures in countries far from Australian shores.

THE WALKING TOUR GUIDE on a hot summer afternoon in the city of London pointed out a terrace town house where Conan Doyle the author of the Sherlock Holmes detective novels had lived. Jimmy had noticed another plaque in the same street with the name Samuel Pepys. Doyle wrote about a fictitious character while Pepys in his diary recorded the real life of the people of London. Jimmy was fascinated by the culture of his own country and of elsewhere. In Brisbane Jimmy had a group of multicultural mates who met for a monthly lunch and exchanged tall stories to each other. There was a Scot, a couple of Germans, a Kiwi, a Pommy, and a few Anglo Australians. His Aboriginal artist mate George would attend when not selling his expensive paintings to wealthy Australians interstate. The group's tall tales seemed mundane compared to what Jimmy's own life sometimes turned out.

NOW HIS MIND REVERTED to the aftermath of his literary London walking tour. Jimmy was en route to the French village of Laroque Des Alberes in the Pyrenees near the Spanish border where he could stay in a friend's villa and eat and drink like the locals. The place was steeped in the history of Roman and Hannibal invasions. The area also buzzed with the gossip of Nazi and SS art looting being hidden in the mountainous territory and secluded derelict buildings which abounded in this Catalan area. Indigenous George had a theory about how the two Aboriginals that New South Wales Governor Arthur Philip brought to the UK in 1792 and who supposedly died there actually had absconded, then made their way to Australia through this Catalan country. If they had died in England where were their bones buried? None could be found. Jimmy knew a London Dulwich Art Gallery curator and they discussed the possibilities over a morning tea of massive scones and cream at the Gallery café overlooking the green expanse of Dulwich Park. The curator confirmed he had heard rumours about missing art treasures and also about black painters who were not African being in the region for a short while. None of their paintings had yet been found. Also, he mentioned that stolen expensive art works were used as a form of currency by criminal groups such as the Mafia in exchange for drug deals. Jimmy now began to realise that George's theory might be credible and he would keep him informed of any progress by smart phone when he was the Laroque region of France.

THE NAMBOUR EXPRESS CONTINUED its picturesque route through the wooded hills and slopes of the volcanic soils approaching Nambour. Jimmy was looking forward to meeting up with his Aboriginal mate George and his wife at their art studio. The rhythm of the train made him relax as he was thinking of his visit to Laroque and the nagging thoughts of missing indigenous art. Stolen art was one thing but if George was right where was evidence of the art of two Australian natives that had accompanied Governor Arthur Philip on his return to England. Anyway why bother about this conspiracy theory it's all fake news.

JIMMY CURSED HIS REFERENCE to Donald Trump and how the world followed his every Twitter post. Jimmy had plenty to occupy his mind with leisurely eating and having coffee in the small cafes and bars in the village. Lately he noticed he seemed to be the centre of attention and receiving furtive glances when dining out. Was he being followed and why? After a morning of social tennis with French and English locals he heard that the local gendarmerie (police) had raided a hill top property looking for drugs. No drugs were found but only boarded up mine shafts and disused sheds. The slopes of the Pyrenees were close to Laroque. So were the coastal ports of Colliure, an artist's town and Port Vendre, a former military base used by the Germans during WWII to transport wounded troops from the north African campaign to French hospitals.

COMMUNITY RESENTMENT STILL EXISTED from the days of the Vichy Government cooperating with the invading German army. Jimmy heard snippets of this while having coffee at a harbour side café in Port Vendre. Tales of the Catheus and black Madonna could be heard in furtive buzzes of conversation as he smelt the aroma of freshly ground coffee beans and just baked pastries. His coffee companion Joan a retired French speaking teacher had been researching the local folklore of how two black men who were not African had come from England. They wanted to return to their home island continent in the far off South Seas.

JIMMY SMILED INWARDLY and thought Joan's ideas a bit like those of George and both were a bit fanciful. Then again the Dulwich art curator mentioned the same rumours. In time he would change his mind but that was much later. Jimmy was enjoying the Plats du Jour (daily lunch special) and was dismissing the theory of two aboriginals painting and travelling through this Pyrenees region. Joan was more observant.

'MORE CARS ARE PASSING ALONG and slowing down as they pass the café.' she remarked. 'Some are taking phone photos as they pass. I can see the reflection as the phone catches the sun. Very strange. Jimmy, someone knows you are around.' She smiled demurely.

He shrugged his shoulders and was not keen on pursuing some sort of conspiracy theory. Joan exhilarated him as she was always thinking outside the square and this challenged him to question his long held views.

On their way back to Laroque using the coastal route which took in some mountain driving he stopped at a deserted property which he knew had former mine shafts and disused outhouses.

'This is the sort of place where stolen art and collectables were hidden and later sold by the local mafia to pay for large drug deals,' Joan uttered.

'Of course,' Jimmy replied, not that he agreed but it was useless to verbally disagree with her. Suddenly, a flash of reflective light could be seen on one of the outhouses. 'We are being followed Jimmy. I told you people have long memories here and do not want the past to disturb their view of the world.' She smiled at him.

They returned to Laroque as Jimmy was leaving the next day going to return to London via Bilbao in Spain. Bilbao was Joan's idea as it was the home of the Guggenheim Museum of modern art. 'Aboriginal Art used dot painting long before Monet and his contemporaries,' Joan had mentioned and Jimmy had not thought the connection had any relevance. Joan knew one of the art curators at the Guggenheim so what had Jimmy to lose. Precisely nothing as he always wanted to see this former derelict ship building town now revitalised and on the world tourist map for art and culture.

MEANWHILE BACK IN THE NAMBOUR HINTERLAND north of Brisbane George the indigenous artist mate of Jimmy was preparing for another of his expensive art shows organised by his wife Penny. George relied on his wife's marketing skills and his art exhibitions always attracted buyers willing to pay a premium for his style of Indigenous art . He had a similar theory to Jimmy's friend Joan in that the two Aboriginals did not die in England but travelled back to Australia via France. He was going to make a surprise visit to Jimmy and Joan in Bilbao as he was familiar with the Guggenheim's art purchases of modern art. His wife would be there at the same time after her visiting lecture tour at a state university in North America. George had an inkling that Jimmy's curiosity and hyperactive imagination over missing art treasures could lead to some undesired outcomes and he needed to keep him in check for his own safety.

In Bilbao it's bright and clear. The regional town surrounded by hills and close to the northern Spanish coastal town of San Sebastian was bathed in sunlight. Jimmy was pleasantly surprised as he caught glimpses of the town's revitalised old architecture and the sweeping view of the striking Guggenheim.

'Wow,' he exclaimed. 'I must see inside that place.'

Outside his inner city Ibis Hotel he took in the sights of the locals bustling amongst the numerous cafes and eateries displaying enticing tapas and the local version known as pintxos. He was within walking distance of the Guggenheim and soon could see the angled outline of the iconic building as it glistened 'silver in the sunlight. When he finally reached the precinct he could understand more fully why this this huge modern building attracts visitors from all over the world. He was curious to see if the interior and art works were as awe-inspiring as the building was from the outside. Also, Joan had organised her curator friend to chat with Jimmy.

The entrance foyer was magnificent, spacious and full of colour from huge Spanish decorations hanging seemingly unattached from the modern angled architecture and struts. All very spectacular but where was the art and exhibitions he thought to himself. His eye caught the lift sign that indicator floors to the art galleries. Modern glass and metal elevators took him to a gallery floor. Nothing boring about this building as Jimmy made his way past a railed galley with views of the city from all areas. His reaction was 'have not seen one picture but this setting is an art gallery on its own.'

To view the paintings he walked along the external narrow passage which curved around the interior of the building amongst the steel engineered struts. Colourful hanging drapes in the vivid Spanish style adorned the entrances to the floor galleries. The passage way was open with metal railings to prevent the paying customers falling to the entrance foyer which was clearly seen from the first floor. The passage way was crowded and as he peered over the railings he felt a sharp nudge from behind which propelled him against the railings and almost half toppled his upper body over the rail. Jimmy quickly moved to the centre of the passage way and tried to catch a glimpse of how or who had pushed into him. Nothing obvious, so he continued on his tour of the contemporary art on another two higher levels. Collections were from Picasso to Monet, and a variety of Spanish modern art featured black Madonnas. The latter fascinated Jimmy as it included some dot style paintings by unknown artists which were estimated to having been done around 18th century.

He had arranged to have coffee with the international curator that knew his friend Joan and that took place in the sunlit café at the front of the Guggenheim. Sipping a strong espresso the pretty Spanish curator made Jimmy feel as if he was young again. She spoke tossing her hair away from her face and had a sparkle in her eyes. Then she mentioned that they had some paintings from unknown artists which were painted in a manner not local to Spain or Europe. They were linked to the stories of the black Madonnas and bore a striking resemblance to Australian indigenous art. But, maybe just gossip she indicated, no real evidence as the artists could not be traced.

Jimmy thanked her for the information and how Joan's inferences on how international art houses had a vested interest in keeping art prices high for established artists. So recognition of some 18th century indigenous artist from the southern ocean would not be good news for the high prices auctioned for collectors at the moment.

The Guggenheim has spectacular architecture internally as well as externally. At ground level is a huge exhibition wing which is used for contemporary multimedia displays. Jimmy was examining a maze made from light building materials which took up most of the vacant space. He entered at one end and was following the snake like curves of surfing waves. Engrossed in how it was constructed he failed to notice a shadow overtake him and then a light shawl was tossed over his head so he could not see. In a flash he ripped it off his head and looked back to see three smiling familiar faces. Joan his French friend and indigenous artist George and wife Penny who had finally joined them after her art lecture tour had finished.

'Mate, you get in a mess when you charge around the globe on some artistic mission. We are here to help,' uttered George.

So Jimmy, George, Penny and Joan all adjourned to the Guggenheim café and ate tapas and had drinks discussing how valid the theory of Governor Phillip's Indigenous invitees actually returned to Australia having sold art work as the first impressionists and never died in England. George reminded the group that the two Aboriginals that accompanied Governor Arthur Phillip's to London in 1792 were the well-known Bennelong and another known as Yemmerrawanne. 'The Pommy tucker would not have been to their liking,' joked George. 'They reckon Yemmerrawanne died there but Bennelong got sick and returned to the colony. Bennelong was no artist but a smart leader of the Wangal clan and would know that paintings were valuable to European society. The other bloke Yemmerrawanne could have been a bit of a natural artist. Penny reckons he painted in London and his works were stolen and would be worth heaps today, even more than my art,' he said with a grin and a wink.

'That's why you are under observation as no collector wants to have to repatriate his paintings back to the country of origin. The Guggenheim could even have a couple of the paintings in their storage and are not game to exhibit them.' The group fell silent.

A YEAR PASSED and the Nambour Express train crawled its way to its destination. George and Penny greeted Jimmy and they drove to the art studio on the outskirts of the town. Set in rolling picture hills the studio nestled amongst some shady trees. Over coffee George uttered, 'Remember that trip to Bilbao and the Guggenheim Jimmy? Joan's contacts were essential in getting that pretty Spanish curator to show us where they archived the collection paintings. 'We found paintings, obviously Aboriginal but not what we thought eh?'

He continued his discourse. 'They were early Albert Namatjira brought to Europe by some German anthropologist and now worth millions. The Guggenheim just got them from a deceased estate as a gift. The young curator was smart, she knew who painted them as she had studied art in Australia during a student exchange while at University. She kept quiet about it as the Guggenheim governing board had Spanish government officials and large corporate art collectors on its art committees.'

To avoid the prohibitive costs of a court case, in which the Guggenheim's vast cash resources would be used to counter repatriation claims, it was better to mediate a satisfactory outcome for both parties. The deal that Penny and Joan brokered was pretty good. The Bilbao Guggenheim would exhibit the paintings and establish a permanent Aboriginal art exhibition display. Also, visiting art student scholarships would be established for cultural exchange between Australia and Spain.

The trio settled into a BBQ lunch and after a few glasses of chardonnay for the girls and Eumundi beer for the boys the conversion revolved around how the recent prices of early Aboriginal art had risen at recent auctions.

'Any paintings by even just one of those two Blackfellas brought to England by Arthur Phillip would be worth heaps now,' George exclaimed to Jimmy and anyone else who was listening. Jimmy after another sip of Eumundi uttered. 'Around your place in Nambour is just like a smaller version of the hilly and secluded Catalan hideouts near Laroque on the Spanish border. Nambour has a druggie scene and this area is a great place to hide stolen art works and sell them when prices are high for a drug deal. You may have some hidden here George and you wouldn't even know it.'

George and Penny chuckled over Jimmy's outlandish comments. George replied, 'Just in case that might have happened Jimmy I will put a security lock on my art paintings storage room.'

After finishing the BBQ lunch off with a delicious array of Nambour cheeses the trio passed through the sales area of the art gallery to where George painted and had a secure storage room.

Penny who was leading the group gave a startled gasp. 'The lock looks fine but the chair in front has been moved. She used a key to open the padlock on the door and went inside the storage room. She immediately pointed to an empty shelf. 'Ha, ha, some bright crim has taken a few of your copies of early dot paintings you were experimenting with and using as demos to students, George.'

So George and Jimmy had no evidence of any Aboriginal art painted during Governor Arthur Phillips trip back to the England by Bennelong and Yemmerrawanne. Just another conspiracy theory. Maybe not, as Jimmy's overactive mind pondered on the possibility that George knew where the missing art was and was cashing in on his own cultural heritage. Then another idea leaped into his head. How was it that the criminals knew about Jimmy's own Aboriginal art and stole some of it hoping to get bucks for it? Then use it to pay for a huge Sunshine Coast drug deal.

Jimmy did not live on the edge but his mind did.

RETROSPECTIVE: From the 2011 anthology:
Can you believe it . . .

BLUEY AND CLIFF'S COASTAL JOURNEY
Lorraine R. Noscova

TIME HAD COME TO START to organise their trip. It was their first trip without their parents. Just the two of them. Two teenage brothers. Cliff was the elder. He knew that he would have to ensure every detail of the trip was worked out. He had always helped his younger brother. Bluey had a problem. His skin was very light which meant that when he was out in the sun even for a short time, he would turn red. Sunburnt within a few minutes. That was why he got the nick name, Bluey. It had been a long time since anyone had called him by his Christian name of Colin. The sunburn would make his usually dry skin even drier.

This meant all travel would have to be done at night which was really when, in summer, they both felt more active, not just because they were teenagers but because they were teenage toads.

By nature in the hot months toads are more active at night as most people who have had to live with toads around will tell you. The croaking noise is loud and their long loud purring trill of their mating call is extremely annoying.

Bluey and Cliff had many relatives who had travelled this coastal trip. They would find out from them the route that would be the safest. They had to leave the safety of their parent's home amongst the rocks at Scotts Point and travel to Queens Beach and return in fourteen nights.

Sometimes the beach is safest when the tide is out. They had to find out the tide times for the nights they travelled in each section of their journey.

They turned on their toadavision to check the weather for the next seven days from the weather toad.

The questions they have to figure are huge.

What night and time do they start?

What do they take with them? Toads are so very lucky when they travel. Only humans have the problem of luggage. Toads have only their dry warty skin to worry about. No jackets, no shoes or boots, no umbrellas to cart with them.

How do they avoid the dangers that lurk on this journey?

They listed the hazards so they could figure how to overcome them.

They had to find out where the safest places would be to rest and stay safe during the day. This depended on where there would be enough food and enough shelter from humans.

What beaches they could travel on and when. They had heard horror stories of toads, even at night, being hit and flung by humans using large chunks of wood.

One of the absolute taboos was to travel during the day. The reasons for this was because there were many humans who attacked toads. They were told under no circumstances travel on the cool of the bitumen of the road no matter how much their feet burned from hopping. The chances of toads surviving even two minutes is nearly unheard of. It is just too dangerous. No toad is game enough to go and scrape a toad off the road to give it a decent burial. They were just left there. Sometimes their close family hold a vigil for a few nights.

Usually it is just said, 'Well he/she was told.'

Bluey and Cliff did not have to travel anywhere near the roads. Their fears were human. Humans on bicycles riding over them. 'Oh, how those humans laugh after their bicycle tyres has splattered one of us. The sound of the bang of a toad bursting, brings cheers and loud clapping and it seems to encourage them to run more toads down, just to hear us pop.'

The two brothers planned to start their trip on the night of the next full moon. At the end of their first nights journey they should reach where Margate Beach ends and Suttons Beach starts. No shortage of food there. It's a grassy area where plenty of small insects thrive. The second day they would eat and rest at the Settlement Cove Lagoon at Redcliffe. They would enjoy dining on the very juicy insects and small frogs that had gorged themselves on the scraps of food and drinks left by humans who swam and played there during the day.

At Eversleigh Road on the northern side of Redcliffe they would spend their third day in the stormwater drain, resting and visiting with friends and relations that lived there.

Onto Osbourne Point the fourth day. This would be the shortest part of their journey. Even though they had more relations to visit there, the chance to rest there meant that they would not be so fatigued when they finally reached the northern end of Queens Beach on the morning of the fifth day.

This would give the two brothers a couple of days and nights to see their northern relations and friends who moved there for the warmer weather and to enjoy the planned festivities. Early on the seventh evening they would start their return journey.

They set out. The full moon lit their way. Outside their home their parents said their goodbyes then sat and watched their two boys hop away.

As planned they reached the southern end of Suttons Beach by late morning. Only a few walkers were on the boardwalk. They did not worry the brothers. Most humans who walk at that time of the morning did not trouble toads. However the brothers knew of many stories that told of walking humans in the hours before daylight, kicking toads, just to see how far they could go. These poor toads often died when they hit land. The ones who survived tried to hop away but were usually kicked again and again till they too died. It was common knowledge in toad communities that if they were unfortunate to get kicked by humans and survive then keep still. Play dead. This was the safest and quickest way to ensure that one may survive. Humans did not seem to worry about kicking dead toads.

Hopping along Suttons Beach the next night was a delight for them. Everywhere there was an abundance of food scraps.

Fresh water dripped from the taps into pools. Lots of fresh spicy insects to eat. They were spicy as these insects also ate the leftover scraps from the human's meals.

Still they had to keep hopping. They had to get to Settlement Cove Lagoon and find a good place to rest where humans could not find them. This Lagoon area, they knew always had lots of humans gathering during the day and into the early evening especially on hot nights. This area too was another toads diners' delight.

Night three. Some humans were still at the Lagoon when it came time for Bluey and Cliff to recommence their trip. Quietly and quickly they hopped away. This was the most dangerous part of their journey. Even at night humans seemed to be everywhere. Some sat on the rocks. Some were walking along the footpath. Some were sitting on the grass. The tide was a long way out so some humans were sitting on the beach.

The brothers hopped along the rocks constantly alert for danger. Exhausted, just before daylight they reached the safety of the stormwater drain at Eversleigh Road. Their cousins were waiting for them and hopped with them to the safety of their abode.

Rested, they set out for Osbourne Point. This trip would not take long at all. They would meet up with quite a few relations and friends. Most of them about their age. All of them eagerly and excitedly looking forward to the two nights and days of open air fun and festivities for all toads at Queens Beach.

Party time.

The evening the events finished and they had to start their way home Bluey and Cliff were a little worse for wear. They were both so pleased that the first section of this return journey was the shortest. Once again Osbourne Point would give them the opportunity to rest and recuperate.

From Osbourne Point to the safety of the stormwater drain at Eversleigh Road was fairly enjoyable and they took their time enjoying the sights.

Leaving the safety of the drain and their family and friends they immediately became alert. No sightseeing this night for either of them. They had to have all their senses concentrating on any kind of danger. The tide was in. The noise of the ocean blocked out the sound of humans walking, running, talking and laughing.

In the early hours of the morning Settlement Cove Lagoon was in sight. Only toads and rats and insects around. No humans. They could relax a little. They hopped to the same spot they had stayed the week earlier.

From Settlement Cove Lagoon till the time they reached the northern end of Suttons Beach, they stayed alert. Hopping along Suttons Beach they once again enjoyed feasting on the meaty insects and drank from most of the pools of fresh water.

When they began the final section along Margate Beach, they both felt a sense of satisfaction from the fact that they had nearly completed this journey. How grown up they felt.

Only thirty more tadometers to go. They rested on top of a sand bag. A homecoming feast awaited them. Everyone they knew would be there.

Can you believe it, it is gatherings like these in a toad's life when they make the most noise.

How wonderful it was to be home. They sat upright on a page of an old newspaper looking at their parent's home. The rocks, logs and greenery all beckoned them welcome home.

RETROSPECTIVE: From the 2013 anthology:
Serendipity

YUSEF BOY

Bernie Dowling

Based on *Danny Boy*, this song was written after race riots on Cronulla Beach

Oh, Yusef boy, the cops, the cops are calling
From Labs to Libs, and down the racist slide.
The summer's gone, and all the goodwill's a dying
'Tis you, 'tis you must go and I must hide.

But come ye back when summer's in Cronulla
And when the rabble's hushed and done with blows.
'Tis I'll be here in sunshine or in duller.
Oh, Yusef boy, oh, Yusef boy; I love you so.

And if you come, and all the deejays are braying,
If I am dead, as dead I well may be,
I pray you'll find the place where I am laying
And kneel and say an 'Allah' there for me.

And I shall hear, though soft you tread above me
And all my grave will warm and sweeter be.
And then you'll kneel and whisper that you love me,
And I shall sleep in peace, asylum come to me.

Oh, Yusef boy, the cops, the cops are calling
From Labs to Libs, and down the racist slide.
The summer's gone, and all the goodwill's a dying
'Tis you, 'tis you must go and I must hide.

RETROSPECTIVE: From the 2013 anthology:
Serendipity

DEEP RIVER

Ronald Holt

NEARLY TEN YEARS HAD PASSED since that fateful night. Yet, even after all that time, no one had come any closer to solving the mystery of what really happened.

As an old detective of 30-years' experience in criminal investigation, I had been assigned by my Inspector to re-examine a number of cold case files and found this one quite intriguing. I had pondered over the confused set of facts for some time trying to make sense of them. Nothing really added up until I accidentally came across the missing piece in the puzzle.

One of the main problems for the original investigators had been that all of the witnesses offered differing versions of the events. All had been drinking heavily that night which had distorted their recollections. I tried to link the areas of agreement to see if anything stood out.

The only certainties were that John Lisicki, the town barber, had died under suspicious circumstances and the autopsy report could not positively identify the cause. The report recorded a high blood alcohol reading as well as other prescription medicines and unidentified substances in his system. While some combinations of alcohol and drugs can be lethal, this did not appear to be case. There must have been something else. Foul play was suspected.

He was a single man in his 40s, lived a quiet life, kept much to himself and, apart from his work, did not have much other community involvement. He lived alone since the death, a couple of years before, of his elderly mother for whom he had been carer. Rumours about his sexual preferences were explored but nothing untoward emerged. On the surface, John Lisicki was a model citizen who was well respected by his clientele. He did not seem to have any enemies and there was no motive for his sudden demise.

Everyone had a theory, of course, ranging from alien intervention to conspiracy, but the truth had remained hidden. Many thought he may have overheard something at work and was killed because it was not for his ears.

The differing accounts extended to what John Lisicki said with his dying breath. Two out of the six witnesses said his last words were 'deep river'. This was eventually discarded as probably being drunken slurred speech due the lack of any such rivers nearby. If that was what he had actually said, no one could work out what it meant.

I flicked through his personal effects looking for any other clues when a slip of paper with his hand-writing on it fell out of an old diary. It appeared to read 'Deep river' but on closer inspection, the break between the two words was after the second 'e' rather than after the 'p'. The second word ended in an 'a' which, when looked at that way, read 'Dee privera'. The 'p' looked like it could be a capital as in 'P'. What was that - a name, a brand, a place or something else? I was champing at the bit to follow this lead.

Criminal histories and driver's licence checks proved fruitless so I turned to the local telephone directory. There it was, Dee Privera, a local resident living in a nearby suburb. Maybe I was on to something. I could not get there quick enough.

The neatly painted cottage was surrounded by a white picket fence and a colourful floral display. It looked like something out of a picture book. *Hardly the home of killer*, I thought as I opened the gate and walked to the front door. It displayed an old faded sign, *Dee Privera, Herbalist*.

My knock with the shiny brass knocker was answered by an elderly lady with snow-white hair, pulled back in a bun. She wore wire-framed glasses and was dressed in a crocheted shawl, a frilly white blouse and long dark skirt. I tried to find a word to describe my first impression but only 'witch' came to mind. That was unfair and I chastised myself. A delightful old grandmother was probably more appropriate.

I introduced myself. 'Good morning. I am Detective Sergeant Colin Sloan from the Criminal Investigation Branch. I am looking for Dee Privera.'

'I am Dee Privera. I have been expecting you although it has taken you a long time to come,' she replied in a soft calm voice.

What did she mean, expecting me? I thought. I did not know myself that I was coming until less than an hour ago.

'Please come in. Would you like a cup of tea?' she asked politely.

I followed her inside, glancing around the room which resembled an antique furniture shop.

I was not used to drinking tea with suspects although Dee Privera was not your usual murder suspect. I replied, 'No thanks.'

She motioned towards an ornately carved dining table. 'Please sit down. You must be here about poor Mr Lisicki. So sad. He was such a nice man. Almost like a son to me.'

I was dumbfounded. I am not usually lost for words but Dee Privera was something else.

I nodded and allowed her to continue.

'Drank too much. I did warn him. It was his ego, of course. Mr Lisicki wanted to stay young so that someday he might find a lady to marry. He had to care for his elderly mother for many years and he never went out much except to work while she was alive. She was very demanding and he never had any real life of his own. His clientele were all men and he was too shy to ask any ladies out. Such a pity. He could have made someone a good husband.'

I observed three coloured bottles on the table and I wondered what they were. I finally found my voice. 'What do you think killed Mr Lisicki?'

'Well,' she said, reflecting upon what she was about to say. 'The newspaper said that he had been drinking before his death. I warn my clients not to drink alcohol with herbal medicines but I have never known anyone to actually suffer any ill effects if they do.'

'I presume Mr Lisicki was one of your clients,' I said, as she continued to ponder the cause of death.

'Yes,' she replied. 'He wanted something to help his shyness and to make him feel and look younger. He was vain about his looks. These are the potions I prescribed for him,' she said, pointing to the three coloured bottles.

I looked at the labels on the bottles. The white bottle read, *Fountain of Youth*. The red bottle's label read, *Passion*, while the third, a green bottle, said it was a hair elixir for external use.

'He had been taking the red and white bottles for some time without any adverse effects. He only started using the hair elixir shortly before his death. He wanted to sell the hair elixir in his barber shop. When I heard of his death, I initially blamed myself. But I knew my potions could not have caused his death, and, as the newspapers suggested, he was murdered, I felt, in some sense, relieved. I thought that the police may come to see me but no one came. I was not surprised when you arrived today even though his death was so long ago.'

'What ingredients do you use in your potions?' I inquired, trying to read the labels.

'Only natural herbs and vitamins. All government approved. My family were Gypsies and the formulas for my potions have been handed down from past generations. I have had considerable success and most of my clients come back.'

'Except John Lisicki,' I suggested.

'Yes,' she looked down as she spoke. Suddenly she looked up. 'Oh, my goodness, you don't think he could have drunk the hair elixir? It was for external use only.'

'My guess is that somehow the high level of alcohol he consumed, combined with prescription drugs and the herbal potions, and maybe the hair elixir, turned into a lethal cocktail. He was pretty drunk. He may have consumed the hair elixir in error.'

'What happens now, Detective?' Dee asked fearing the worst.

'I will have to ask you to come to the station to make a statement sometime but in the meantime I will have these potions analysed in the lab.'

'I never meant to harm him. He was such a nice fellow.'

'I know. His death was probably an accident caused by what he chose to ingest. I do have to report to the coroner but at last we may be able to put his mysterious death to rest.'

As I walked back to my car holding the coloured bottles, I had a chuckle to myself. Not that John Lisicki's death was a laughing matter but at the thought of what the boys back at the station would think. Would I get a reputation of solving a cold case murder mystery where hair elixir was the probable cause? Deep river, Dee Privera, I mused – the missing piece in the puzzle.

RETROSPECTIVE: From the 2012 anthology:
Sweet and Sour

THE HAUNTED HOUSE

David MacLaughlin

I AM JUST AN ORDINARY HOUSE and all I want is peaceful co-existence with the Homo sapiens that live here. Made from local timber, I am laid back and comfortable, in the style of a Queenslander. I creak and groan naturally, nothing put on; it's all to do with the temperature variances, especially at night. My windows are wooden casements which stick in summer and rattle in the cooler weather. All in all I like how I am, and all I ask is a little consideration from my human inhabitants.

However, the lot I have at the moment are really over the top. A family with kids! So noisy, not just some of the time but all of the time. I cannot get a decent sleep some nights with these kids and their loud music. If I had teeth they would rattle. The father of the household 'revs' his car before he leaves for work early and it nearly blows my roof off. The mother never stops talking on the phone, mostly gossiping with her female friends.

Then there are these obnoxious cooking smells, she fancies herself a gourmet cook.

Well the kids, the little darlings, the baby wets my nice timber floors and puts his sticky hands all over my walls. Yuk! The two older ones have junk everywhere. The bikes, their sporting gear, all over the place; their rooms are full up with stuff, even the ants have moved out, as there is no room for them!

That dog is a pain. They all pat it and hug it; don't know why. It is just a mongrel dog, no real breeding in it. He scratches and leaves his fleas all over me and his loose hair keeps falling out. They seem to be a nice family but they slam my doors and screw things into my walls to hang pictures. Their taste in art is appalling! I can't stand having cheap badly painted original landscapes on my walls.

The boy has a drum kit. It would be ok if he could play it but he just belts it and I vibrate all over – so inconsiderate of him. This can't go on for much longer. I will go ballistic and have a mental breakdown. Drastic action is needed.

If I become haunted for a night, they might calm down or leave! I will pick a night when it's wet and windy, rattle a few doors and scare the kids and that dog. He will bark and stir things up. I do not have any ghosts living here. That's all fake stuff anyway, but spirits would be great to scare them. I can flash the lights on and off. That will have a similar effect. I hope that they will get the message and be more considerate.

My chosen evening comes. It is raining, and that dog has shaken his coat all over the veranda floor. It is windy too and my casement windows are creaking nicely. The baby is asleep. The adults are out. A baby sitter – a neighbour's older offspring – is there to keep an eye on these rowdy kids for the night. Eventually, by 1am, there is silence from these humans and the dog. All are in bed and finally asleep, but not before they had kept me awake for hours with loud music. The drums made me vibrate all over.

The wind increases in intensity. The leaves on the trees brush the house and the branches bang against the casements. I wait for a particular strong wind gust, then, with a flourish, I manage to creak open the widows. The wind rushes in, knocking their junk all over the place. The baby sitter, a know-it-all female uni student, gets up, closes all the windows and gets back to bed. At least the noise gets the others disturbed. I flash the lights on and off, moan, and creak. That seems to work. The dog starts howling and barking and the baby sitter, looking a bit perplexed, shuts the widows again.

I have never had so much fun. My mates the possums start racing across the tin roof making a great racket. Nothing seems to bother the baby; it keeps sleeping. The other two kids hide under their beds. After a while, feeling a bit silly, they climb back on the beds and so to sleep, perchance maybe to dream... But I won't let them sleep as they have kept me awake all night and that annoys me.

I open and close doors in the house, making them bang as much as possible. That does the trick. They all jump up; scamp to the kitchen with the dog in pursuit, knocking a flower vase off the table in the process.

The baby sitter wants to know does this happen often. 'All these weird noises and flashing of light, doors banging, dog howling, possums going mad on the roof, and windows creaking open?'

'Never happened before,' the kids say.

And the baby is still asleep.

The baby sitter, using her intelligent university brain, makes the startling revelation that this place is haunted. 'Wow, you live in a cool house, a haunted house. Wish I lived in one, not just a boring ordinary house like my oldies own,' she says.

The children blink. The oldest speaks for them, 'It was scary, eh, but kind of cool. We won't tell Mum and Dad.'

I groaned and shook the wall. They all squealed like they were on a roller coaster (scary but safe in the end). I twigged. They did like me scary. I was stuck with them.

After that episode I became a celebrity. When the adults were out, I would put on a show for anyone left, maybe no wind or rain but flashing lights, the possums, and dog howling all in harmony sounded really good. I like those little noisy monsters being around the place.

It's good being haunted

JACKALS CAUSEWAY THREE KILOMETRES
Jenny Woolsey

SEEKING SOLACE AND SOLITUDE, I had driven four hours to this quaint leafy one pub and one take-a-way town. I had plucked Jackalston and its surrounding area from a tourist magazine, having needed time to think and wallow in my self-pity. The article claimed the natural phenomena I was about to see had healing power.

Pressed up against the safety fence, I looked over the edge of the cliff and stared at the tessellating hexagonal basalt blocks at the bottom. They looked like a giant's black tiled bathroom floor, cracked from the brute's weight. I tried to conjure up the supposed healing power and pushed the final volatile argument with my fiancé out of my memory.

As I scanned the grandeur before me, a yellow t-shirt near the edge of the clearing caught my attention. It was a person, maybe another jilted lover, but it looked like they were lying prone, face down. I squinted but it was too far to tell if there was blood. What if? A sudden chill ripped up and down my spine as I shoved my hand over my mouth to stifle my scream.

I stood transfixed, as if I'd been cast in bronze, looking for movement below, but the tree branches and thick leafy foliage obscured my full view. Hairs rose on my arms as goose bumps populated my skin like tiny anthills, and macabre thoughts raced around my brain. I curved my hands around my mouth and yelled as loudly as I could, 'Hello down there!'

The wind whipped my cheeks and flyaway wisps of hair stung my eyes. I abruptly pushed the blonde strands back behind my ears. The figure remained where it was.

My hands began to shake like maracas and I clutched the fence hard, turning my knuckles white. The causeway was probably 500 metres or so straight down. I looked around for an information board. To my right a forestry sign read, 'Jackals Causeway 3 kms.'

I flashed my eyes around the picnic area. There were two empty wooden tables with benches, and a bricked bbq in between. If I remembered correctly, there'd been one car in the parking lot. There didn't seem to be an information board.

As a nurse, I knew I had to get down there and apply the DRSABCD aka Danger Response Send for help Airway Breathing CPR Defibrillator, Action Plan if the patient was injured.

In my well-worn Nikes I strode down the narrow dirt path, dodging random tussocks of grass. The path twisted down the cliff like a wriggling snake. Long bladed swooshing grass lined the edges and blocked my view. As the incline began to level out my heart pounded and my thoughts were wish-washy: What was I getting myself involved in? Maybe there was a murderer down there . . . or the patient had committed suicide . . . or they were abseiling and fell . . . or maybe they were just sleeping and it was nothing at all. So many possible scenarios.

I came upon a wooden bridge which traversed a fast-flowing creek. Leaves raced like formula one cars down it. I took a step and the board beneath my shoes moved up and down. I stopped and noticed the nails were coming loose. Being careful, I held the iron balustrade and soft-toed across.

Crack!

The wood below my feet gave way with a splintering snap. I instantly plunged down into the creek, the cold water sending a #7 on the Richter scale, shockwave through me. I felt the surge of the beast wanting to swallow me whole. Water shot up my nose and filled my mouth as I sank towards the muddy bottom. I had to get up to the surface or I would drown. As panic started to claim me I pushed myself back up towards the surface, my head re-emerging above the torrent. I was spun in the water and saw I was now downstream from the broken bridge, being swept along with the current. I yelped as submerged branches scratched and tore at my legs. I tried to think about what to do and not the things or wildlife that might be in the water with me! My instinct was to paddle to the edge, but the pull was too strong and I kept bobbing up and down as the angry monster took me further with it.

'Help!' I screamed, as I swallowed another mouthful of the muddy soup.

Downstream I went, telling myself that I needed to keep calm, and scan for something to hang on to. I could see a large bough bent over the creek, with its smaller branches touching the water. I dove towards it, clutching a handful in both my hands. Some of the twigs snapped and the leaves crushed in my tight grip. Holding on, I kicked my legs around seeking something solid for a footing. My feet found a rock which I used to lift myself higher up in the water. I then flung my body onto the bank.

Exhaustion wracked me and tears filled my eyes. That had been so close. I covered my eyes with my hands and sobbed . . . and sobbed . . . and sobbed. Not just because of the accident but also from my broken heart. A vision of my confrontation with Daniel appeared before me. A fortnight before, I had used his phone to ring the hospital, as my phone's screen was cracked and in being repaired. I accidentally clicked on his messages instead of the phone icon, and a few erotic words in a message caught my eye. My stomach churned as I read the multiple conversations. Scrolling back, it became apparent that Daniel's weekend in Sydney for business a few weeks before was really a tryst with the Belinda woman in these texts.

At first I couldn't believe it. Daniel loved me, he was my Prince Charming and my soul mate. We were going to be married in a year and had booked the beautiful gardens. I had spent hours dreaming about the day and starting to look for a dress . . . but then it all made sense. Daniel had lately been using an abrupt tone of voice with me, making excuses why he couldn't take me out on dates and stalling on the venue booking.

It had taken everything within me to keep calm and bring the messages to his attention, and to my dismay he admitted his infidelity straight away. He said she came onto him and he couldn't resist as she was hot. The volcano in me exploded and I yelled at him. How dare you treat me like this! Get out of my life! I never want to see your dirty face again. Daniel had left my unit and my fairy-tale.

I cried until there were no tears left.

I sat up, water dripping off my face and clothes, my lungs sucking in oxygen. I brought my knees up to my chest and hugged them. The closeness of my own death experience caused my body to shake. I stayed where I was until the tremors had subsided, then I straightened my torso, and watched the blood trickle in tiny streams from numerous cuts on my arms and legs. I didn't want to wash them with the creek water as they might get infected. My phone which was in my pocket before the bridge catastrophe was now at the bottom of the creek, along with my backpack which had been torn off when I plummeted.

I studied the layout of the creek and its direction. I tried to see if the picnic area was above me but overhanging weeping willows and other tall thick trees blocked my view. The creek was probably moving to my destination or close by, but I wasn't sure, and I didn't have a map or a compass to check. The most logical thing to do was to go back upstream to the bridge. This was the bush, and that meant traipsing through the trees and high grass that licked the creek. Nasty cobbler pegs caught their rides on my socks, shorts and blouse, jabbing my skin like a multitude of sewing needles. My legs were concrete and a dull ache filled my skull as I thumped around tall and taller green spiky pine trees and bright yellow balls of wattle. Eventually I arrived back at the bridge and glanced at the large jagged hole where I'd fallen.

I lent up against a gumtree and pulled the acupunctural cobbler pegs off my clothes where they had been torturing me. How far was there left to go? I stared back at the bridge. Maybe I could shimmy across the structure and backtrack to my motel. I would inform the owners and let them deal with the situation. I didn't need to be involved.

I shook my head. Life and death often wager on the speed of measured medical assistance. I had to go and see if they had a pulse.

I picked up speed, jogging slowly; my wet shoes squelching. I rounded another corner and thump! I landed hard on the path, my right knee crashing first, with my hands splayed out in front of me.

'Ow!' I yelped, as I rolled to my bottom. I stared at the bruise and redness that was appearing on my kneecap. I shook my hands which were grazed and stung. I twisted my head to see what I'd tripped over. There behind me was a large pile of sticks and rocks in the middle of the path. Uneasiness stirred in my stomach. Could it have been deliberately put there?

I gingerly pulled myself up to my feet. My knee ached and it hurt to bend. I looked again at the scattered pile. Maybe it *was* a trap and I needed to ignore my training and go back to the motel. I hobbled over to a nearby tree stump, plonked down on it and rubbed my knee which was all I could do with no first aid kit.

A sound like someone crying interrupted me. I strained to hear more but the wind picked up, whistling through the trees masking any other noises. I was sure I wasn't imagining it and it seemed like a child. I had to go and see. There may be more than one person in trouble.

I picked up a stick that I could use as a hiking prop to take the pressure off my knee. If this was the way to finding solitude and solace, I would have preferred a yoga class. I gave a bitter laugh.

The rest of the way was unremarkable, though my senses were heightened. The path wandered between more gumtrees, wattles, tall grass, cobbler pegs, and scattered bushes with pretty pink wildflowers. A couple of rustles in the grass made me jump. One was a bush turkey, scratching around, strutting off when he realised I was in his territory; another a large goanna scurrying away. Both scared by my intrusion into their world.

A set of wooden steps came into view. At the top another forestry sign announced, 'Jackals Causeway.'

My heart pounded in my chest as I walked down the steps. There were so many and they creaked under my feet so I went as slowly as I could. I didn't want to be heard, or fall again. The further down the stairs, the louder the crying became but I still couldn't distinguish whether it belonged to a distressed child or adult.

At the bottom, a tall tree with a thick trunk gave me a screen to peek out from. Checking for danger was the first step of the DRSABCD Action Plan.

I couldn't see anyone. I surveyed the area and examined the place where I was sure I'd seen the yellow clothing. There was a water bottle and a small black bag, and a small red puddle which had soaked into the basalt blocks. I scratched my head and looked around some more. The person must be hurt, and around here somewhere.

My hands were sticky with sweat as I took a step out into the opening. Then another, then another. The hexagonal basalt blocks rose and fell beneath my feet.

'Hello!' I called.

A high-pitched cry made me spin, and as I did, I slipped off the block I was on, landing on the pebbles in a crevice beside it. My head smacked the basalt block and a sharp pain ripped through my skull. I covered my head with my hands. I tried to stand but I couldn't.

And then everything went black . . .

A FARAWAY VOICE entered my consciousness.

'Lady, can you hear me?'

I groggily opened my eyes, staring up into the most beautiful emerald eyes I'd ever seen. They were framed by shoulder-length wavy brown hair.

'Um, yeah,' I mumbled, a sudden warmth spreading across my face.

I tried to pull myself up, but dizziness sent me back to my horizontal position.

'Don't move.' The guy's voice was a soft comforting purr.

'There was yellow. A person,' I stammered, 'and crying.'

'Shhhh,' the voice cooed. 'Sam, how long did the ambulance say they would be?'

'They said they were on their way. Shouldn't be too long,' a deeper male voice replied.

Blackness enveloped me again.

A BRIGHT LIGHT FLASHED into my eyeball and brought me back to the present.

'Where am I?' I asked, though the bed and pale blue curtains opposite me gave a pretty good clue.

'You're in Helensville Hospital. You hit your head out at Jackals Causeway and they brought you here.'

I nodded; a sharp pain in my head causing me to wince.

'Do you need something for the pain?' the nurse asked.

I nodded, my throat too dry to talk.

She left and I pulled the crisp white sheet up under my chin and felt the back of my head where the pain had speared me. There was a huge lump, a haematoma, which commonly occurred with an injury to the head. I would ask the nurse if I had concussion but I guessed that would be an affirmative. The events that happened before my last fall at the causeway flashed in my mind like a slideshow and I shuddered. That meant at least I didn't have amnesia.

'Glad to see you're awake,' a vaguely familiar voice said, causing me to slowly turn my head towards him. I winced.

My stomach flip-flopped as I locked eyes with those emerald ones I'd seen in the causeway.

'Um, yep, I-I just woke up,' I stammered, putting my hand up to my hair.

'I'm Jeff,' he said. 'I helped you in case you don't remember. You had a huge whack to your head.'

'I'm Tess,' I said.

Jeff nodded and sat down. 'I know. How is your head feeling?'

'It feels like I've been smashed with a baseball bat,' I said, 'and thanks.'

Jeff looked down at his fidgety hands, then back at me. I wanted to melt like hot chocolate under his gaze.

'I'm glad I was there,' he said, leaning forward in the chair, his elbows on his knees. 'Did you fall in the creek too? I noticed you were all wet and had cuts on your legs. The ambos patched you up, and they put planks across the bridge to get across the creek.'

I nodded. 'Yeah.' I said. Tears dripped down my cheeks. 'I got pulled down the creek and I gr-grabbed a tr-tr-ee to get back on the bank.'

Jeff's eyes furrowed and he passed a tissue to me. I dabbed my eyes.

'Geez,' he said, his eyes round like the lenses on binoculars. '

'Yeah, hiking usually isn't my thing. I only went down to the bottom because I saw a person from up top, in a yellow shirt lying on their stomach, and they weren't moving. And I'm a nurse so thought I should help them,' I told him. 'And, as I got closer, I also heard crying. Did you see them?'

'Oh,' Jeff said, shifting in his chair.

'What?' I asked, raising my eyebrows.

Jeff's face went white.

'What?' I asked more sharply.

'You were right, but it was all for a film I'm making.'

I gasped. 'Oh no!' I cried, screwing up my face as a rush of tears sprang from my eyes. 'I almost d-drowned in the creek, my phone is destroyed, I-l lost my backpack, I tr-tripped and fell . . . and fell . . . and fell . . .' I sucked back the tears and fixed my eyes on Jeff. 'All to save the person . . . and it was an actor?'

He nodded and shifted some more in his seat.

'That could have been funny except I nearly died, so it isn't,' I muttered.

'I'm so sorry,' Jeff said, his face pale. 'We were going to be quick and usually no one is around at that time of day. Oh geez.' His words caught in his throat. 'I really *am sorry,* and I will replace your phone and cover any other costs.'

His dull eyes and downturned mouth told me he spoke the truth.

Jeff reached out his hand and touched mine. A zap of electricity penetrated my skin. I flicked my eyes from our hands, up to his face, wondering if he had felt it too. His eyes closed slightly, and his smile softened his expression. I think he had.

Neither of us spoke. Our eyes locked like two magnets, and I found myself toppling into those beautiful irises. He did not turn away but instead brought my hand to his lips and kissed it. In that instant I felt a connection like I'd never had with Daniel. Maybe my happily ever after was never to have been with Daniel, and I'd been brought here to be shown that.

I sighed and felt my body relax. In a weird way the Jackals Causeway may just have brought the healing I needed.

RETROSPECTIVE: From the 2017 anthology:
Redemption

FINDING ALISHA

Jenny Woolsey

'NO! DAD COME BACK!' Alisha cried, as she bent over the motionless body that lay on the velvet quilt in her parents' bedroom. Her long blonde hair soaked up the tears that drenched the pale face. 'Why Dad, why?' she moaned as sobs wracked her.

The day of the funeral Alisha felt completely numb. There had been no emotion. She'd gone through the process, been kissed by distant relatives she didn't know, listened to 'I'm so sorry's', even tipped a handful of dirt onto the oak coffin with its wreath of white lilies and baby breath. The coffin her mother had mulled over and taken hours to choose. 'Would your father like the oak or the pine?' she'd asked Alisha. 'And what handles? The silver or the gold?'

Alisha didn't care. Her dad was dead. Everything else meant nothing.

In the first term of Year 12, Alisha's report had shown all As.

'Keep this up and you could be dux,' Mr Allan the Head of Department told her.

'I'm so proud of you darling,' her father said upon hearing the news. 'You could be the first doctor in the family!'

But that fateful night, just before she blew out the seventeen candles and sliced through her chocolate birthday cake, what she knew as happiness was destroyed. Her father had staggered around the lounge room and collapsed on the floor. Alisha dialled 000 and her mother attempted CPR.

Distress crushed any joy in the household. The paramedics did all they could but pronounced her father deceased, and laid him on the bed for the funeral directors to come and retrieve him.

Part of Alisha perished with her father.

'I don't care that I'm getting Ds,' she told Mr Allan after he enquired about the deterioration in her marks.

'School is here to help you,' he said. 'You can have special provisions.'

But Alisha gave up on her career dreams, she slept a lot, arrived late to school or wagged it. The dark cave of her room was her sanctuary.

'I just want Dad back,' she told Billie, her closest friend.

'But you can't throw your life away,' Billie replied.

'Why not?'

'Your dad wouldn't want you to. He wanted you to be a doctor.'

'I want to be dead like him.'

Alisha saw Billie starting to hang out with other girls. Her negativity wasn't understood.

'Great, I've lost my best friend too. She didn't want to stay with a loser. What's the point?'

Alisha stopped going to school altogether.

'You're throwing your life away. Your father wouldn't want that,' her mother said.

'I don't care.'

'Maybe it's time you went and saw someone,' her mother suggested.

'What? A shrink?'

Her mother nodded.

'No way! Everyone thinks I'm crazy. That'll just prove it.'

'We need to do something to help you.'

Alisha grudgingly attended the appointment.

'It'll just take time,' the psychiatrist said. 'You have PTSD. The medication will help.'

'Great, I am crazy,' she said with sarcasm.

Alisha's flashbacks lessened but her enthusiasm for life did not return.

'Come on, let's go out and do something. You'll feel better,' her mother said, opening up her curtains.

Alisha blinked as the sunlight hurt her eyes.

'No! I don't want to go anywhere!' Alisha snapped, yanking the curtains back together.

Her mother hauled the curtains back open again. She grabbed Alisha's arm and tried to pull her up off the messed up bed.

'Leave me alone Mum! I'm not getting up. I'm not leaving my room!'

Tears fell down her cheeks.

'If you're going to stay in here, at least have the light on,' her mother said quietly, flicking on the switch.

'Fine,' Alisha muttered.

The day the autopsy report came back, Alisha's mother sat her down at the kitchen table and taking a deep breath told her, 'It says he died from a drug overdose.'

'What? Why on my birthday? Why did he do that on my BIRTHDAY?' Alisha yelled at her. 'Did he hate me?'

'No, he loved you. He was depressed. I wanted him to get help. I'm sure he didn't mean to. Maybe it was an accident,' her mother told her, wringing her hands together. 'You were his princess, Alisha. He loved you from the moment we knew we were having you.'

Day after day passed by. Alisha stayed in her self-induced imprisonment, absorbed in online fantasy worlds.

'Alisha get off your phone! You need to hang the washing out. I've asked you five times!' her mother snapped.

'Go do it yourself!'

'Get up and do your job! This can't go on. I'm sick and tired of this!'

The wicker washing basket flew across the room and hit Alisha in her face. Blood trickled down her cheek.

'Sorry,' her mother squealed.

Alisha jumped up off her bed. 'Leave me alone! I don't want to live here anymore!'

She stormed out to the dining room and picked up the porcelain vase from the dining room table. She knew it was special. Her father had given it to her mother for their last wedding anniversary; their twentieth. She threw it to the floor and watched it smash on the tiles.

'I bet you poisoned Dad,' Alisha landed her final, twisted blow. 'You said he was a waste of space because he sat on the couch all the time. You killed him and I will never forgive you!'

'What are you talking about? That's insane! Go to your room until you calm down.'

Alisha rushed to her bedroom, grabbed her wallet, some clothes and toiletries and stuffed them into her school backpack. She surveyed the hallway for her mother. The toilet door was shut. Alisha left the house, ran to the train station and jumped on the first train. It was going south to Fortitude Valley. Alisha stuck in her earbuds and gazed out the etched glass window as the trees and houses whizzed on by.

At the end of the train station mall she'd turned left. The buildings loomed over her, sneering at her with their shadows. Buskers with guitars who collected coins in hats, glanced her way. There was no purpose to her wandering. She had no idea where she was going, not that it mattered. Inside she was angry. Angry at her mother. Angry at her father. Angry at the universe.

She had heard stories about the Valley. There had to be someone on the streets she could hang with for a while until her head cleared and she worked out what to do.

'Hey girlie, you new round here?' a scrawny guy with a wild sea of red hair asked her, as she strolled past him. He was casually leant up against an urban clothing store. 'Yeah, do you know where I can stay?' Alisha asked him.

'You a runner?' he asked her, a wry lift to his lips.

Alisha nodded.

'All the hostels are full. You can stay over there.' He pointed his dirt-stained finger behind her, 'At the back of the park is a drain. That's where me and a few others hang out. But keep out of the way of the coppers or they'll take ya home.'

Alisha nodded. 'Um, do you have any money? I'm really hungry.'

'Sure but what are ya gonna give out to get it?'

Alisha stared into the eyes that had instantly lost their sparkle.

'I do-don't-don't give out,' she said, turning to walk back the way she had come.

'Ha-ha-ha. Just testing ya. You have to be careful here on these streets. There's lots of guys who'll want to take advantage of ya. You being a pretty girlie. Here,' he said reaching into his pocket, pulling out three two-dollar coins. 'It isn't much but it'll get ya something from the 7-Eleven. The Salvos bring a food van around later. Ticko by the way,' he said sticking out his hand.

'Ticko?' Alisha said, raising her eyebrow, ignoring his invitation.

He gave a lopsided smile and flopped his hand back to his side. 'You?'

'Alisha.'

A week turned into a month. Her anger mixed and gurgled with her depression, and spewed like an exploding volcano inside of her, consuming her brain and body. She didn't have her medication. Nightmares of her father's lifeless body and his depressive moods before he passed haunted her.

Ticko became her best friend. 'I'll look after ya. I get how you're feeling. My oldie died too,' he said, giving her a ring he'd found.

A month turned into six months.

'I'm cutting my hair short,' she told Ticko. 'Time for a new look.'

'Lookin' good Babe,' he had complimented her. 'You'll need tatts to cover those cuts on your arms.'

Twelve months passed. Alisha stared at her gaunt face in the mirror at the public toilets. The girl who stared back, did not resemble her. A vision of her father's face filled the mirror and she punched it.

'Damn you, Dad.'

The glass cracked and slithers cut her fist. Blood dripped into the basin.

Outside the take-away kiosk and on the pavements she searched for dropped coins.

'Hi darling I'll give ya some money if you sleep with me,' a guy said, interrupting her.

'Get lost,' she told him. 'I'm not a whore.'

Alisha sat in the gutter outside a donut shop. Her hair matted and her clothes worn. The sweet smells stirred her hunger. She counted her coins. She didn't have enough. She wondered if she should become a whore.

'Hey there,' a pleasant masculine voice said, interrupting her thoughts. 'Do you need some money?'

'Yeah. A couple dollars if you have it.'

'I'm Kai. I've got a van over there where you can have a shower or wash your clothes, if you want.'

Alisha looked to where he pointed. There were some other street kids there already. 'Thanks.'

'Um, did you go to Beerburrum High?' Kai asked her.

'Yeah, why?'

'Are you Alisha?'

'Yeah, why?'

'I was in your biology class.'

'Hey. I don't remember you.'

'Are you staying around here?'

'Yeah.'

'Where?'

'Over in that drain,' she pointed.

'Okay. Well I'm here every Thursday if you need any help. I'll see you next week,' Kai said. He took his mobile out of his pocket and rang someone.

Alisha wandered over to the others at the van, took a shower and ate. It felt good to be clean and full. She'd lost a lot of weight. Then she meandered back to the drain to tell Ticko about the van.

'Ticko, where are you?'

Alisha walked around the concrete tunnel.

'Ticko!'

Alisha rushed over to the wall where a man was slumped over his backpack. She pushed him backwards and felt for a pulse. Alisha's howl like a tortured wolf filled the air.

'No, Ticko, no!' she shrieked. 'Not you too!'

Alisha took off. Tears streamed down her face, and soaked her embroidered t-shirt. Her sandal snapped and she flung it off her foot. She fled from the smell of more death.

The Storey Bridge rose up before her. Alisha stared up at the curved metal giant. She thought if she climbed it, she could fling herself off and all this pain would be over. She could join Ticko and her father.

Alisha took some steps towards the narrow opening between the beginning of the bridge and the road. She slipped sideways through it. The brown shimmering water swam before her eyes.

'On the count of three,' she whispered to herself.

'Alisha? Alisha?' A voice spoke to her.

She stared blankly at the lady.

'Alisha. Are you Alisha Evans?'

The woman whispered, 'Alisha, it's me, Renee. I was your neighbour in Beerburrum. I'm sure it's you.'

Alisha stared into the green eyes of the woman. They looked kind though tinged with sadness.

'Renee?'

'Yes, it's me.'

Tears welled in Alisha's eyes and tumbled down her cheeks. She collapsed into the woman's arms and sobbed.

A blaring siren was the last sound Alisha heard before she slipped into unconsciousness.

Alisha blinked her eyes and stared around her. The walls were cream and pale green. There was a side table and an oil painting of a bouquet of flowers on the wall opposite her. The sheets felt hard and rough. It had been a long time since she had been in a bed.

'Where am I?' she asked into the silence.

She brought her hand up to flick a strand of hair out of her eye. There was a hospital name tag on her wrist. Alisha stared at it.

She pulled herself up to sitting then swung her legs over the side of the bed and tried to stand, but wobbled with dizziness. She grabbed the table.

'You're awake,' a woman in a navy uniform said to her crisply. 'No getting up yet. Hop back into bed.'

Alisha slowly laid back down and stared at the ceiling.

'Where am . . .'

But the nurse had disappeared. Alisha slipped in and out of consciousness. Strange and psychedelic dreams whirled and swirled around her manic subconsciousness. Ticko and her father, yelled and drowned, and rose as angels.

'Alisha. Alisha, Honey.'

A voice as soothing as warm milk, penetrated her mind.

Alisha's eyes fluttered open and stared into the face.

'How are you, Honey?'

Alisha noted that the hair of the woman was greyer than the last time she had seen her and there were wrinkles and bags under her eyes. She saw concern in the brown irises.

'Grandma?'

'Yes, it's me honey. Just rest.' Grandma reached for Alisha's hand and held it in her own. The warmth spread through Alisha's veins.

For a week Alisha lay sedated, and each day Grandma sat with her, holding her hand and stroking her hair.

'Let me brush your hair like I used to do when you were little,' Grandma said, picking up a brush off the side table. 'Can you sit up?'

Alisha slowly hoisted herself up while Grandma gently pulled the bristles through her hair.

'That's nice Grandma. How long have I been here?' she asked.

'Oh, a small while.'

Alisha relaxed as Grandma began to sing; her mind travelling back to enjoyable childhood times, baking cookies and playing in the backyard.

A sharp knock startled them both. The door opened slowly.

'Mum!' Alisha screamed as tears sprang from her eyes and gushed down her cheeks.

Alisha was crushed by her mother's arms.

'I've missed you so much.'

Alisha stayed in the warm embrace.

'I've spent every day trying to find you. If it wasn't for Kai and Renee I may never have. I could have lost you too,' her mother said as she released her.

Her mother sat on the chair beside the bed. Alisha grabbed her hand. It was squeezed tight.

'Kai?' Alisha asked, confused.

'Kai met you in the Valley. He and Renee help the homeless. Renee followed you to the bridge and rang the ambulance. And I'm so happy she found you,' her mother said wiping her red weepy eyes. 'She said you were about to jump!'

'I think so. I don't remember,' Alisha said.

'It's okay. You're getting the best help here.'

There was silence in the room.

The nurse came and checked Alisha's vitals. 'Will I be able to go soon?' she asked the nurse.

'Maybe, if you have somewhere stable to go to.'

Alisha turned to her mother. 'Mum can I come home?'

'Yes of course! I've moved in with Grandma, so you can come and live with us both.' Her mother looked towards the nurse.

The nurse nodded.

Alisha looked at Grandma who smiled. 'Wonderful!'

'I have something for you,' her mother said, taking a gift box out of her handbag.

Alisha hesitated

'Go on, it won't bite.'

Alisha lifted the lid off.

She stared at the crystal figurine of an angel holding a heart. 'It's beautiful,' she whispered.

Another knock on the door, made Alisha jump. She gasped.

'Kai, come in,' her mum said to the young man shuffling awkwardly into the room.

'Um, I just wanted to see how you were,' he said to Alisha.

'I'm okay. I'm going back home.'

'That's good,' he said smiling. 'Wo-would I be able to come and visit you?'

Alisha's eyes grew wide. 'Sure.'

Home was at Beachmere, in a quaint cabin in the caravan park.

'I like it here. I like the beach and no one knows me,' Alisha told her grandma.

'That's good. Don't forget to take your meds and you have counselling at one today.'

Alisha nodded.

Kai visited often.

'Why are you coming to see me?' Alisha asked one day.

'I like you, and I had a secret crush on you at school.' A bright red flush filled his cheeks.

'Really? I didn't think any boys liked me.'

'Of course they did! You just had your head stuck in the books and didn't notice.'

Alisha gave a harsh laugh. 'Fat lot of good that got me. Now I have nothing.'

'You have me!' Kai smiled then nudged her.

'That's true,' she said smiling back at him.

Nine months later, Alisha's mum handed her a large yellow envelope with her name typed on the front.

'What's that?' her mother asked.

Alisha pulled out the handbook and said, 'It's uni information. I've decided to try to get into paramedics. Maybe I could save someone's life one day. I've been thinking about Dad and I'm sure he would like that.'

'Wow. You've been keeping that a secret. Your Dad *would* love that.'

Alisha smiled.

'I know that you can conquer the world if you want to. You're smart and you're beautiful and you're strong. You can do anything you put your mind to. And I'm *so* happy that you're here.'

Alisha put her arms around her mother. 'I'm getting my life back on track and I want you to be proud of me.'

Her mother cupped Alisha's face in her hands, as tears spilled down her cheeks. 'I am already proud of you. And I love you with all of my heart and no matter what happens I always will.'

NOT OURS TO SEE

K.J. Sauffs

I LOST EVERYTHING I loved when planet Earth, no longer able to tolerate the abuses against it, fought back.

For many years there had been constant rumblings, with deadly natural disasters and climate events increasing around the globe.

'It will soon settle down,' said some experts.

'Our planet is in its death throes,' said others.

The Internet was inundated with stories arguing all the possibilities, and it seemed to me that 'the end is nigh' philosophy outnumbered all others. As to whether this meant that the whole planet would soon explode, or, that it was only the human race that was doomed was a tie.

While the suicide rate increased, the majority of the human population continued on living as normal a life as possible. There was a lot of fear of course but little panic. What would have been the point of panic anyway? We didn't really have any viable options. We couldn't evacuate the planet because we didn't have that technology, and we most definitely couldn't stop whatever was happening inside our precious globe.

A month ago news came Yellowstone super volcano had erupted. Followed by a massive earthquake that almost wiped out Continental America and the north of South America. Footage from satellites and drones showed the destruction of major cities and less populated areas. It looked like a giant had used a pitchfork to turn the soil and leave only rubble behind. Enormous sinkholes had opened up and swallowed entire towns.

Niagara Falls collapsed and became a basin with most of the surrounding suburbs falling into it. Those that didn't were raised into the air only to fall back and smash upon the unsteady ground.

Volcanoes around the world erupted in a chain of explosions. When the Pacific Rim of Fire joined in, we knew that humanity was now on the brink of extinction. The sky was darkened by volcanic ash and our once tropical climate began to chill.

With no basement to shelter in my husband Nathan and I did our best to seal our house. Along with our sons Matthew, 10, and Joshua, 4, we wore scarves across our faces to protect our lungs. I thought we were delaying the inevitable but said nothing. We still had running water because as yet we had not been affected by strong earthquakes. With our large stockpile of food Nathan thought we might be able to survive. I had my doubts.

I was outside on the fateful day that a sinkhole opened up under our house. I can't remember why I went outside, I guess I probably just needed a break. When the shaking began, I dropped to my knees and before I could even think to try and get back ground beneath me started to rise and I instinctively clung on.

Up and up it rose to form a rocky crag, made to seem all the higher because of the land that had simultaneously dropped away. There had been no time to think or react to the disaster unfolding around me. If there had I think I might have let go and be done with it; but that inborn survival instinct that I didn't know I had, kicked in and I held on for my life.

How long the upheaval lasted I couldn't say. When it stopped, I was left on a ledge near the summit of a newly formed mountain with my legs dangling above the abyss where my old home and family now lay, crushed and mangled. Thoughts flitted across my mind like manic hummingbirds.

My life, my world, was gone.

I reached into my jeans' pocket for my mobile phone in the hope that it would still work, not as a phone but as a photo album. Perhaps I could have one last look at my lost loves before the battery died. Telling myself it would hurt more to see them alive and smiling, I threw the phone away. It was now a useless remnant of a dead civilization.

Memories started to flood in.

Meeting Nathan when I was still in high school, the fun times we shared, the stress of a teenage pregnancy, both of us giving up our dreams of going to university and getting full-time jobs instead. The joy of Matthew's birth, and later Joshua's. Our marriage and life together had been mostly good and I didn't regret a thing.

I didn't cry.

The scale of this tragedy was so catastrophic and much too big for my mind to fully comprehend.

I felt the familiar stirring of the new baby in my belly.

I'd known I was pregnant for a week now but hadn't got around to telling Nathan because he was so caught up in trying to make sure his family was safe. I hadn't wanted him to worry more than was necessary. I'm one of those fortunate women that do pregnancy the easy way, no morning sickness, no complications. It was easy to keep it to myself for a while. I had planned to tell him before I started showing.

I wonder now what the new conditions I might endure will do to my unborn child. When I think about the future I wonder if the struggle is worth it and maybe I should take us both out now. Pushing myself off that ledge would be such a simple thing to do.

How could I give birth on my own? What if I died before the baby could fend for itself? Was I dooming it to a slow and lonely death, to then be torn apart by crows and such? Wild animals would one day become a major threat to our survival. How could I keep it safe?

A hand grabbed my shoulder.

I was still in high school, slumped across my desk with a little drool forming in the corner of my mouth.

I had fallen asleep during science class.

Mr Bonner had been droning on about volcanoes and that, combined with the warmth of the afternoon sun spilling into the classroom, had worked as well as any sedative. My best friend Becky had pulled me out of my dream and back into reality before I was discovered. I wiped the corner of my mouth with the back of my hand. Sitting up slowly so as not to attract attention I blinked a couple of times. The brightness of the day was in stark contrast to the gloom of the nightmare landscape I had left behind. Becky was struggling to stifle her laughter as the last bell rang.

'All right off you go then, no homework tonight.'

The class cheered.

At our lockers Becky said, 'Oh my God, Amy, that was hilarious. I was so tempted to let you get caught.'

'It's so close to graduation I doubt Mr Bonner would have done much. He would probably have laughed, or made a daggy joke at my expense.'

'Yeah, he's a pretty cool guy . . . for a teacher.'

We both laughed.

'And,' I said, 'He's one of the few who understands the futility of giving us homework at this point.'

'No more lessons, no more books, no more teacher's dirty looks.' We sang together as we grabbed our school bags and skipped out of the building arm in arm.

Later when we were at Becky's house, her sitting cross-legged on her bed, and me in an armchair, I told her about my dream.

'It was so real. I felt the grief and could smell the smoke in the air. I could hardly breathe.'

'Wow. Do you think it means anything? Was it like a prophecy or something?'

'It kind of felt like that, yeah. Only I'd met my husband in high school and there's no way I'm dating any of the boys at our school.'

Becky nodded. 'They're all so immature. How many Nathans are there anyway?'

'Three that I can think of. And I'm not remotely attracted to any of them.'

'Well then this is probably nothing more than a really epic dream.'

'But I can't shake it off. Look.'

I put my hands out in front of me to show her that they were trembling. What I didn't tell her was that I still felt the pain of losing my husband and children. They had seemed so real to me and so was my grief at their loss.

'Some dreams do that.'

'So now you're a dream expert?' I said.

'Maybe.' She laughed.

Then went on to say, 'Anyway, the future isn't fixed yet, so all you have to do is avoid boys called Nathan and, to be on the safe side, don't have sex until you're twenty. No Nathan, no teenage pregnancy. Wait till you're twenty before you have sex, also no teenage pregnancy. Hey-presto change-o, no extinction event. Easy.'

'You're probably right. Besides, I fell asleep listening to Bonner go on about volcanoes and eruptions and all that stuff, so that probably put it all in my head. Also, if I make sure I get into university instead of settling for an office job . . . '

'There's nothing wrong with an office job.' Becky sounded a little defensive and I remembered she already had an office traineeship lined up with a major insurance company.

'Of course there isn't, I didn't mean it like that. My Mum loves her admin job at the medical centre. What I meant was, that by sticking to my career plan, that would be another way of changing the future I saw in my dream.'

I paused as a thought came to me.

'Maybe I should study geology. I've got good marks in science.'

'Oooh, that would be cool. You could specialise in volcanoes. What do they call a volcano specialist? Volcanologist, vulcanologist?'

'One of those.'

'That's what your dream was about.'

'Huh?' I said.

She gave me an exasperated look and said, 'You've been trying to decide what you wanted to do for ages now and this dream has shown you. Become a scientist and help save the world.'

'I don't know about the saving the world part but I might look into the geology thing.'

'Good that's sorted. Now let's get changed and meet the others at the shops.'

The others were our usual group of friends that we socialised with out of school, we had planned to meet up with them in the food court of the local shopping centre. We were the last to arrive and there was the usual teasing, Becky got ribbed the most because she was usually late to everything.

While they all chatted, I went to get a milkshake. The guy behind the counter was new to me and very cute. We made eye contact and for the first time ever in my life I felt the electric shock of instant attraction. I looked at his name tag. Nathan. My stomach dropped. Grief fell away and was replaced by excitement tinged with fear.

Unnoticed by me, Becky had come over and was now standing behind me.

She whispered to me, 'It can still be changed, just remember no sex until you're twenty and make sure you get into uni.'

I turned to her and said with a smile on my face, 'I'll make sure to use protection every time.'

'Uh-uh. Total abstinence is the only way to be one hundred percent sure. The future of the world and all humanity is dependent on your education and sex life.' She patted me on the shoulder.

'So, no pressure then?' I said.

GREETINGS
Karine Dupre

From the edge of the world, my friends, I welcome you!
Take your sunscreen, your sunglasses and your surfboard, the waves are waiting for you
As much as the bleached hair, tanned boys!
Live fully, navigate through sharks and dolphins although
Bluebottles might be the only encounters in the large sea.
The continent is vast and I can easily promise you dozing nights in the long distance bus,
And wake-ups amid stars in skies so dark you would wish to get lost;
Or wake-ups with the darting sun, cracked red soil, flies buzzing,
Camper vans and roos' skeletons along the road.

Come my friends, on this side of the world, tilt your head, bend your body,
Down under, the sun is warmer and the smiles brighter!
They have been dancing for thousands of years and the fascination is still there
Despite the dreams that don't meet and the land so difficult to share.
Not more, not less than in any other, this country spits, roars, grumbles, mumbles.
But also cares.
Come my friends, the grass is certainly not greener here
But the beer and barbecues are plenty to share.

Friends, why are you waiting?
I know the travel is long and it is far far away
But on this side of the globe, you will meet all colors and all sounds,
Even the birds have an accent.
Escaped from Africa, race the camels and forget the ibis, digging the bins;
Chopstick your dumpling, fork your steak, pack your swag,
The valleys of wine are waiting for you, blue mountains and all,
In comfortable convertible.

Friends, let me know,
I have been in and around, to the west and the east, to the tip and the top.
I have seen the rain pouring and drowning the cattle;
The wind dancing with trees and dropping them dead after the first waltz.
I have seen blisters on the land, blisters on the walls, blisters on their lips,
And the ants still building, despite all.
I have seen the planes, circling around and around, not giving up even with
The flames licking them hungrily.
I have seen them, infinite chain, carrying the bucket,
For water, for the gold coin, for fairness.

Truth is, my friends, I have fallen in love
And from the edge of this world I believe
In these open arms
But
The suitcase is packed
The tickets are bought
The house is empty
As I need to go before coming home.

RETROSPECTIVE: From the 2014 anthology:
Alpha and Omega

THE ONE ABOUT THE FARMER'S DAUGHTERS
Bernie Dowling

75km from Birdsville, Queensland, September, 1993

THE RADIATOR HOSE hissed like a punter encouraging a racehorse or discouraging a comedian. Steam swirled from the hose raising the air above beyond its previous 40-degrees. In disgust I slammed my cheap straw hat into the red dust.

For three hours I sat, listening to the radio, in the driver's seat of the motionless EH Holden ute, with both doors open and a plastic bottle of warm water for company. The radio played wailing country music and inane pop songs.

The playful ditty *I'm Gonna Be (500 miles)* came on. I do not mind the quirky song by Scottish identical twins Charlie and Craig Reid. But I was not in the mood, being a lot more than 500 miles from hometown Brisbane. And why were they playing a 1988 release/ 1989 Australian hit in 1993 on a radio station with the call sign of 'latest hits and country bits'?

I remembered why. That year of 1993, cultish American film *Benny & Joon* popularised the Scottish lads' song and launched it into the American Top 100. The song was born again in the USA and, blessed by Hollywood, circumnavigated the globe.

Me, I was going nowhere. The high excitement of my first trip to the annual two-day Birdsville horse-racing carnival had sustained me over the 1500 kilometres I had travelled from my humble home in the Brisbane suburb of Hendra. Every serious Australian punter was expected to make, at least once in their lifetime, the trip to way out in western Queensland, on the edge of the Simpson Desert. There is the Queensland Outback and then there is Birdsville. The racetrack is no Royal Ascot. The prizemoney is nothing flash. Punters have been forever flocking in their thousands for the annual Birdsville races *just because*, an addiction hard to break when you cannot even classify it.

I looked skyward but descendants of the birds which gave the town its name were nowhere to be seen. A few metal birds had flown overhead carting the early birds of the 6000 people set to join the 100 citizens of Birdsville for the races. It was Thursday and the races were on Friday and Saturday. I wearily noted dusk perched above the western horizon and contemplating a plunge.

The Japanese four-wheel-drive, which pulled up behind me, wore more dust than the bush highway. The driver climbed from the cabin but he could have stepped from the pages of Australian history, or at least a Hollywood version of it. He was mid-40s, tall and thin. Beneath the pristine Akubra hat, his confident face was as red as the dust at his feet, except for his chin's sandy stubble, neatly clipped but untamed by a razor.

He wore a Jackie Howe, a navy singlet, evenly coloured, unstained and creaseless, under an unbuttoned short-sleeved denim shirt, above pressed moleskins and polished leather boots, with red dust surreptitiously creeping up the edges of the soles. He told the teenage girls, both pretty-faced blondes, to stay in the 4WD. He strolled towards me. 'Have an accident?' he said.

'No thanks, just had one,' I said.

'Thought so.' He looked at me, stared into my eyes actually.

I looked at his blue eyes briefly before lowering my glance.

'Better get you home,' he said.

'I live in Brisbane.'

'Hnnh, don't suppose you have a tow rope.'

'Not on me, no.'

'Hnnh, thought so.'

He drove the 4WD to park in front of the ute, took out an ancient thick grease-stained rope and hitched the two vehicles together with some pretty fancy knots. He returned to the 4WD driver's seat, beside the teenagers who might have been smiling at me but were more likely smirking. He started his engine, killed it, and returned to the ute.

'You know to put it in neutral?' he said.

'That's how I got here,' I said.

He stared into my eyes again refusing to blink before he spoke. 'You say the stupidest things. I'll put it down to sun stroke.'

The farm house was fifteen minutes down bush tracks after we turned off the highway. The house was three times as long as it was wide, verandas all round, the exterior off-white in colour, tinted ochre over the years by dust.

Inside was spotlessly clean — high ceilings, hallways leading to lots of rooms. A delicious smell rode the heat haze from the kitchen. In the bush, many still have dinner before dusk, after a hard day's yakka on the land.

The girls, who looked to be in their late teens, smiled at me from tanned faces set with blue eyes. Everybody but me had blue eyes; I had to make do with grey.

The young women took plates from a cupboard and cutlery from a drawer to a solid rectangular wooden table in the middle of the large kitchen. The dining room, beside the lounge, was empty of furniture, empty of everything, actually, except space. Eight wooden chairs, with padded brown leather seats, pushed against the durable kitchen table.

The man looked across at me and nodded towards the head of the table. Not sure what he was indicating, I stood still. He shook his head, moved, and roughly pulled out the chair to the right of the head one. Having finished laying the dinner ware, the young women gently withdrew chairs, one to the right of me and one opposite. Neither girl sat down. I realised they had not said a word between them. I wondered if they were mute.

The man pulled out his chair at the head of the table and the three of them waited for me. I sat down. They sat down.

I tapped the impressive table. 'What sort of wood's this?'

The man looked warily at me. 'Ironbark.'

'There is worse wood to have a bite on,' I said.

He ignored that. 'We don't normally wash up before tea unless we've been working,' he said. 'But you can if you don't mind wasting water?'

Tea means dinner in some parts of the bush, though it also means the beverage. After a couple of decades in Australia, new chums understand most of the lingo.

'I'm sweet,' I said. 'I'll just end up dirty again.'

'Hnnh,' he said.

The blondes went to the stove and placed hot food from two saucepans into large ceramic dishes. They opened the oven and brought out a loaf of hot bread which they placed on a plate.

Using a ladle, one blonde motioned to place its contents on the man's plate. He pushed a palm towards the ladle. 'Him first.'

I inhaled the aroma of rich beef stew as she held the ladle before me. 'You're not vegetarian, are you?' she inquired sweetly.

Ah, she speaks. Perhaps the other one does too.

The man answered for me. 'Course he's not. Does he look vegetarian? How tall are you? About six foot, I reckon.

'About that,' I said.

'You're skinny, that's probably drugs, not vegetarian food.'

You know how in the movies someone says, 'I don't like your tone', but no one ever says it in real life. I didn't like his tone. But I did not say it.

Silence seemed the best option so I stared down at my plate covered in large chunks of beef surrounded by onion rings, diced carrots and thick gravy. I smiled gratefully at the blonde who moved to serve the man.

The other blonde came to my side to put large servings of mashed potato, mashed pumpkin and boiled peas around the edge of the plate. We nodded at each other as she moved towards the man.

The four of us soon had our meals, including side plates of buttered hot bread. The man nodded at me and I ate. They ate.

'How far are we from Birdsville?' I asked.

'Haven't been there for years,' he said.

I looked at the girls who tittered. The so-far-speechless blonde opposite me obviously had the gift of sound.

'They haven't moved it since you were there last, have they?' I said. I heard both girls take in breaths.

'You're a real joker, Mr Steele Hill,' he said.

'You know me?'

'I looked at your driver's licence while I unhitched the tow-rope. You should keep it in your wallet not in the glove-box of your car.'

'Then you wouldn't have found it.'

'Might have.' He tossed my licence across the table.

The girl nearest me tapped my forearm. 'We are the Graves. Dad's George Grave. My sister's Isobel and I am Francine.'

Nods all round.

'As you know, I'm Steele.'

I tapped the table again. 'Ironbark and Steele, made for each other.'

Francine and Isobel laughed politely but George hung tough.

'You did that one already.'

I was going to correct him but instead put my hands out in a gesture of misunderstanding.

'Ironbark and Steele, it's the same joke as having a bite on Ironbark. Dogs bark and they bite.'

I looked at him to see if he was serious because what he had just said did not make sense. I had implied no connection between the table and a dog. It would have been quite clever of me to do 'ironbark and bite to eat' but I could take no credit for it. The way it was going down with my toughest audience member, I would not want to. I had little opportunity to appease George Grave with an appeal of unintentionality because what he said next startled me.

'You calling my family dogs?'

'No, I did not mean any of that. My jokes are very shallow,' I said.

'Shallow Graves, now.' He thumped the table with his fist and his daughters exchanged concerned looks.

'We didn't have to stop for you,' George said.

He had me worried, no doubt, but the thought that he had spoken gravely caused a tiny smile at the edge of my mouth. I really need to stop finding humour at inappropriate times.

'I know you didn't have to stop,' I said solemnly. 'And I'm glad you did. I've driven all the way from Toowoomba and the ute's packed it in. I was just trying to lighten things up.'

'Toowoomba, you said you were from Brisbane.'

I might have said that but now I did not want him to know where I lived.

'I thought you might not know where Toowoomba is. So I said Brisbane.'

'Hendra's a suburb of Toowoomba?' he asked. 'Hendra, that's what it says on your licence.'

'Yes,' I said. 'I mean no, Hendra is not a suburb of Toowoomba. But it does say Hendra on my licence.'

I waited. He looked at the daughter on his left and back at me.

'Only been through Toowoomba twice, quite a while ago. Only been to Brisbane twice and never been to the horse races. Can't remember if I went through Toowoomba on the way to Brisbane.'

I was not going to tell him he probably did.

'Every Australian should go to the racetrack at least once,' I said. 'If you are ever in Toowoomba, I'll take you to Clifford Park.'

'Might keep you to that when I visit Isobel, like I keep promising.'

'Visit Isobel?'

The blonde on his left answered for him with a big smile. 'I am studying drama at Toowoomba Uni.' She speaks, too. 'Second year, I have been living in the City of Flowers for eighteen months.'

For some reason, I felt I was in the middle of a tense protracted hand of cards, playing poker.

'That's right; it's uni holidays, isn't it?' I said. I discreetly wiped a bead of sweat from my eyebrow and looked to my right. 'What about you Francine, you studying in Toowoomba?'

Francine put her knife down and rested her chin on one fist. 'Fraid not,' she said.

I deserved this consolation.

'I am studying law at the University of Queensland. Quite a commute from the northern suburbs of Brisbane where I'm boarding.'

That would be those northern suburbs, one of which is Hendra.

'I know what you're thinking,' George Grave said to me. 'How does an old bush brumby like me raise two beautiful talented daughters?'

That was not what I was thinking: more like, are a mob of crazed blowflies running amok in George's top paddock?

'Are they twins?' I said.

'Would you like them to be twins?'

That question could not possibly have a correct answer.

'We're twins,' Francine and Isobel answered together.

Dad was not done with me, yet. 'I would hate to be the man who wronged either one of my daughters. By the way, Mr Funnyman, have you heard the one about the banker's daughters?'

I hadn't but I did hear the farmer's daughters cough in unison. 'No, I haven't,' I said meekly.

'This destitute beef cattle farmer visits the big city and goes to a banker's house. The banker, who has two beautiful daughters, invites him in and breaks open a bottle of single malt whiskey for the destitute beef farmer and himself. You with me so far, Mr Joker from the Big Smoke.'

Francine's voice was nervous beyond what you might expect of a daughter enduring an embarrassing parent. 'Dad, please,' she said.

Her sister Isobel chimed in. 'Dad, you're terrible at telling jokes. Leave Steele alone.'

This made George mad. 'I am not allowed to tell one lousy story in my own home. You think that too, Mr Hill?'

'It's awlright by me, George. Is this one of those guess-what-really-happened riddles? Like the bloke hangs himself on a block of ice, sort of thing,' I said.

'Why would any bloke hang himself on a block of ice?' he said. 'Out here, we use a tree.'

'If you can find one,' I said.

'I'm sure I could find one.' He swatted away a thought with a back-hand sweep. 'Wouldn't waste it on suicide.' He looked directly into my eyes. 'A lynching's another matter,' he said.

I glanced nervously across at Isobel, serenely placing in her mouth a forkful of mashed potato, wrapped in gravy. I guess she was used to dining with a certifiable madman.

George was warming to his subject. 'They hung Westley Allan Dodd this year. First one in 28 years, they tell me. He asked for it.'

I was keen not to ask for it inadvertently. 'What did he do to ask for it?'

'Don't you read the paper, Mr Funnypages?'

I do not read much beyond the racing form guide though, of late, I sometimes have this silly attraction for the arts pages. Even with my lukewarm commitment to media, I surely would have heard of a lynching in Birdsville. Maybe the locals kept it to themselves.

'They hung him in Washington State Penitentiary. Dodd was an American murderer, rapist, and a child molester,' George said.

Sounded all round, not a nice man. 'So that's what you meant by he asked for it,' I said.

George raised his eyes and shook his head. 'My words are not good enough and you gotta put some others in my mouth, Mr Funnylines. They asked Dodd how he would like to die and he said by hanging.'

'That showed some guts,' I said. 'I would have said old age.' George curled the side of his lip in a snarl but all he said was, 'Hnnh.'

We ate in silence for a while until George said, 'He asked for his hanging to be televised live.'

'Dodd did?'

'You're catching up fast now, Mr City Slicker.'

'And was it?'

'Course not. That animal Dodd, all he wanted was fame. But all the clear-thinking executioners wanted was to see him dead. Without a fuss.'

'I can see that,' I said.

'Would people fuss over you, Mr Funnypot? How many hours you drive by yourself before Fate brought you here?'

'Seventeen.'

'You take some of those speed pills?'

'I slept overnight in the back of the ute.'

'Hnnh,' he said.

I had lost my appetite. I nodded at my almost finished meal and the girls began to clear the plates. They brought apple pie and ice-cream.

'I see you get electricity out here,' I said.

'Cost us an absolute fortune because we had to pay for the connection for twenty kilometres,' George said. 'But a generator's too noisy. I don't like noise.'

'Me neither,' I said, wishing I was at a rock concert at The Zoo in Brisbane's Fortitude Valley. 'How come you had so much food prepared for dinner?'

'For tea,' he said. 'On account of the other young bloke.' He put a knuckle against one cheek and stared ahead. Must be a genetic gesture as Francine had done similarly earlier.

'We had another visitor,' Isobel said. 'Once.'

I may have looked uneasy. I felt it.

Francine touched me lightly on the shoulder and looked at her sister. 'Don't sound so dramatic, Issy. Another young man broke down last year and we had hardly any food in the place. It was embarrassing.'

George snapped out of his reverie. 'Embarrassing,' he agreed. 'For all we knew, it could have been his last meal.'

I coughed. A piece of beef must have gone down the wrong way. 'You a cattle farmer, Mr Grave?' I asked.

'Used to be, just like the one who visited the banker and his two daughters,' he said. 'That was before the wife passed on.'

I heard the girls tittering again and looked to find they were trying to hide smiles. Maybe George was not the only Grave of concern.

'I'm sorry,' I said.

'She passed on to Alice Springs and from there down to Adelaide. Ran away with my best mate.'

'You must miss him.'

'Miss who?'

'Your best mate.'

'Didn't I just get through telling you he ran away with my wife? Why would I miss him?'

'I'm sorry,' I said again, rather than tell him I was recycling a venerable old joke.

'He was a bank manager,' George said. 'They went to the Birdsville races together and they never came back.'

I looked at him, trying to decipher whether he was making it up as he went along. There were far too many coincidences between my trip to Birdsville and his sorry tale, not to mention his unfinished joke about the banker and his daughters. George's body language gave nothing away.

'Is your mate the banker in your story?'

'Could be.' He pushed away his empty dessert plate. 'Getting late, time for me to take in the blanket show.'

The blanket show is bedtime, the last show of the day. The expression is so old it probably referred to the last show on radio before retiring rather than on television.

'What time is it?' I asked.

'Seven o'clock. We have quite a few guns around the place if you would like one, Mr Hill?'

'Why would I want a gun?'

'Comfort. Though guns are a popular way to top yourself, out here, for those too scared for a hanging. The brave ones stroll into the dam.'

'I'll pass on the gun. You didn't finish your banker's daughters' story.'

'It'll keep. Don't you girls have our guest up late; he's got to get to the races tomorrow.'

George Grave ambled down the hall but turned after taking his hand from a door knob. 'The last young bloke did not make it.' He entered his bedroom.

Isobel removed the plates and Francine boiled the jug for coffee. 'Where would you like to sleep, Steele?' Francine asked.

Hendra, I thought. 'Anywhere,' I answered.

'You have a choice,' Isobel said. 'My room or Francine's.'

'What about the couch?'

'If you like,' Francine said. 'Or there is the guest room.'

This whole family gave me the creeps with their unfathomable way with words. I tried for a straight answer. 'Did your Mum really run away with George's best mate?'

'It's hardly a thing you'd make up,' Francine said.

And he was a banker?'

'Yes,' Isobel said.

'And you two are twins?'

'You're on a roll,' Isobel said, speaking out of turn. 'We should go to the races with you, tomorrow.'

'That's if I get there.'

'You'll get there. Dad's got lengths of every thickness radiator hose you can imagine in the 4WD,' Francine said.

'And heaps of water. He could have had you on your way to Birdsville within minutes, if he wanted to,' Isobel said.

'Why didn't he?'

'He likes you,' Francine said.

Buddha, he likes me.

Isobel pranced across the room to flick the hair above my temple. 'That light plane spotted you hours ago and radioed Dad.'

'We could have picked you up ages ago,' Francine said.

'But Dad said you were probably a city slicker who needed a survival lesson,' Isobel said.

Francine had moved to the other side of my face. 'A lesson best taught by the boiling sun,' she said.

Something else made sense, now. 'So that's how you knew to prepare extra dinner?'

'Of course,' Isobel said. 'Out here, we keep heaps of extra food. You might not be able to imagine it now but the Diamantina River does flood.'

'You are gullible, Steele,' Francine said. 'You really believed that story about the food and the other man.'

'Of course not,' I protested. 'I was just being polite.'

'We didn't feed him,' Francine said.

'Dad didn't like him,' Isobel said.

'He likes you,' Francine said.

I had no idea what that meant. What I would like to find out was if the whole family was bound to this Australian version of the Bates Motel. 'You girls are studying those courses at uni?'

'You're a suspicious man, Steele,' Francine said.

'Are they all like you in Brisbane?' Isobel said.

'I'm from Toowoomba.'

'I forgot,' Isobel said.

'You don't really want to come to the races with me?'

'Yes, we do,' they said together.

'Your father said he'd never been to the Birdsville races. But that's where your mother ran away with the banker.'

Between them they explained. George never had any inclination to go to the races. But his wife wanted to go, seeing they lived so close, only 85km away. George asks his best mate. You know how it goes: take my wife. His best mate does.

I was curious if George tracked them down but didn't ask.

'Don't ask,' Isobel said.

'What?'

'You were going to ask whether we are virgins because we have lived in the Outback so long,' Francine said.

'But don't,' Isobel said.

'Don't ask,' Francine said.

'Let's play Trivial Pursuit,' Isobel said.

We did, for hours. They were more trivial than I or better at pursuit because I never won a game. They should put more horse-racing and rock-music questions in that board game.

I did take the guest room. It was a long time before I found sleep. I kept dreading a knock at the door, no matter whose hand it belonged to.

I awoke and blundered into the kitchen to see George sitting at the table with a bath towel, a hand towel and a cake of soap in front of him. He wasn't drinking or eating or talking to anyone — just staring into space. He handed me the towels and soap.

'Don't waste the water,' he said. 'I might fix your ute, while you wake up. Good car, the EH, but only a fool would drive a 30-year-old one from Brisbane to Birdsville.'

'Toowoomba,' I corrected. 'And they're all 30-years-old.'

'Yours will see 31. Were you hoping to see 30?'

'Hadn't made any plans but I guess I had expectations.'

'Everyone has expectations. I'll put some breakfast on the eastern veranda. You know where the east is?'

'I know it's where I came from.'

I found the eastern veranda after I showered and changed into T-shirt and shorts. A smaller ironbark table held a glass of orange juice, a pot of coffee, pitcher of milk and hot buttered toast. I drank the juice and was enjoying the filter coffee and toast when a soft hands massaged the back of my neck. I turned. She was wearing blue pyjamas with white rabbits on them.

'Isobel, that's nice.'

'I'm Francine.'

'Fifty-fifty chance and I am wrong. You girls don't really want to go to the races with me.'

'I am Isobel. I thought you might have backed your judgement a bit longer, Steele.'

'I'm no good at games.'

'We'll see.'

I looked out over the veranda and I did see. Nothing. A couple of big dams, both shy on water, four paddocks, two barns, hale bales, even a bravely battling vegie garden. But not one lonely solitary Buddha-forsaken cow.

'How many hectares out here, Isobel?'

'Dad talks in acres, 15,000. How many hectares is that?'

'I don't know, a lot, more than 5000, I think.'

'Well, that's the family farm.'

'But you're not farming anything, Isobel.'

'Oh, I see. We should farm something, have a negative annual income and owe the bank more money. Why didn't Dad think of that? It takes a bright city boy to come up with such a master plan.'

'I'm not going to make it to the Birdsville races, am I, Isobel?'

'Why ever not? Such suspicion in a man not yet 30.'

'Are you and Francine really twins?'

'You're obsessed with that and we answered you last night. Maybe Dad's right and you are stupid. I don't know what he sees in you.'

'Are you the twins in George's story?'

'You are getting nowhere with these questions, Steele, though I am answering truthfully. Maybe you need to think laterally like the person on the ice block. More coffee?'

'You're playing with me.'

'Perhaps.'

'Did your Dad kill your mother and her lover?'

'You'd have to ask him.'

'Is the bank about to foreclose on the property?'

'No.'

I stood up. 'I am going to ask your Dad to finish his story.'

'No, don't do that. We are still playing.'

'Game over,' I said. 'Where's Francine?'

'You wanna play with me?' Francine said from down the hall. She wore a two-piece white nightie, revealing until she tied a light dressing gown around it.

Isobel was annoyed. 'Steele wants to know how the story ends when Dad visited his brother in Sydney.'

'His brother? His brother's a banker, too?'

'Investment banker,' Francine said. Dad reckons they're the worst kind but he and his brother were always close?'

'Were?' I said.'

'Are. Are close,' Francine said. 'Down in Sydney, they just had a few a drinks. Dad gave his nieces presents and stayed a few days. Hardly earth-shattering.'

'His nieces are twins and his brother's a banker,' I said.

'Having twins runs in the Grave family,' Isobel said.

'And your mother?'

'She writes to us all the time,' Francine said. 'Phones when we are away studying. Dad pretends he doesn't know a thing about the phone calls.'

'The farm makes money doing nothing?'

'Dad writes comedy scripts for film and television. 'He even writes bits and pieces for U.S. TV. They keep Americanising his jokes but he does not watch television so it does not bother him. His income fluctuates but in the end it pays well enough to send us to uni and prevent him from flogging a dead horse, um, cow,' one of them said.

'He doesn't write comedy scripts? That can't be true,' I said.

'Please yourself,' Francine said. 'I bet he's been taking notes since he went to his room after dinner, which he does not call tea, and which we usually have a lot later. And which we always wash up for, except yesterday. And he doesn't go to bed at 7pm.'

'And when you say he likes me?'

'As a character,' Isobel said. 'He says he wants to use you.'

'And all that ominous flirting you pair were doing with me?'

'What can we say?' Isobel said.

'Like father like daughter,' they said in unison.

The girls decided to give the races a miss which was a bit of a shame as I found them quite attractive now I was fairly certain they were not planning to kill me.

George insisted he fill the ute's tank from his petrol supplies. 'They tell me many visitors to the Birdsville races fly in,' he said.

'Flying to Birdsville sounds good,' I said. 'Next time I'll take a different route.'

'Which one?' George said.

'Probably Natalie. She stood by me during the money drought.'

George said I was a stupid clown and the family waved me on my way.

FROM THE EDGE
Raelene Purtill

Inspired by the true story of *An Innocent Man* by John Grisham

FOR TWENTY-TWO YEARS Colleen O'Brien never missed a visit to her daughter's grave. Not on April 10th, Debra's birthday; nor on December 17th, the anniversary; or even the second Friday of the month, Colleen's day off. On every significant occasion, she bought daffodils, Debra's favourite, and walked to the family plot on the hill behind St. Martins.

With each step, she found comfort in her memories until she arrived at the grave site. At that point, it was a strange set of emotions which claimed her - a mixed-up cocktail of sadness, sweet memory, and anger. And she would drink of it until she became numb, until the anger subsided, the memories blurred all together and the sadness drained away.

But today was not Debra's birthday, nor the anniversary of her death, nor even Colleen's day off. Today the sadness and anger did not go away, but it rose like a bright hot sun to burn her. Today she stood- there was no kneeling in submission or acceptance today – she stood at the edge of a muddy great hole. A muddy great empty hole.

Today they had exhumed Debra's body.

Dark soil lay scattered over the lawn embossed with tyre marks from whatever machine had desecrated the site. The collapsed headstone was flat and cold and as a final insult- some disrespectful cretin had placed a Coke can on it.

She had been at work when Susan told her about cranes and coroner's vehicles and police doing something up here. Colleen threw down her headset. It bounced off the desk and hung abandoned as she dashed from the office. No daffodils, no comforting memories; it was panic that pulled her up the hill today to find it was all true.

The edges of the hole blurred. She could slip in there herself and no one would notice. She could cover herself with that dark, brown mud and disappear forever. She could join Debra in a place where it wouldn't hurt anymore. But right now, it hurt and right now she was ready to hurt someone else. Not herself, not yet, although she was sure that would come. Her tears mixed with her mascara, so when she wiped them, she appeared as a warrior with war paint on her face. And her prey was that lying toad of an investigator who promised Debra would be left in peace.

She paced the warpath to the old stone building which housed the police station. In the first weeks of the investigation it was Colleen's second home, and she knew it well. In those early days when Debra was missing, she climbed the steps with hope, expectancy and respect for the work of Patrick J. Brady. Today the man would be lucky if he survived the next hour. She slammed through the revolving door and shouted his name from the lobby.

'Detective Brady!'

Her voice echoed through the atrium and brought a young sergeant to her side.

'Can I help you, Ma'am?'

Colleen gasped. The woman could have been her daughter. Mousy hair pulled back in a bun, sharp, dark eyes holding a question, her bright mouth ready with a smile. Colleen squashed the reaction and said, 'Where's Patrick Brady?' The name soured her tongue.

'Please wait here.'

The girl directed her to a seat, but Colleen remained standing. She turned her sight to the street outside, in an effort to regain her composure. She had begun to crumble against the reality of a personnel officer doing her job and the fact she was on Brady's turf now. She could not let him win. She would not let his cause destroy hers. She was here to fight for the remains of her daughter, for the remains of her own sanity.

'Colleen.'

She turned on him. 'You should have told me. You promised you would tell me.'

'How did . . .?'

'A work colleague told me.'

He frowned.

'She said there was equipment and I knew, I just knew . . .' Her look accused him. He rubbed a hand over his bald head and down his neck where he ran a finger around the collar of his business shirt. 'It all happened so fast. We couldn't wait.'

'Couldn't wait to make a phone call?' Colleen's frustration turned inward. She groaned. 'I should never have let you get to me. I should have held my ground. I said no, I should have meant it.' She sat, her head in her hands. He moved in beside her.

'You did the right thing when you finally agreed to it. As soon as we get the results, I'll let you know.' He raised an arm to her shoulder.

She shrugged it off. 'No apology?'

'I don't see why . . .'

'You don't see, do you? All you care about is your case. One more arrest. Are you going for detective of the month?'

'You need to stay calm, Colleen.'

'How could you? How could you disturb my little girl?'

'This new testing will help us find her killer.'

'What?! Who did you put in gaol then?'

Brady licked his lips and lowered his gaze. 'There's been some new evidence.'

So, he was innocent, just as the papers were saying, just as he protested. An innocent boy, a grown man now, who had lost twenty years of his life, a victim of justice.

She narrowed her eyes and spoke slowly. 'What new evidence?'

'Should I say new technology, which has caused us to re-examine the evidence. And we need Debra's help.'

'Don't condescend to me. I know what you're up to. My girl is just ... just a guinea pig in your new experiments.'

They plunged into silence. Brady adjusted his collar again. 'In that space, Colleen's brain vibrated against her skull. She could hear the nerve endings pop. She rubbed her temples.

'Why couldn't you just leave her alone?'

The detective's face blurred and went far away. His voice became indistinguishable from the rushing disorientation that engulfed her. She staggered from the revolving door and stumbled into the street. Swept along by the Friday lunch time crowd, her senses were bombarded by the smell of fragrances and body odour and Yum Cha. Light reflecting off glass and metal made her eyes ache. A siren pierced the afternoon air. The bitter taste of Brady's betrayal stung. She could sense cold fingers of madness stroking her arms. She stepped off the footpath.

Across the street the neon light of the pub competed against the bright sky. She entered and had to wait for her eyes to adjust to the darkness. Adjust to the darkness – hadn't she been doing that for twenty years? Do you ever really get used to it? She had fought it and she fought it now. When everything came into focus, she found an available seat at the bar.

On the way out, she stopped by the drive-through next door and bought a six pack to continue at home. The endless street, the endless night, her endless life lay before her, like that muddy great hole where her treasure had been.

Graves were supposed to be permanent. Debra's grave had been Colleen's security, the permanence she craved, and it had been violated. Where could she go now?

A church bell rang out on cue. She laughed. She'd given up finding solace there a long time ago. Could she try again? She slid into a pew at the back and listened to the choir rehearse at the front. She allowed the song to float above her and she swayed to the rhythm of it.

'Come to me all who are heavy laden, and I will give you rest.'

Rest.

It had eluded her for twenty years.

Rest.

She slid the six pack under the seat and stretched out, her jacket became a pillow for her head.

The organist found her after choir practice. 'Wake up.'

She sat up.

'Move along. You can't stay here.'

The combined effects of opened graves, confrontations with condescending cops and a long afternoon with long bottles of wine, rose to Colleen's throat and erupted onto the tiles. At the sight of her vomit splashed on the man's shiny shoes, she laughed. He lifted her by the back of her dress and pushed her out the vestry door before him. She found herself abandoned on the street, clutching her six pack.

The nap had cleared her head and she wandered home where she crawled onto her bed and dreamed she fell from the edge of a black hole. When the sun warmed her face, she stirred and reached for the beer carton. By lunch, she needed something stronger and tripped downstairs, steadying herself at the bottom before lurching into the kitchen. From under the sink she grabbed two bottles of wine and a couple of extra cans. With her arms full she bent to the bench and took the car keys in her teeth.

She floored the accelerator and her Datsun squealed underneath her. While she waited at the T-junction, she opened the window so the world could hear *Fox on the Run*.

Colleen roared, her voice tuneless and bitter. One hand on the wheel, one hand holding a beer. The amber liquid soothed her throat, but nothing else. She gained a rhythm: swig – toss the can from the car – sing along – grab the next can – change tape, next song – accelerate – empty – toss, sing - and it gave purpose to her otherwise meaningless actions.

So it went until her headlights lit up a country exit. She hurtled through the night along a narrow road with undefined edges, going nowhere.

This was not how she had planned her life. Somewhere, somehow twenty-two years ago she had been betrayed and abandoned by whatever forces controlled the universe. Fate, or God, or that other unseen thing – the killer climbing the stairs to her daughter's apartment.

The headlights of an oncoming car became the light of reason. How did she come to this? How did she come to betraying and abandoning herself to rage and drink? She slammed on the brakes and pulled over, where she opened the car door and vomited. With the dregs of her last can, she rinsed and spat. The pressure in her bladder became urgent. She relieved herself in a bush. And with that relief her sanity returned. She drove back toward town.

Sheila and Dan found her at Big Bob's service station.

'Colleen, where have you been?'

'What's going on with you?'

She filled her mouth with a burger and swallowed it with the help of black coffee, but she didn't answer. There was no point, not to her answers, not to her sister and brother-in-law being there, not to any of it.

'You're coming back with me. Sheila will drive your car.' 'Good ol' reliable, controlling Dan. Now there was another voice in her head: *'He's concerned, not controlling. Go with him.'*

'No', she said aloud but she was answering the head voice, not her brother-in-law.

'Don't argue.' Dan again. 'Finish your coffee.'

The road did not look familiar. 'This isn't the way home, Dan. Where are you taking me?'

'Hospital.'

'What? No. Let me go.'

She opened the door beside her, and the road rushed by underneath. Reality again. Reality and panic. She pulled it shut and sat back. The tears came then, unbidden, unending, and exhausting. She wiped her face when Dan pulled into the emergency bay knowing that they had not really ended. Now she had let them come, they would invite themselves again at unexpected moments.

She signed the admission forms as if someone else had control of the pen. It was her name scrawled there, but she didn't recognise it. Dan and Sheila helped her into the ward, but they were strangers to her. Their voices came from far away as they arranged pillows, put shoes in the bedside cupboard and talked like she wasn't there. Perhaps she wasn't. That's it. I'm not really here. This is some weird dream; but then Sheila said, 'They shouldn't have taken Debra's body,' and Colleen came back to that empty hole in the ground.

From her bed, she imagined she paced around the grave waiting for Debra to return. Only when her daughter rested again could she come back from the muddy edge.

SIX WEEKS LATER she and Detective Brady were there. Neat, green turf surrounded the site. The headstone was clean and upright. She knelt and placed a new vase of fresh daffodils, then stood to admire the effect: a splash of contrasting colour against the grey slab.

'The DNA tests have provided new evidence,' Detective Brady said.

'So, twenty years in prison for an innocent man?'

He nodded.

'I've done my time too.' Like Debra, she had been disturbed for a while but now she was tidy, neat and all put back together.

When they turned from the grave, Colleen was aware she was stepping consciously and deliberately toward something new and away from the edge.

RETROSPECTIVE: From the 2012 anthology:
Sweet and Sour Ken Armstrong illustration

TREASURE IN THE SNOW
Jeanette O'Hagan

HUGE WET SNOWFLAKES SWIRLED on the mountain wind, clumping on my eyebrows and piling up on my shoulders. The snow came thicker and faster, blotting out the sky, smothering the light and deadening sound. Only a few tanis of the path in front of my horse's ears remained visible, and the precipitous drop beside us was transformed into a churning cloud of white.

I pulled the cloak tighter around me. 'We should turn back and find the shelter we passed earlier.'

The silvery-skinned lady rode on, head and shoulders hunched against the bitter edge of the wind, one arm cradling her large treasure bag against her body.

'Turn back if you want.' Her words came back in snatches. 'You've done your duty. No one will blame you for leaving.'

What she said was true, except I'd sworn as her guide to protect her.

'Lady, we can wait until the storm stills and make the journey then.'

She looked over her shoulder, her gaze sweeping the path as though looking for unseen pursuers. 'If this snow blocks the pass, it could be days or indeed a cycle of the golden moon before passage is possible. Go now, if you wish. I cannot turn back.'

Slide it. I put aside all thoughts of warmth and focused on the small section of icy path before us. My horse's hooves slipped on the icy scree. A rock dislodged and slithered over the precipice's edge. It gathered other rocks and snow and sent them blundering down the cliff below with a muffled roar of an avalanche. I reined my horse in at this stark reminder that with one slip we too would be broken on the sharp rocks in the ravine far below us.

She'd promised me precious stones worth five hundred kapoki to help her on the journey, enough to set me up with a house or a lifetime's use of a plot of land. Much good it would do me if I fell over the mountain's edge or was buried deep under an avalanche. And how many more stones did she carry in her treasure pouch? Wealth unimaginable.

She turned and her forest-green eyes met mine. She didn't say a word; she didn't need to. My cheeks and neck burned with shame at the direction my thoughts.

'At least dismount, Lady. We should lead the horses on this steep icy path,' I said, my voice gruff. I wanted to ask what the hurry was, why her journey couldn't wait until a more seasonable time, but something in her look, the way she held herself repulsed such questions.

She hesitated, then swung a leg over and slid down the mare's steaming flank, all the while cradling her treasure. Her pale lips were blue-tinged with cold, and her eyebrows and the glimpses of hair beneath her hood like mahogany.

I slipped off Seeker and whispered gentle words to calm him before pulling out a flask of maize beer from my pack. First, I took a swig of its warmth before offering a sip to my charge.

The day was fast going and we had to reach the other side of the pass before nightfall. 'Come,' I said. 'We need to hurry.'

She nodded. 'I sense his coming with the shadows.' And I wondered if she was crazy or maybe that was me.

We pushed on through the storm, careful to keep the horses on the outside edge. Their bulk sheltered us from the worst of the wind. Already, my limbs were heavy with fatigue and a strange dream-like state settled over me.

The wind strengthened, dumping more snow. My face stiffened like the skim of ice on an exposed pond and with each step the drifts deepened. Soon all I could see was a driving wall of freezing white, the sharp mountain peaks mere ghostly shadows.

For all that she was a fine lady, she didn't complain. Head down like the mare, she trudged on without tiring, her cloak wrapped tight and carrying her burden snug against her chest.

We shuffled on in a wold of icy white upon white, the silver disc of the sun halfway down the sky behind us. Darkness would come later to these heights but it would come. We needed to be on the uplands by then. Despite urgency, we could go no faster.

The path steepened, a sign we were nearing the height of the pass and the promise of a waystation beyond it. I breathed a long sigh of relief, the air clouding from my breath.

Sudden shadows fell over us and a strange screeching noise filled the air above me. The horses pulled away, eyes white and ears flinching backwards. I threw up an arm in defence as a great shadow swept down over us. My heart thundered against my ribs. I spun around, peering into the swirling, white wind.

'By the two moons, what was that?'

The lady continued to walk on. 'An illusion. It cannot harm you.'

Her words seemed to come from a long way away, high-pitched and weak. All around me dark shadows flittered and swooped. Flame-red eyes, feral and hungry glared at me. Slavering teeth and sharp curved claws rent gaps in the mist.

'There are monsters,' I yelled.

'Calm yourself, Pathfinder. The shadows will only harm you if you open the door to fear.' Her voice was like a beacon in deep darkness.

A great shape swooped down upon her and I thought it would swallow her whole. She did not falter but kept walking, eyes fixed ahead, and it broke against her like a wave against a rock, shattering in a swirl of foam and air.

Shivering so hard my jaw ached, I clutched Seeker's bridle to follow the lady. Great shadowy shapes rushed at me, I closed my eyes, any moment expecting the rending of my flesh, but only the ice-sharp wind buffered my face. The air was full of foul voices but I kept going, not willing to be out-done by my charge.

After a while, only the snuffling of the horses, the soft thud on their hooves and the cold whistle of the wind filled the silence. The shadows were gone.

By now the snow was almost to my knees, my clothes soaked and icy, and each step was a torture. If we didn't find shelter soon, we would die.

We followed the path as it turned yet again drawing back from the edge, climbing up to disappear between two peaks. At last, the wind slackened and a flickering golden glow painted the steep rock faces, guarding the pass.

'Looks like a campfire.' It seemed unlikely. Perhaps travellers had come ahead of us on the trail and managed to light a fire out of the full force of the storm.

'This way, my Lady.' I shouted against the wind and lurched into a shambling walk towards the red-ochre light promising warmth and safety, the sudden urge to get to the other side of the pass like hunger upon me. We needed heat and shelter to avoid a frozen white death.

'No!' She caught my arm with an unexpectedly strong grip and pulled me to a stop. Even as I turned to rebuke her, the gravel beneath my boots shifted and one foot slid down until it found only air instead of the solid path I was expecting.

I fell to one knee and threw out my arms in an attempt to catch something solid. My chest tightened and terror shot through me. I could feel myself slipping into the abyss.

'Catch.' The lady threw me a rope and looped the other end on the horn of the mare's saddle, urging it to walk. Bit by bit, it pulled me back from the edge.

The wind dropped and when I turned, I looked straight down into the ravine, with a foaming white water below. My limbs shook like leaves in a gale.

'That is not the way, Pathfinder.' Even as the lady spoke the golden glow fizzled out, leaving the howling wind and the blanketing grey-white snow like a shroud winding around us.

'The path, what happened to it?'

'It was never there. Another illusion sent by Man of Shadows to deceive us.'

Whoever that was, or maybe I was going addle-brained with mountain sickness. How stupid could I be? How many times had I travelled these paths, but never before been so mislead or confused in the middle of the wildest storm? First the shadows in the wind and falling snow, now a fire and light that was not there. Perhaps the cold and the thin air at these heights had dulled my mind. Or was this a dream and soon I'd wake in our adobe hut, my wife lighting the fire and preparing the dawn meal to the clatter of the neighbour's pots and calls of the village yarma herd boys. I shook my head, snow falling in clumps.

'Forgive me, Lady, for leading you wrongly.'

I brushed my hands of dirt and ice and stood shakily to my feet, no longer sure what was solid ground and what was illusion.

She smiled and touched my arm. 'I fear it is I who have put you in danger. But if we stay strong, we will win through the forces sent against us. The Maker of Light will show us.'

Her words sent a chill down my spine. What forces? It made no difference for we could no longer go back to shelter with the depth of snow now behind us. All we could do was forge a path ahead. And we needed to be quick about it. The snow storm lulled for a few moments and in the west, a sullen red light lit the clouds as though soaked in blood.

We continued up the trail, each lost in our own thoughts. The path climbed steeply and wound to the right, now between rough walls of stone. Beyond it, our way would bend downwards and into the lee of the wind and to the way station where we could camp for the night.

A dark hooded figure stepped out of the flurry of snow where the path widened into a saddle between two rocky tors. He leaned on his staff, blocking our way.

More mirages, phantoms to confuse me. I put my head down and kept walking, stopping only when the metal tip of the staff nudged my chest.

'Not another step or you will die.'

My legs went to chilled water. I am a guide, a trader, not a warrior, though I will fight to protect my charges if need be.

'Let us pass, sir, for we are travellers along the Royal road, and we mean you no harm.' Who was this stranger blocking our path, stopping us from reaching safety?

'My business in not with you, mountain guide. Step aside and do not interfere. When I've finished my task, you may go.'

I drew a long knife from my belt, keenly aware that what other weapons I had were secured to Seeker's saddle. Yet I could not allow this stranger to harm the lady.

'Come, friend. Why put your life at risk for a stranger?'

I bristled. A mountain guide was only as good as his pledge. If word got around that I'd failed to protect one of my charges, who would hire me and what would be left of my honour?

'Hard to be a guide if you're dead.' The stranger's cool voice chipped at my certainties. As if to tease me, he came in fast with his staff, a blur in the wind, and knocked my knife from my hand, sending it sliding down the path.

The certainty that I couldn't subdue this opponent grew like a malignant seed within me. And for what, to save the life of this silvery-skinned outlander, a southerner at best, a demon and sorceress at worst. What was she doing in our lands anyway?

'Step aside, good guide, and I, once I'm done, will share her treasure with you.' The man's silver eyes were mesmerising.

Maybe she was a sprite, an Adelphi, who lured me into the storm to destroy me. I have heard of such things, though never before experienced them. I swallowed hard, feeling the pressure to obey.

'Friend Pathfinder, I absolve you of your duty to protect me, if only you will promise to take my treasure to safety. Let me deal with this Man of the West.'

It was as though the lady's musical voice awoke me from a dream. I could not let this man do whatever he willed on her, for it suddenly came to me that his intent was evil.

'Fool.' The flame-haired man pulled out a small silver dagger from his robes and sent it spinning toward me, all the while muttering in a strange language. I ducked. He sent two more blades in quick succession. The third dagger nicked my arm causing a fiery sensation.

The winds stirred and whipped around us, and our horses turned and bolted down the path.

Now he swung his staff at my legs and I staggered backwards, suddenly dizzy.

The woman stepped in front of me. 'Begone, Man of Betrayal, go back to your hiding hole. Your time is passing, Killer of Innocents.'

The man laughed. 'My time is ascending, Rutiah, Mother of Fools, and when I come into my full power, I will eliminate all your kind, starting with you. How convenient to find you all alone and vulnerable?'

The lady hugged her bundle. 'Have you no pity. No, I know you don't. Was your heart always so shadow-filled?'

He blinked and stared at her for a moment.

'Then do what you will.' She turned and bent over me. 'Let me see your wound.'

'Watch your back,' I whispered. The fire spread from my arm to my shoulder.

'He will do what he must,' she said. 'But if I don't treat this, you will die.' And she poured a liquid on the seeping wound and gave me some dried leaves to swallow. 'I have no time to steep it in scalding water,' she said, 'this will have to do. Help will come, you'll see.'

The man leaned on his staff, his face a sneer. 'This is entertaining. You waste your time, for he is already as good as dead from the poison and you will soon follow.'

It was as though the lady did not hear him. She took strips of cloth and bound my wound.

Then came the strangest sound, a keening from the swirl of snow and ice above the peaks. And three large, white-headed eagles flew down and attacked the man.

He wielded his staff against them, sending dark balls of mist flying at them. They ducked and feinted, diving and attacking with beak and claws, and driving him down the path to the edge of the mountain. 'Go, Man of the West, you are not welcome here.'

I blinked, thinking that whatever poison was on the dagger was taking full effect for I could swear the eagle had spoken. And then they were gone and three figures emerged from the snow with the same strange slivery skin and dressed similar to the lady's flowing clothes.

'Love of mine heart, why didn't you stay in the haven until we could come,' the taller one said, taking her hand.

'It's by the Maker's favour we came this way at all, Matu,' another, a woman of similar appearance said.

'The haven was compromised. Shanta is no longer safe for us,' the lady said. 'I could not stay longer and risk our little one.'

'Come, no time for talking, let's get to warmth and safety.'

The first man turned, and putting his fingers in his mouth, he whistled. Moments later the horses trotted back up the path, the mare, Melody, first and Seeker following.

'Thank you, Man of the Mountain Paths, we can take it from here,' he said.

The strange events, my injuries, and the end of the danger finally took their toll on me. My legs buckled under me and darkness swirled around, taking me with it.

Warmth suffused my limbs, my fingers and toes tingling at the return of sensation. And somewhere close, musical voices spoke words I did not understand. I cracked open my eyes and saw the orange-red leap of flame. The acrid-sweet scent of burning pine cones and wood filled the small wayside house. Had it all been a dream?

I sat up and rubbed my thawing hands. A searing pain flashed across my upper arm beneath a neat bandage. Four strange people were in the lodge with me. My heart quailed. Were they demons, stealer of souls? But how could that be?

'He's awake,' the lady said and her laughter filled the warm space. 'Eldest daughter, give him some more of the green broth.'

'Why?' I asked.

'The poison on dagger was a strong one. It will take time to counteract its effects.'

She came closer to me and when she did, I noticed the pouch snuggled against her chest, though now it was open.

'Your treasure, you did not lose it,' I said.

'No.' She smiled. 'Because of you she is safe.'

'Me? I did so little.' Though why a she?

'You gave us time.' The tall man came and put an arm around the lady, his dark eyes star-filled, 'What is your name, Pathfinder?'

I cleared my throat. 'Kuman.'

'Kuman, Man of the Mountains. I am called Jazadek, and this little one is Rasel, our youngest daughter. He pulled a cloth to one side, and at last I could see, a tiny fist with five perfect fingers waving at me. A silvery-skinned baby, no more than a few weeks old snuggled inside the pouch.

'How may we repay you for your services?' Jazadek asked

'You have already given me my life. For saving such a treasure as this little one, that is enough'

Jazadek smiled and touched my forehead. 'You restore my confidence in the children of Tamrak with your deeds. For this we call you friend.'

The baby turned her dark eyes toward my face and gurgled in agreement.

RETIRED OFFICERS

David J. Bell

At intermittent times they meet and dwell
on days of yore, those once important men
who held great sway o'er lesser man's career.
From soaring in high halls they since have fell
to reminisce on power of word and pen
in distant past. They now instil no fear,
for time has left these geriatric souls
as lingering shadows. There is no dispute,
in season, they were towers among their kind;
elected by like men with similar goals.
But now, they sit by quiet bars in moot
and ponder passing feet and swirling wind.

FEATHERED HOOVES
Chris Radge

PAIGE SHOT HER ARM OUT like a boom gate across Trudy's chest. 'Wait,' she whispered urgently and dragged her down behind the dense bush.

'P, P-aige.' Trudy said gulping down deep breaths pointing toward the clearing.

They had only been running for a short distance, but trying to keep up with Rue and Nitro seemed near impossible. They weren't fillies anymore. Far from it, they were dressage and show jumping horses with well-established ancient Egyptian lineage.

Twenty minutes earlier, Paige and Trudy had gone to the sand enclosure to rub down and congratulate the pair on yet another blue-ribbon win but the enclosure was empty. There should have been at least a dozen or so horses frolicking and rubbing themselves down in the sand. Paige spun on her heel and scanned the surrounding area. There, at the edge of the forest pranced all of the missing horses. She whistled for Rue to come back but the horse ignored her and flicked her head from side to side in what she could only call elation. *What's gotten into that horse?* she thought and noticed all of the escaped horses were acting the same.

'Um, how'd they get out there?' Trudy interrupted her thoughts and whistled to her own horse Nitro with no effect.

Paige saw a flash of black and squinted hard to see what had lured her horse away. Another swish of Rue's head and she saw him, head high and nostrils flaring and the ebony coat of the unbridled stallion glistened in the afternoon sun. The carrots she'd brought slipped from her fingers. Their eyes locked and the world went still, and any thought of getting the horses back had left her. She stood mesmerized starring at the perfect specimen of horse flesh until he flicked his own mane breaking the bond.

Paige's eyes cleared and she saw Trudy kicking up sand as she ran toward the guard rail preparing to jump over.

The stallion started to tap and drag his white hoof across the dusty ground. She raced after Trudy who was now on the other side of the fence and jumped to the second rung and flipped herself over in one fluid motion landing on both feet like the high school gymnast she was. She looked up in time to see the stallion rear, turn, and gallop away into the forest with the rest of horses following.

That's how the girls found themselves hiding behind a bush, desperately trying to catch their breath. The horses had stopped abruptly at the bottom of a cliff with nowhere to go. The stallion pushed the horses forward toward the rock face but they skittered away corralling themselves into a tight group. If it was possible for a horse to have an expression of frustration, Paige was sure she saw it on this fellow. He reared and tapped again at the ground but the herd of horses did not move. Finally, the stallion walked toward the shimmering rock.

Paige blinked trying to refocus on what she couldn't believe. The black horse was now half engulfed by the rock with just its flank exposed. She turned to Trudy and saw her own dumb founded expression.

Swinging back around Paige watched the black stallion emerge smaller than it had been moments earlier. 'What the . . .' she said not believing her eyes, how could she, the stallion was now pony size. Her hand flew to her mouth to stop voicing the surprise bubbling to the surface. Trudy's face turned white as chalk and she swayed trying to stand.

Paige pulled her back down again and said, 'Are *you* seeing what I'm seeing?'

'A, um, arh, a', Trudy babbled.

'That arh, horse has wings.' She voiced for her.

Trudy nodded once with a look that belonged in a comic strip. Finger to her lip Paige made a shushing motion and said quietly. 'Let's just watch for a moment.'

The small winged stallion circled the skittish horses moving them closer to the shimmering rock. It looked like a circus act with this little horse trying to make the others do his bidding. He flapped his wings forward toward the group and they finally started to move forward filing in one after another with Rue and Nitro bringing up the rear. There was no time to waste. 'Okay. You ready?' Paige said anxious to follow them.

'Arh, ye . . .'

But Paige felt a hand on her right shoulder. It couldn't be Trudy, she was on her left and before she could turn around to look, a large calloused hand was clamped across her mouth stopping the squeal that was ebbing to the surface. Her eyes darted to the left to see Trudy staring at the person holding her captive. Paige's eyes pleaded to her *help me*, but Trudy did nothing. Instead a deep hushed voice said.

'If you promise not to scream, I will let you go.'

What choice did she have? She nodded once and was turned around. Standing in front of her was Nash the handsome stable hand all the girls secretly wanted as their boyfriend.

'Wa, what are you doing here?' Paige asked in her own hushed voice.

'I heard you whistle and saw the two of you chasing after the horses,' he said.

Silently Paige pointed toward the scene in front of her but was taken aback when his expression didn't change. He just nodded scanning the scene in front of him.

'I've seen this before when I was a young boy. It's what has kept me here in these stables all my life, waiting to see this again.'

'Huh?'

'My first experience with the winged horses was when I was very young. I'd seen the black stallion coerce the mares from their enclosure and I ran after them only to see the last horse enter the side of the mountain. I'd run to where the rock had shimmered and beat on it, but nothing happened. I sat there with my back against the rock for hours until it was almost dark,' he said still watching the horses. 'I returned the next day and the day after that but the shimmering never happened again, until today.'

'So, this has happened before?' Paige asked, her eyes darting from the horses back to him.

'Yes, about eight years ago', he said. 'There is a legend about ancient winged horses, the descendants of Pegasus, the white winged stallion of Medusa and Poseidon and their secret mountain entrance but only a few have ever witnessed it.'

'So, have any of the horses ever returned?' Paige asked.

'No.' He looked at his riding boots.

Her heart constricted. *No, not Rue.* That stallion could not have her horse, her friend, the one she told all of her deepest secrets to. The one constant thing in her life that never changed, and her mind was stabbed with the memory of her father dying four years earlier and the upheaval of moving to Egypt to where her mother's family lived. One positive thing was she'd met Trudy and made friends with Nash who made every inch of her tingle whenever he looked her way.

She shook the memory away and stood. The stallion turned and looked at each of the teenagers in turn. But it was too late. The last of the mares had entered the shimmering rock. The small stallion nodded once and fled towards the shimmering wall. But Nash was fast, his long legs carried him quickly to the mountain and thrust an arm into the shimmering entrance. He'd waited a long time for this chance and he wasn't letting it get away now.

'Come on girls, quick. This won't last too much longer,' he called as his body was slowly engulfed by the shimmering rock wall.

The girls were almost there. Only his hand was now visible bidding them to take it. Forming a human chain, Paige grabbed his and Trudy's hand and they were dragged into the dark cave.

'How'd you know we'd be alright?' Paige's hand tingled at his touch. She wanted to hold it longer, wanted to rub her thumb along his and . . .

'Paige. Earth to Paige,' Trudy said in a harsh whisper.

'Um, well?' Paige dropped his hand waiting for the answer she could tell by their voices had already been answered.

'I didn't. But I've done a lot of research.' He continued with a grin. 'This mystery has consumed me for years and I knew we only had moments before the gateway closed. I'd read, if an object with a beating heart was in the opening of the entrance it would stay open for longer.'

'Okay Einstein, now what?' Paige said as the sound of hoof beats faded in the distance.

He shrugged and realised nobody could see him. "I hadn't thought that far ahead. I'd given up even finding the entrance until now.'

Trudy pulled out a lighter and the cave lit up with shadows. 'What?' She shrugged. I use it to melt the end of rope when it frays.'

Paige rolled her eyes and said, 'Sure you do', and left it at that. *We'll sort that out when we get back. If we get back*, she thought.

The tunnel looked like polished black onyx and they could see another light fifty paces ahead. Like moths to a flame they were drawn to it. Coming closer Trudy extinguished the lighter and crept to the edge of the light. Their soft gasps echoed in the tunnel and some of the tiny winged horses turned towards them forcing the trio to scurry back into the safety of the blackness.

Minutes passed before they felt safe enough to peak again. In front of them was an environment perfectly suited for any horse, wings or not. There were rolling mounds of lush green grass, a running stream and a brightness like sunshine. But there was no sun. *How . . .* Paige thought and noticed light refracting off crystal like stalactites. She traced the light phenomenon to a hole in the ceiling where more crystals acting like mirrors bouncing the light back and forth until it reached the first stalactite. *So that's how they got photosynthesis to work down here, clever. But that doesn't to explain the entrance, wings and their size.*

As if reading her mind, Nash said, 'So how do they reduce in size? Not to mention those wings. I can see why they have too, there are so many tiny horses in here some with, but many without wings, and some carrying foals.'

'Is that why they stole our mares? To mate with! How disgusting' Trudy said stepping forward into the light.

It was then Paige noticed she too had shrunk. *Um.* Moving beside her friend she sized herself up. *Yep, me too*, Paige thought.

Nitro and Rue started to trot toward them but the stallion blocked their way. He wanted his new concubines for himself, but as far as Paige was concerned, they weren't his to keep and she stepped further into the open cave system to fight for their freedom. She didn't know how yet but she would figure it out, she always did. Paige squared her shoulders, hands on hips and planted her feet.

'Now now.' She heard it in her head. 'Wha . . .?' and the look on her friends' faces said it all. They'd heard it too. *So I'm not going batty after all.* Paige realised it must be something about this cave that gave them the ability to communicate with the horses through thought.

'Now now, nothing! Paige stated flatly. 'We want our horses and we will be on our way,' she said even though she had no idea how she was going to achieve that.

These girls have been foretold to be the mothers of future Pegasi Knights,' the stallion thought to us.

'Pegasai Knights, seriously.'

'Have you ever heard of King Arthur and his round table?'

'Of course.'

'Well this is similar, and Pegasi are the knights.'

'So, do they' she waved her hand around to encompass the two mares, 'have a say in this?

'Yes, they have already been formally asked. I would never bring a mare here without her permission, foretold or not.'

'Why, other than the obvious reason, do you need them?' Nash joined into the conversation.

'Because our lineage needs replenishing. The great wars of twin verse dragon saw many fatal injuries.'

'The who and what now . . .' Trudy stammered.

'The Great Wars! They happened a long time ago before you were born.'

'I have never heard of these wars of twin let alone a mythical dragon,' Trudy said

'Look where your standing, is this not mythical?'

'Well, um, yes I suppose it is.'

'We, the Pegasai are the protectors of the great council of Atlantis and we . . .'

'Oh, come on,' Paige interrupted, 'Do you expect us to believe there's an Atlantis now?'

'Haven't we established that you are standing in a mythical place with tiny flying horses? Is that not proof enough?'

'Arh, um, I suppose it has to be. Still we need to be with our horse friends to make sure they are ok with everything that is happening.'

'*Very well.*' And the stallion stood aside so Rue and Nitro could nuzzle their friends.

'Are you alright Rue?' Paige asked

'*Yes, Paige friend, I am,*' Rue thought to her friend. '*This is our destiny. It has been known for millennia that some of us hold the ancient blood and one day would be called upon to build our population once again, and we are honoured to do so.*'

'But what about our friendship, will your ever return?' Paige said in a little girl's voice.

'*We will return, but it won't be for many human years. You will have children of your own and I will have mine.*'

'It just seemed so all of a sudden.'

'*For you yes, but for us, we've known the time was coming and we are happy you can see us in our true form now.*'

'Your true form?'

'*Yes, to be able to fit in with the equine.*'

'It's interesting, I always felt we had a special connection. Did you feel that with Nitro?' Paige said to Trudy.

'I did actually. It was like Nitro was reading my mind, and now I know she actually was.'

'What about you Nas . . .' Paige looked around to see Nash with outstretched arms walking towards a heavily pregnant nut-brown mare.

'Tricky, you're alright. It's so good to see you again and look at you, going to be a mummy soon I see.' The horse nuzzled into his shoulder as he stroked her neck.

The black stallion communicated again. '*I have something for you. It was also foretold there would be one, The Minder, who would enter this cave and when this happened the egg would be transferred to her.'*

'But there are three of us,' Paige stated.

'Yes, the Minder and her closet friends.'

Paige looked at Nash. He had become a good friend over the years of competing but nothing really special. Maybe they were meant to become besties after all. You know the power of three and all that. 'Ok, but are we able to return to see our friends here once again?'

'Yes, take this.' The stallion pushed a black egg-shaped stone towards her. *'As long as you have this you can re-enter the cave.'*

Picking up the stone she placed it in the zipped pocket of her jodhpurs.

'So, this egg, where is it?' Paige asked.

Every horse in the cave looked to the centre of the ceiling. There, cradled in the crevice of the largest stalactite was a luminescent maroon ostrich size egg.

'And how pray tell do we get that?' She answered her own question almost immediately watching the black horse's majestic wings flap as he knelt forward.

'Please young Minder. It would be my honour.'

Paige hesitated only for a second and mounted him grabbing fistfuls of his glossy mane as he took off.

It was exhilarating. The breeze whooshed past her as he expertly navigated the beautiful but dangerous stalactites. It felt right being on the back of this winged horse, her training and instinct clicked into gear automatically squeezing gently with her thighs to help her stay seated. The flapping of the wings gave a similar motion of galloping and she fell in sync easily with the movement.

The crowd below watched the pair who looked to be one beast. If this had been the great wars they would have been inseparable.

They reached the egg in moments and the stallion hovered in one spot as she reached out both hands to retrieve the precious egg but it was wedged hard. She pulled harder but could see loose shards of crystal had wedged the egg into place. Releasing the egg she reached for the closest shard. 'Ouch.' Paige pulled her hand back quickly.

'*Look,*' the stallion said. '*The shards are releasing. This proves you are in fact, The Minder. Only the blood of The Minder will release the egg.*'

'You could have told me that sooner,' she said sucking the metallic taste of blood from her finger.

'It is now yours to take young Minder.'

She reached out both hands again and lifted the egg slowly toward herself. She hugged the egg with one hand and grasped the horse's mane once again.

'Keep it safe, Youngling,' the stallion said. 'The fate of the council is up to you now. We will be here to protect you but you need to travel this journey yourself and with your confidants.'

Gosh, that sounds imminent, she thought forgetting the stallion could hear her, and he nodded after bringing her back to the ground without so much as a bump.

'Till we meet again, Minder.' And he nudged her towards the entrance.

'Goodbye Rue. Keep well my dear friend,' Paige said.

The three friends turned and set off for the end of the tunnel where shimmering light lit their way to the promise of adventure.

YELLOW
Karine Dupre

I AM AN OLD LADY.

In less than five years I will celebrate my centenary. One century with them, under the sun, the rain, some snow as well, and so many sky colors. I have looked at the trees raising, the lake receding, the hill getting inhabited. I have seen the footpaths becoming roads, the bitumen overtaking the tiny sandy pebbles and timber and bricks disappearing in favor of concrete. I have heard the icy lake growling at the end of every spring, and seen the fishermen running while the ice broke. Few were not fast enough; sometimes.

I have felt the sun warming my skin, blistering it and right after, the rain coming down on me, infiltrating any cracks and splits.

I carried tons of snow with still much more laying all around me. Snow becoming slushy, dirty, day after day and magically white again in just one night. I have seen children, and older even, rolling in it and building igloos. They also built candle nests to welcome visitors during the long and dark winter nights.

Many rested on my sides. They sought a bit of respite, a bit of meaning from their hectic life. Too many things to juggle with; too many things too fast. Around me, they dreamt of gardens, small carrots and peas. Some threw seeds and watched them grow, year after year. Sometimes, flowers were cut and bouquets were ornamenting my kitchen. Fruits were plenty also, but children, worse than any horde of crows, would rip off almost all of them before I had time to taste any. Especially the berries. Raspberries and redcurrant never lasted very long.

And poets came along as well. One boat in each hand, they offered me the ocean, to me who had only seen the lake. They made me travel, to me who will never leave. Others deposited in my heart the laughs of children, with swings and sand pits in building zig zag pathways from one house to the other.

The grills tickled my nostrils, the barbecue was lit many times. The mustard sausage in hand, we also sang or we listened to the one who scratched the guitar or violin. It was almost dark, the mosquitoes were coming in, the bottles were beginning to seriously litter the ground, but no matter, they were all staying, because the sun would finally rise soon and there was nothing more beautiful than a shared dawn.

I have seen things, indeed.

But few know what really happened.

Younger, I was impressive, taller than most. We shared home with several families. Downstairs, the hairdresser took care of all the heads and more than just hair; she cut short all the states of mind that might send one off the bridge. She had the gift of hope, giving you hope even if your life really was just a collection of miseries. On the first floor there were four families and on the second as well. A beautiful u-shaped staircase, very large, majestic, adorned with a round window, connected the two levels. And I, spruce, resplendent, proud of hosting so many tenants, could not prevent anything.

It was said that he was just coming out of jail; that he was an ugly fellow, one who spent every single coin in these liquors that drive you crazy. He had the little room upstairs, on the forest side. The same light, summer and winter; a small stove for heating and eating, just a tap for the water. His great luxury was the cold room, in fact the uninsulated part under the extended roof. Many wished they had a cold room, when no one had a fridge. Small, thin, a sailor's tattoo on the arm for a job he never pursued, he lived on these daily jobs that the factory proposed, or that the seasons offered.

On the same floor, also on the forest side, she lived. Nobody knew much about her. The room she occupied was barely larger than that of her neighbor but some of the floor timber slats creaked. So you could hear her getting out of bed, her back and forth small steps in front of the stove that had to be resuscitated, the water that had to be boiled.

It is said that he pushed her into this beautiful staircase. It is said that she was looking for it. It is said that it is not true, that she just fell, just an accident, and broke her neck.

But I know.

And I cannot say anything.

The hairdresser left and the rumors began to run.

Years later, when my first wrinkles appeared, when the neighborhood was still filled with these tiny houses that will make its reputation, the shouting began. This time, it did not concern us directly. But from every window, through every skylight, we could see that it was going to end badly. Their house adjoined ours at the back, at the edge of the forest that goes back to the primary school. They were there, both flaying each other, trying to love what was left. For him it was more and more his bottle and for her, her memories of him. Too many times she came to seek refuge under my porch. Too many times I opened her my door, hoping she would step over the threshold.

It was on a winter evening, this season that drives the men from here so crazy, that I found her in the snow, so close to my entrance door.

I could not say anything.

The rumor rumbled.

Then, one by one, they all left me. I begged them. I reminded them of the breathtaking view, the calm and serenity, the poems of the neighbor, the songs of the other. Nothing changed their mind. They had heard too many stories, the rumor had swelled.

My body went decrepit. I lost my splendor, my bowels started to rot. Nobody took care of me. On the contrary. Little brigands started to play with what I had left, dirtying every object, smashing and breaking everything that could be. I stank of vomit, inside of me everything was stained. They squatted at my place. No more poetry. It was rather the absence of life, the short paid intercourses, messy, abject, the desperate search for shelter to try to go on with life, at least until the next day. No wonder she came to me.

I saw her coming out of her little pink house, going down the road towards me, looking at the lake on her right. I saw her climb the little path that leads to my stairs trying to avoid the bedrock and its falling stones. I felt her weigh on every step. Heavily. And to look again at the lake, that lake she also could see from her bed. I heard her open the first door, watch for a sound that did not come, then open the second door. From her bag she pulled out the rope. Turning left, she opened the last door and looked at the beautiful tiled stove. She touched a few tiles, right where these rascals had put some rifle leads on a brawling night. The knot was already done. Conscientiously she unfolded the little stool that she always took with her to the community garden. Her small plot was the one running along the lake. Hanging the rope from the ceiling hook, where the habit had been to hang a beautiful chandelier, she was still looking at the lake, her beautiful lake. The stool was kicked.

The search went mad. They could not understand. And no one thought of asking me. You understand, I was so old, so damaged. And I was really embarrassed; I did not stop her. I could not say anything. What was the point?

So I let time destroy me. I thought the end was coming, I did not care. Let them all go to hell. Yet.

One day, they arrived, one after the other. To come see me. The talkative fatty with his ear stuck to the phone. Tall ones, little ones, singles, couples, families, retired, youngsters, some who did not see anything, some who understood right away. Some who were afraid, had heard about the rumor. Some who could not stand the smell.

And then, there were these two.

Eyes full of stars, who spoke between them a language that I did not understand. These two caressed the patina of my railings, gently scraped my sides, shook my stomach a little, gently lifting a few shreds of skin. They went around, listened to the wind in each flower and in each stone of the garden. They brought their dreams and their future.

This is when I realised that I would still have stories to tell and they would learn, very slowly, what I could not have said.

I became someone's house again.

FROM THE EDGE

Vera Murray

As I open the garden gate,
A cockatoo screeches,
Dropping macadamia nuts,
Too hard to crack.

Frangipani leaves whirling,
Some spinning in the wind.
Others spiral in their wake.
Ready is the garden rake.

As my cat Stacey stalks,
Loudly a parrot squawks,
Making gum leaves shiver.
In disgust, my cat then walks.

Beside the pile of garden waste,
A midget mouse and a worried worm,
Stare at each other, face to face,
While a nearby ant line slows its pace.

I hear, but faintly, Mum's voice raised,
Above the grating sound of grandpa's rocker.
No longer from the edge do I look,
As through the front door myself I lunge,

MISTAKEN IDENTITY
R. William Penshorn

JEFF BAKER WAS AN EXPERIENCED SURVEY CHAINMAN who was employed by Jones and Co, Surveyors. He was a clean shaven, good looking, capable young man as well as being quite popular. His smile was quite noticeable because of the spacious gap between his front two teeth. He was an off-sider to several of the company's surveyors from time to time and always did what was called the 'western run' with Surveyor Phil Dennis. This was a trip usually done twice yearly which normally went as far out as Charleville but at times to Quilpie and Eromanga. Jeff enjoyed being in the west but was always happy to return to the coast. He was a keen fisherman.

At other times he worked with Surveyor Arthur Molyneaux. They both enjoyed a beer and often would have a few together at a pub after a hot day's work. On a particular road centre line survey where Jeff assisted Arthur at the north coast, they stayed at a place known as Laguna Guest House. While there, they often joined the guests in a game of darts after dinner. Jeff excelled at the sport. Dart Cricket was a favourite game. Guests divided into two teams, Batsmen and Bowlers. Bowlers would have to hit the numbers one to eleven in numerical order while batsmen would attempt to make the highest score possible. The bullseye and triple twenty were the most aimed for targets. Once the eleven were hit, players changed over. The batsmen became the bowlers and vice versa. The highest scoring team of course, was the winner. Drinks always followed and everyone had a good time.

Arthur was happily married to a pretty woman named Mildred. She was quite a looker and had won a beach beauty competition not long before their marriage. Mildred was employed as a nurse in a local hospital and remained doing so after their wedding as Arthur was so often out of town with his work. Nurse Mildred Molyneaux had a very pleasant personality and was very popular among the hospital patients as well as the staff. She and Arthur met while he was a casualty for a short stay after being bitten by a black snake. He had been working on a bushland survey. Romance blossomed.

One of Mildred's favourite hobbies was to collect antiques. She was delighted one time when Arthur returned from an out of town job where his party had camped at the same location as one of the early Australian explorers. Lots of old bottles and other relics were on the site. Arthur took a selection home for a pleasant surprise to his beloved wife.

Jeff had an Italian girl-friend named Gina Martinelli. She was quite a good looker and would have given movie stars like Sophia Loren or Claudia Cardinale a good run for their money.

Jeff and Gina became engaged to be married. There were some celebrations held at Jones Co Headquarters. Everyone was happy for them.

Three months later Jeff sadly announced to his workmates the engagement was all off. 'She's a hot head,' he said. 'Too fiery for me. That's the way it is.'

After that, Jeff seemed to be down in the dumps for several weeks until one morning he arrived at work seemingly more cheerful, to announce to his mates that he and Gina had sorted out their problems and the engagement was back on. Everyone seemed to be very pleased for him.

The couple were married within the next six months. It was a happy wedding, conducted by the well-known minister, Reverend Reginald Gunson.

Many of Jones and Co. employees attended the wedding. Patsy Michaels, a pretty receptionist from the firm, sang Julie Rodger's old hit song *The Wedding* at the ceremony. She sang beautifully and received much applause, especially from the younger single men.

Jeff and Gina put a deposit on a good quality suburban house and seemingly happy, moved in together. Jeff confided to some of his workmates that things sometimes became a bit stormy within the marriage. He made it clear he found Gina's foul temper a bit hard to handle. 'But,' he added with a chuckle, 'the good times more than make up for it.' That always caused laughs all round. He was well aware that his male work mates quietly looked upon Gina as someone very desirable. He was pleased about that.

One evening when Jeff and Gina's second wedding anniversary was almost due, Arthur sat with his wife, Mildred in their living room, enjoying a drink while watching the TV news. A pretty announcer came on and caught Arthur's attention, even more so when he heard what she had to say. Her report said a man had gone missing, feared dead. His fishing boat had been found washed up on a rocky outcrop on the south coast.

'Listen to this Mil,' Arthur said. They were aghast to hear the missing man's name was Jeff Baker. 'What a shock that is,' Arthur remarked. 'He has probably made his way to shore somewhere. He was a fine swimmer and always as fit as a fiddle.'

'We can only hope for the best,' Mildred replied in a shaky voice. 'I liked Jeff quite a lot. It, it's unbelievable.'

'Unbelievable is right,' Arthur agreed. He placed his arm around his wife.

Jeff's body was never found. A memorial service was performed which many of his work mates attended. They all offered their condolences to Gina who quite naturally was most upset. She was dressed in black with a matching veil, yet tears could be seen rolling down her face.

Sometime later, Arthur was sent to north Queensland to work on a railway line project. Jim Newman a newly employed young chainman was appointed to go with him. Jim was a fit and healthy handsome young man who was a member in a Lifesaver's club on the Gold Coast. 'There won't be much surfing where we're going,' Arthur told him.

'I'll manage,' Jim replied, 'You can't win 'em all.'

They arrived on site and set up a camp west of Townsville. Quite often on Friday nights after work they would drive into the Queen's Hotel along the Strand in Townsville and have a few quiet ales.

On one of those nights, Arthur heard a familiar voice somewhere in the bar room. He looked along to see who he believed to be was none other than Jeff Baker. That person was with a few of the local patrons, participating in a game of darts. All carried a schooner of beer in their free hand. Arthur watched the manner in which the man in question tossed the darts and he felt almost certain it was Jeff. Arthur mentioned to Jim who he thought it was.

Jim shrugged. 'I wouldn't know, I never met him,' he said.

The man had the same noticeable gap as Jeff did in his front teeth, similar to what the English film star Terry Thomas had. Unlike the clean shaven Jeff Arthur knew, this man wore a beard and moustache.

Arthur approached him, smiling with his arm extended, prepared to shake hands. 'What are you doing here Jeff?' he asked. 'I thought you were dead.' Arthur gave a small chuckle.

The man ignored Arthur's hand, looked him fair in the eye. 'I'm afraid you've got the wrong bloke Mister. My name is not Jeff. I am John Meredith.'

'Come on mate, it's me Arthur,' said Arthur with a persuasive expression.

'Sorry Sir, I can't say I know you,' John Meredith insisted.

Arthur shook his head. 'It's got me stone stumped,' he said. 'They say everybody has a double. Yours is like an identical twin or was, I should say. The one I am mistaking you for is supposed to be dead. Jeff Baker, his name was.'

'Sorry to hear that,' said John. 'Everyone makes mistakes.'

'Sorry to have bothered you er, John,' Arthur replied, feeling a little sheepish.

'That's quite okay,' John said with the hint of a smile. Arthur returned to be with Jim.

'He reckons he's not the bloke I thought he was, but I still think he is,' Arthur said.

Jim shrugged. 'Could it be a case of amnesia do you think?'

'That's a possibility but something tells me there's more to it than that,' Arthur answered. They did not cross paths with John Meredith again after that meeting.

A few months later, after the job in the Townsville area was finished, Arthur was back home with his adoring wife, Mildred. They sat together in the living room, enjoying a cold drink while watching the latest news on TV. Their attention was aroused when an attractive female news reporter came on to say, 'A man has been arrested in far north Queensland today for faking his death and living under an assumed name.'

'Did you hear that Mil?' Arthur interrupted.

'Listen,' Mil replied.

The reporter continued, 'The man, Jeff Baker, posing under the name of John Meredith, went missing from what was believed to be a fishing boat accident two and a half years ago. Investigators have reported that his wife inherited a large sum of money out of his life insurance.'

Arthur looked at Mildred. 'What did I tell you?' he said, 'Can you believe it?'

Mildred looked at her husband, shook her head and gasped, 'It's unbelievable, Arthur, just unbelievable.'

DIGGER'S WEAKNESS
R. William Penshorn

Digger enjoyed reading Girlie books
His wife always frowned upon that.
Digger always sneaked a magazine along
No matter where he was at.

He folded them into a newspaper
So that they would not be in sight,
And take a sneak-peek whenever he could
Whether it be in the daytime or night.

He said he read them for the articles.
Believe that if you can.
The truth is he loved ogling centrefolds.
Digger was a red-blooded man.

One Sunday he went to church with his wife.
A magazine was tucked under his arm.
He thought a sneak-peek at the semi-clad babes
Could do nobody no harm.

While the congregation stood to sing songs of praise
His secret was placed in his hymn book.
While they were singing, he peeped at the pages.
His wife smelled a rat, took a look.

There was hell to play then, she screamed, 'Digger you fiend'.
The Minister rushed on down to her aid.
Then he spotted the book and his eyes almost popped
When he saw the centrefold maid.

'Oh my!' He sighed as he gaped at the page
'God's finest creation, I say'.
He shook Digger's hand and then spoke to him,
I must subscribe, who and what do I pay?

Digger returned home feeling a little bit smug.
He'd brought pleasure to the Minister's life.
But the day did not end up the way he had hoped.
He had to deal with the wrath of his wife.

AMEN.

RETROSPECTIVE: From the 2015 anthology:
Inspired By . . .

THE ORPHAN WALLABY

Vera Murray

MUM Ronsa, the rock wallaby, clung closer to the wall with baby Bozo snug in her pouch as the flood water whirled and pounded around the rocks below. Ronsa's eyes searched the route her husband Davey had taken when he left to locate long grass for their next meal. He had not returned.

Without warning, a whirlpool of fast moving water swung around and upwards, almost throwing them into the melee. As it withdrew, Ronsa quickly and desperately jumped across the closest rock and on to a higher ledge. This enabled her to scramble further up and on to the road above.

As Ronsa bounded along the road in fear, truck lights blinded her. She was flung off her feet as the vehicle brushed her aside. Pain overwhelmed her as she rolled over and over to lay unconscious, on a grassy verge. Baby Bozo, filled with fear, found he could no longer hold on inside his mother's pouch. He was flung out into the cold wet air. He instinctively extended his paws out in front of him to protect his face as he rolled into long grass. 'Mummy, mummy!' he cried as loud as he could, but there was no answer.

He tried to scramble back up the slope and on to the road to find his mother, but it rose too sharply. With a cry of dismay he felt he would never see her again. He frantically tried to climb, but his feet kept slipping on wet slimy mud, until his legs hung loose and his hands could no longer hold on. Bozo felt himself slide downwards. He tried to grab a tuft of tall grass but failed. As his body reached ground level he continued down a tunnel-like hole in the ground. He closed his tear-filled eyes until he stopped moving. He lay there in pain, trying not to cry. Hearing voices he opened his eyes to see the two occupants of the hole gather around him.

'Look, we have a little brother,' said the tiny voice of an infant meerkat.

'He's crying,' said the other as he looked into Bozo's face. 'Don't cry. You're shaking. You're cold. We'll keep you warm.' Immediately their warm bodies were pressed against him.

'What's your name? Mine's Gilly and this here with me is my sister Wandy. What's your name?'

'Bozo,' muttered the little rock wallaby as he took in a deep breath, 'and I'm an orphan now.'

As Gilly was about to ask what an orphan was, Wanda spoke. 'Look Gilly, what funny feet he's got, and, he's got funny biggish ears and nose, not like ours.' They both giggled.

A shadow blocked the entrance to the nursery. They turned to see their babysitter Boolie peering in. 'What's all the giggling about?' she asked.

'Our new little brother looks funny,' Gilly and Wandy answered in chorus.

Boolie entered the nursery and scratched the side of her neck with one of her paws in wonderment when she saw Bozo. 'I'm off having something to eat and look what happens. Tell me, where did this strange baby came from? It's deformed. Who put it in here when my back was turned?'

Gilly and Wandy looked vague.

'Right! I'll find out, I will indeed.' She gave another quick glance at the babies before returning to her outside position of guard.

When the group returned that evening Boolie questioned every female to try to discover whose baby it was, but every one of them, wide-eyed with surprise, denied any knowledge of a deformed baby. Boolie decided she would wait and keep watch to see who in the group took extra interest in the baby's welfare. That one, she decided, would be the mother. Weeks went by and Boolie was no closer to getting an answer.

Meanwhile, Bozo grew bigger and taller than his meerkat 'siblings'. He began to go on trips with them, at which the elders showed them how to recognise signs of potential danger, and, as important, how to find food. Bozo astounded them by not digging for food but eating grass. 'He must be still sick and green stuff makes him feel better. He'll gradually discover that insects and the like are much better fare,' spoke up Boolie when questioned. On these daily runs Bozo kept looking around for any sign of creatures like himself, but he saw none.

One morning the camp was on alert. Alarmed voices told Bozo that those on lookout duty saw a group advancing towards them, and only the defence group would stay outside to protect them from a possible invasion. Bozo was ordered back inside one of the burrows so he would be safe. Curious, he waited until he knew the guards would be checking the other end of the settlement. He then peered out.

He heard thump-thump of heavy feet. There was something familiar about the sound, so he crept out, leapt across the narrow open area before him, and quickly hid behind a large tall clump of grass on the other side of their area.

As the sound of advancing footsteps grew close, Bozo, feeling more nervous, drew back, deeper into the scrub. The visitors were almost directly in front of his hiding place when he heard a voice say, 'He must be around here somewhere. He wasn't found near me.' Bozo sucked in his breath. It sounded like his mother's voice. Then another voice Bozo was convinced was his father's, spoke. 'Are you sure?'

'Yes. It was up on the road we just jumped down from, and where I showed you I was hit, and where that Good Samaritan found me, and, looked after me until I recovered.'

Now convinced they were his parents Bozo leaped out of his hiding place to flop down before them. 'Mother, Father,' he cried. Within seconds he was receiving a warm and weepy embrace from his parents. He briefly told them about the meerkats who adopted him. 'You must come and meet all my friends.'

His parents, eager to thank their son's saviours, walked with Bozo towards the meerkat guards. Seeing Bozo with his arms held away from his body they relaxed, and informed their leaders, who came forward. After a brief conversation they welcomed Bozo's parents.

After considerable discussion and exchanging of information, it was finally decided that the area they were in could be shared between the grass-eating wallabies and the meerkats, especially as Bozo would always be considered as a member of the meerkat family.

Boolie, watching on, sighed with contentment, for the mystery of the 'deformed baby' and its strange eating habits was solved.

INSPIRED BY the TV series that covered meerkats' lives in the wild.

MARTHA'S HEAD
Bakthi Ross

FROM THE EDGE OF BREAKING, a tremor, an involuntary rush in her mind, urges her to get to someone to warn them, but she backs away again. She should not react to pressure. It all could be someone who wants information, but they do not know anything about it. They are playing all sorts of games to get her reaction.

The big cliff, she could fall if she reacts. Who could come to her rescue? No one. If anyone came to rescue her it would be another link and that would lead to another. We would not want that. Do we? The untraceable link should never be broken. What if a few people are dead because of this reason. It is not a big deal, people die every day for many causes.

Martha's black eyes stare at the big cliff. It is a steep rugged slope and on the bottom, a little river runs. Only she could see the white hermit lily, between two narrow cliffs, anchored to the ground in a remote secluded wild area.

A long legged crane on the river stands with a fish in its mouth, satisfied to eat its catch.

Martha knows if she falls over the cliff the river would not save her. The river was full of rocks. She probably would smash her head on the rocks and die.

Life hasn't been good for Martha. She had to live a life of someone else and could not live her own life. Her life was full of drama. She feared for her life. If someone recognised her they probably would kill her. She faked her death many times. Many empty coffins were buried in many places. Her name had been changed many times and now she could not even remember what her own name was.

A tombstone to remember one's life and name but it stood there like a fake stone. Some of the tombstones had versus written that could bring tears to your eyes, but it was an empty coffin. She cried for her own death.

She even visited her own tombs and left flowers, but she did not know why. She cried inside for being dead and living someone else's life. It was hard, because she always had to look over her shoulder. If anyone walked behind her, she feared someone was following her or stalking her or remembered her.

She has no peace and cannot rest or let her guard down. Some days fear consumes her mind and in those days she cannot eat nor rest. Martha spends such a day in a panic state.

So many sleepless nights, is it worth it, she asks herself. If she went back home to face the music, she would get killed and that would be the end of it.

Carrying on a fake life becomes so hard. Every stare from people, she becomes suspicious.

That cliff with the long-legged crane looked so good, but from the edge something stopped her. Her mind thought all sorts of things. Martha was thinking like a crazy person. Not a single normal thought came to her mind. Every thought was about someone or someone looking at her or someone following her. There was no end to these sorts of thoughts. When you live a life of a mentally ill person, the conscience and the paranoia take over.

No one can convince her of anything. She could not believe anything. Her mental state has gone beyond reality. If you say something she comes up with such a question that would surprise a highly qualified psychiatrist. Such suspicious thoughts and thinking. No one could convince her otherwise. Eventually she will fall off that cliff. That is where her mind is leading Martha.

The psychiatrist's job was to make her see reality. It may have been a big secret-agent life she lived and had to kill people many times. But now she cannot cope with her own killings. It seemed okay then. Now getting killed by her own conscience without even a bullet, she cannot cope. It is a mental and emotional stress. The strain is too high.

Can we get through to her somehow? thought psychiatrist Cester. Every question he asked, everything he said, she would come up with an answer that would make the psychiatrist look suspicious. She could not trust anyone. Her own mind become such a problem but she did not realise it.

She would walk out of the psychiatrist's office with her face that tells the psychiatrist, he was also part of the plot to kill her. Her stories would start to build up on anyone, even the ones she met for the first time. They did not know her and had no clues about her life, but she built them into her own suspicious thoughts and followed them around and made up so many stories about them. You would not believe how Martha can make up so many stories.

Her mind was one of the most interesting minds psychiatrist Cester had ever come across. Most mentally ill he helped. This was far far-gone a mental state. Whether he could reverse it, he did not know. He had to question his own ability and accept that anyone could become part of someone else's mental illness.

Cester also became a part of her story. Now he too would be trying to kill her or get her. You could not tell anything to her. She would twist it into another suspicious thing.

If you asked, 'Did you go out today', she would ask, 'Why? Do you think I went out to kill somebody?'

Even though psychiatrist Cester did not think any of these things. She would say so many things he did not know where to begin or where the problem was.

A total suspicious mind. Every question, Martha would have a suspicious answer. She was always right was the sort of mentality she had. Her thinking cannot be changed. She has depression she cannot overcome. Everyone was a suspect in her eyes. She was limited in her thinking and showed lack of freedom. That limitation made her lose reality. Her mental disorder questioned others more than herself. She always influenced others with her thinking and never listened to their reasoning.

Some of her thoughts were so funny that the psychiatrist actually had to take Martha to the person she was complaining about and made her talk to them so her weird thoughts about them would clear off her mind. They weren't thinking about Martha at all but she had built up so many stories about them in her mind. Martha was reluctant to accept psychiatric reasoning.

Martha's mind was gone to the edge of its limits. It was a matter of time before she would fall off the cliff.

One day she talked to me as if I am the one having problems and she was the psychiatrist. She made my life miserable with the things I had to see from her point of view. I had to even pay for the sessions with her. With this trauma I left my work for a while and went on a holiday. Even I couldn't cope with her as a psychiatrist.

While having my holiday, I was relaxed and thought about the sessions with her and her 'she can do anyone's job' sort of mentality even though I saw the faults in her. She could not accept anyone could solve her problems. She was so determined that she can do my job and I am the one in the wrong. She did point out some things that I did not see as a problem in me. Her game was that everyone had to see her as the good person and she comes across as a good person while she told me about their faults. Some would not see them as faults but she does. Then I thought she may have to be perfect and do everything to its perfection. That became an obsession and she could not control it.

As a psychiatrist I could not end it there. She has more problems than I can identify. Since she tried to do my job, whether she was a real spy and having these fears I couldn't work out. She could have many personalities and created these thoughts and she acted on them. Even if it involved killing a person. Not even a minute taken to see whether there is any truth to it. Martha could not identify the real thoughts from the fake ones. Her mind was like an instruction from a computer, it did not have any senses and reacted to the codes of the program and killed, abused and vandalised. No sense of any emotions and remorse.

You would not see her cry, you would not see her smile but her gazing eyes in a determined venture to tell people that you have to be perfect. Do not take a tissue provided in the public places to wipe your nose, because that seemed as stealing in her mind.

The extent you have to go to for perfection is the only thing that kept her calm and stopped her from doing bad things against these tissue-taking thieves.

She could not look from the edge to save herself.

KEEPING CALM AND CARRYING ON
Scarlett Reed

A FLURRY OF PEOPLE MOVE about the hospital. A new batch of wounded allied soldiers were brought in overnight, and the number of casualties has exceeded the hospital's capacity. Men who can stand are clustered in groups, smoking cigarettes with shaky hands while they wait to be seen by overworked doctors and nurses. The corridors are lined with stretchers for those who can't mobilise and the groans of injured men echo down the once barren halls. British Intelligence has relayed that the Luftwaffe have planned an attack on London tonight, so I've organised some medical students from my department to take fire-watching shifts on the roof when the raid begins. Looking at my watch I notice that shift change must have already occurred, so I might be able to catch Ava before she goes back to the nurses' quarters. I delve into the deep pockets of my white coat and pull out a packet of Chesterfields and my lighter. I flick the lighter open and emblazon the wick. Leaning into the flame an ember forms and I breathe deep to inhale the smoke.

I turn the lighter over between my fingertips. The crude scratching on the polished silver reads 'live today to die tomorrow'. Flipping it over 'ER' is cursively engraved. Edward Reeves. My younger brother, another casualty in the war against Adolf. Nobody expected it to last this long, and nobody seems to know when it'll end.

As I walk through the double doors into the general ward I scan the blue uniformed women and spot her leaning over a soldier with a gunshot wound, filling in his details onto a sheet of paper on a clipboard. I loiter around nearby beds, picking up charts and glancing blindly at them while staying within earshot, but it sounds like Ava will be a while yet. I pluck a pen from my pocket and tap the chart in my hand.

'Excuse me, Nurse, could I have a word with you for a moment?'

Ava gives me a startled look then lowers her eyes. 'Oh. Yes, Doctor, of course.'

I guide her towards the doorway and lean in closer, pointing my pen at the chart as I speak. 'I need to see you after your shift.'

'Elwood, I can't. You're married. I can't do this anymore.'

'I know. I thought about what you said and you're right. I think I have a solution, a compromise . . .'

'Doctor Reeves!' Dr Dancovitch's voice booms across the room and all eyes are on us for a moment. 'Are you going to commandeer Nurse Adams's attention? Or can she continue with her patient assessments?'

Ava blushes and scurries back to the waiting soldier. I return the chart to the end of the bed, snatch up a freshly rolled bandage and move to a soldier with a head wound. The ward falls silent and movement ceases momentarily as the air raid siren blares. It won't be long before the Germans are bombing us overhead. As I triage patients my eyes keep being drawn to Ava. Occasionally our eyes meet, making me think, or maybe hope, she's also watching me work.

An explosion close to the hospital radiates a shudder through the ward. Everyone stops and gasps, worried faces looking at each other for reassurance. Out of the sudden silence a shrill scream and we all turn our heads to the sound. A patient has woken shrieking as he claws at the bedsheets, trying to remove them. Soldiers either side of him hold him back.

'We have to get to the trenches!' the patient screams while fighting off the two men.

The two officers try to settle the man back into bed. I hear whispered words of reassurance. The patient isn't cognitive to time or place so he continues to throw himself out of bed to take cover, grabbing at the soldiers' holsters for a weapon to defend himself.

I grimace as I reach for a vial of tranquilizer and a syringe. As I'm drawing up the dose of medication a gunshot echoes through the room. I turn towards a groan of pain. I watch as a wardsman grasps his thigh and falls to the ground. Dr Dancovitch rushes over to him and applies pressure over the bloody wound.

'Esther, get gauze and bandage!' Dancovitch's niece drops the linen she was holding and runs out of the room. 'Reeves!'

I turn towards Dr Dancovitch's voice. His face is contorted into a deep snarl.

'Don't just bloody stand there! Put him down for Christsake!'

The patient is screaming, waving a gun in the air, out of the officers' grasp.

I turn my attention back to the medication in my hand. I draw up double my intended dose and pull the needle out of the vial.

BANG!

Another shot. I run over to the patient who is struggling against both men. I plunge the needle through his clothing into his thigh. The patient's screams lose their intensity and within a few moments his body slackens. I scan the room. Nurse Margie and a wardsman are rushing toward a nurse who is lying on the floor. I frantically look around the room for Ava. My heart lurches and my breath catches in my throat. I throw the syringe on the bedside table and race to her. I fall to my knees, pushing others out of the way so that I can turn her over onto her back.

'Ava!'

I shake her. No response. I look her over for damage. A small blood stained wound to the abdomen. I put my hand on the wound and look up at a nurse. Without saying a word she nods and runs off in the same direction as Esther. I feel her wrist for a pulse.

I can't feel anything.

My heart is pounding and my mouth is dry. The nurse returns with gauze. I move my hand away so she can apply pressure to the area. My shaking hand moves to her throat to seek her carotid artery. My fingertips desperately probe for a pulse. Perhaps it's the adrenaline pumping through my system, but I can't feel anything. I lean forward and put my cheek close to her face. I can only stand this proximity for mere seconds.

'Dr Dancovitch!'

My mind is swarming with possibilities and I can't focus.

A trolley arrives, I pull Ava's body up into my lap. I hold her for a moment then wrap my arms under her legs and lift her up onto the trolley. Dr Levi Dancovitch approaches with a stressed but controlled expression. He touches her neck. Margie pulls a compact mirror from her apron pocket and holds it out. Dr Dancovitch holds the mirror under Ava's mouth and nose. The reflective glass doesn't fog. My heart is in my throat and the world feels as though it's crashing down around me. I take several deep breaths to push down the rising sense of loss and grief, but that's an impossible task so I stumble towards the exit instead.

The corridor is filled with soldiers. I trudge past them in a daze, blindly seeking a place of privacy. As I reach the men's lavatories a sob escapes my lips. I feel relief momentarily but my body is no longer my own. Tears flood my eyes, welling over and running down my cheeks. It was an abdominal shot – how can she be dead? Was it the shock?

No. Even if she died from shock she would have lingered longer. What could I have done?

I wrack my brain for every life-saving intervention I could have provided. My brain is spiralling out of control.

If I had drawn up the tranquillizer faster, would she have lived?

I put my head in my hands and weep uncontrollably. My brain is being cruel to me. Asking me questions like – what could I have done differently? How could I let this happen? It was an abdominal shot, not fatal. Not fatal. How could she have died so fast?

'Dr Reeves?'

My ears register a female voice. I hadn't heard the door open. I lift my head and see Ava's best friend, Margie, standing before me.

I wipe my face on the sleeve of my lab coat. I try to look composed, but Margie's expression of sadness and concern reflects my failure. We're standing a few feet from each other in a silent impasse. The knot in my throat is growing so large I'm struggling to swallow.

Margie approaches and places a hand on my shoulder. Her makeup is smudged and her cheeks are wet with tears. It is my undoing. I bring my hand to my face to cover my eyes as fresh tears spew forth. Margie presses her body against mine and wraps her arms around my waist.

My sadness evaporates momentarily. My first thought is how unprofessional this must look. A nurse hugging a doctor in the men's lavatory. If anyone were to walk in there would be a scandal. I'm about to push her away when I hear a sob. Hearing a woman crying affects me at a primal level. I wrap my arms around her and focus on comforting Margie. The burden of Ava's death doesn't feel as heavy knowing that I'm not alone in my grief.

'There was nothing you could do.'

Hearing her say that makes me almost believe it's true.

'She died so fast. I don't understand . . .'

Margie tightens her grip around me and sobs again. 'Nor do I.'

She releases me and takes a step back then looks at her uniform. Her white apron is covered with blood – transferred from my clothing. I look in the mirror and notice a smear of blood on my cheek. Ava's blood.

'You should get changed.' Margie is untying the bow of her apron.

I look down. My coat, shirt and pants are splashed with dark red. Margie bundles up the soiled apron.

'I need to get back to the ward, Elwood.' She turns and walks towards the door.

I turn to the basin and run the tap to wash the blood off my hands and face. I hear the door click close behind her.

I pull out a fresh set of clothes from my locker and throw my soiled clothing in the bin – there's no point bothering to clean clothes I couldn't bear to wear again. My reflection shows bloodshot eyes and I look weary beyond my years. I'm only twenty-eight but a middle-aged man stares back at me with grief etched into his features and auburn stubble on his chin.

I push Ava's death to the back of my mind and shift my focus to the injured soldiers lining the hospital corridors. Whenever my mind drifts back to her lifeless face I chastise myself silently. Compartmentalise, Reeves.

I walk back to the ward. Ava's body has been removed. Dancovitch's niece, Esther – who shares his dark hair and slim features, is on her knees wiping up a pool of dark blood off the floor. I have seen so much blood as a doctor and the sight of it has never fazed me, but knowing it is Ava's makes me queasy and the memory of her death floods back to me like a tsunami wave. I turn my back on the scene, I can't stay here with the incident still bombarding my mind. I glance down at my watch and see my shift is already over. I remember that the only reason I was staying back was because I wanted to speak to Ava. The image of her lifeless body hits me with such force that if I don't move forward I will most certainly fall back.

* * * * *

I WANT A WHISKY, but the barman says they're out so I settle for a pint of ale. Damn rationing. The image of Ava's lifeless body keeps flashing before my eyes. The only thought that gives me solace is that there was nothing I could have done. I still can't understand how she died so fast. I've seen many soldiers with multiple gunshot wounds who have lasted longer. Did I want that though? For her to linger, confused and in pain? Of course not, but there would have been a chance that I might have saved her. Or at least said my final goodbyes to her.

I loosen my jaw and allow the amber liquid to slide down my throat in one long effortless swallow. I motion for the barman.

'Are you sure you want another?' A look of concern crosses his face.

'I'm not causing any trouble, and my day has been long and hard.'

The barman hesitates for a moment then pulls me another pint.

'You should slow down before you fall down,' he says as he turns towards a group of uniformed soldiers who are flagging him down.

I pull a cigarette from my packet and ignite it with a flick of my brother's lighter. 'Live today to die tomorrow'. Edward's inscription is particularly apt tonight.

I feel a gloved hand on my shoulder and a feminine presence beside me at the bar.

'I feel like a drink after today too.'

Margie motions to the bartender. She climbs onto the wooden barstool beside me. 'How are you feeling?'

I draw on my cigarette. 'It keeps replaying in my head. It happened so fast, it's all a blur.'

Margie nods

The barman approaches Margie.

'Gin and tonic, if you have it.'

'Yes madam.'

'Put it on my room,' I interject as Margie reaches for her purse.

The barman nods, serves her a drink then moves away.

'You've got a room?'

'I can't go home tonight. My wife is trying to fix our relationship. I can't handle that while I'm processing Ava's death.'

'The ward sister has given me the day off tomorrow. To grieve.'

I look at Margie's composed features.

'You seem to be handling it pretty well.'

The alcohol seems to be affecting me more than I anticipated. My words spill out almost as I'm thinking them. For a moment I think she hasn't heard me as she continues to caress her glass and looks deep in thought.

'I don't think I've realised she's dead. I just feel numb.' Margie delves into her purse and pulls out a cigarette. I pick my Zippo off the bar and hold it to her cigarette. Margie leans into the flame and puffs lightly.

'I have to pack up her belongings tomorrow and take them to her mother in the East End.'

We sit in silence for a few minutes then drain our glasses and order another round. During this silence my mind comes back to why I wanted to speak to Ava. I wanted to tell her I'm going to leave my wife after the war.

'I don't think I can go back to the nurses' quarters tonight. Last time I was there she was alive and well. All of her belongings are there just where she left them.'

I can understand why she doesn't want to go back. If I was surrounded by her belongings I would go mad with grief.

'I have a suite upstairs. You can have the bed and I'll take the couch.'

I know it's improper to offer such an arrangement to a single woman but I want to help. My words have once again bypassed my reason and shot straight to my mouth.

'Thank you. But I'll take the couch.'

I had expected her to say no. I look at her naked ring finger and consider how it would look to others if she came up to my room with me. I put my hands under the bar and slide off my gold wedding band. I place it on the bar and slide it discreetly toward Margie.

Margie gives a tight lipped grimace. I don't think she had considered the social implications of my offer. She picks up the ring and puts it on her wedding finger.

'Thank you.'

I give her a curt nod then motion to the barman for another round of drinks.

* * * * *

MY LEGS FEEL A LITTLE WOBBLY as Margie and I walk up the stairs towards my suite. My decision for another round before the bar closed wasn't the greatest. I hold open the door for Margie to walk through and I notice her gait is also affected. Margie collapses onto the couch and I sit next to her. I cross my feet on top of the adjacent coffee table. She lights two cigarettes and hands one to me. We're all talked out after hours in the bar, realigning a relationship that was only defined by our mutual association with Ava. Now there's just the silence of grief and comfort.

Margie removes my wedding band and glides it onto on my left ring finger.

'What about in the morning when you leave?'

Margie chuckles. 'I'll keep my hands in my pocket.'

I clasp her hand and give it a squeeze. 'You've been a welcome distraction this evening. I feel better for having you here with me.' I release her hand. 'You're a lot like her in some ways.'

Margie stubs out her cigarette and turns to face me. 'How so?'

I stub out my cigarette in the ashtray and turn towards her. 'You're easy to talk to. You have the same sense of humour.' I look at Margie's face and that's where the similarities stop. Margie has a heart-shaped face with soft angelic features. Her full lips beckon me, promising to remove all the pain and sadness I currently feel. I touch her face and rub my thumb over the border of her lips. She doesn't flinch away from my touch. I lean in and kiss her. Margie returns my kiss and pulls me closer to her.

* * * * *

MOVEMENT IN THE ROOM wakens me. Margie, dressed only in her undergarments, is moving around the room collecting her clothing. I sit up in bed and she turns to me.

'How's your head?'

I am surprised by her question. The atmosphere in the room is heavy.

'It's been better. Nothing a little aspirin won't cure.'

Margie slips into her dress, and sits on the edge of the bed to fasten her shoes.

'Did you know your wife once accused me of sleeping with you? She said I looked the type. I guess she was right.'

My eyebrows peak. 'My wife?'

'Yeah, she confronted Ava and me outside the hospital. She shook me up while shouting accusations. Ava told her the truth to stop her assaulting me.'

My mind reels. 'How did I not know this?'

'You and Ava broke up soon after. We assumed you knew.'

I sit there dumbfounded. How could my wife not tell me? I consider confronting her, before realising I don't care enough about the relationship to try and repair it.

Margie turns to face me. 'I appreciate you letting me stay here last night but we can never do this again.'

'I feel like I should say sorry.'

'That's guilt Elwood. I feel it too. We did the wrong thing by Ava.'

'We came together because of her.'

'We shouldn't have taken things as far as we did.'

'So, what do we do now?'

'We go back to our prescribed relationship and we don't mention this again.'

Margie bows her head and her hand reaches up to wipe her cheek.

I think it has finally hit her. Ava isn't coming back and Margie can't confess she has done wrong by her. And nor can I.

Margie collects her coat and leaves the hotel suite without looking back.

* * * * *

I'VE READ OVER THIS PATIENT'S CHART for what seems like the fifth time. I can't concentrate. I keep thinking about Ava. Conjuring more complex and detailed fantasies about us reuniting or reliving memories and moments with her. I would have cherished her more if I knew my time with her was so short.

'Reeves!'

I snap back into reality. Dr Dancovitch towers over me. While his features rest naturally with a look of displeasure, in this instance it seems purposeful. He shoves a chart into my hands.

'This is the third medication error you've made this week, Reeves. Where's your head been for the past few weeks?'

I open the chart and read through the medications.

'Oh.'

I had written one ounce instead of one fluidram for a strong opioid medication. The dosage would have killed the patient.

'Oh indeed! It's fortunate my niece was caring for this patient and she brought it to my attention.'

I should feel bad, or at least offended, that a subordinate is disrespecting the hierarchy. Instead I feel numb and apathetic. I've been going through the motions of my professional duties while my head is reliving the past.

I am on my final round before I hand over to the next shift. The pep pills I took earlier in the shift to help me concentrate on the task at hand and get out of my own head are losing their effectiveness. I need to get home and sleep, but I can feel eyes watching me. I look up to see Margie approaching me, the fabric of her nurses' uniform enhancing her blue eyes.

'Dr Reeves?'

She gestures for me to move away from the patient's bedside. I put the chart at the end of the bed and move with her into the centre of the ward.

Margie leans in close and whispers. 'I need to see you after your shift.'

My eyebrows peak with surprise. Margie's last words to me on that morning several weeks ago still ring in my head. *We can never do this again.*

Perhaps she has reconsidered. This moment isn't ideal. I feel fatigued, but if I reject her now I may never get another opportunity.

'I'm finishing up now. I can meet you at the hotel bar in an hour.'

She nods. My colleague walks onto the ward and gives me an expectant look. I excuse myself and go to hand over my patient notes to him.

* * * * *

CLEAN SHAVEN AND SMELLING FRESH I wait at the bar for Margie, swirling the rare treat of a Scotch whisky around the base of my tumbler. A foreboding sense of guilt washes over me – I know Ava would disapprove of my affair with Margie. I shouldn't be here but it's hard to resist Margie's company when it alleviates some of the grief I feel.

The hum of soldiers' voices dips for a moment and in unison all heads turn towards the doorway. Margie spots me and glides through the crowd, ignoring their appreciative gazes. I wave to the bartender and I order Margie a gin and tonic. It arrives as she approaches the bar.

Margie glances at the stool beside me then surveys the room. 'Can we sit in a booth?'

I nod and pick up both drinks as we make our way towards a vacant booth. Margie's expression is sombre, perhaps she's feeling as guilty as I am, but I'm certain she'll loosen up after a few drinks. We slide in close together. Margie reaches for my packet of Chesterfields that I've placed on the table. I look at her hands and notice a gold band on her wedding finger – that encourages me to rest my hand on her thigh and lean in to kiss her.

'I'm pregnant.'

I stop before my lips reach hers – frozen momentarily as I process her words. I pull back and my hand jerks away from her thigh. Her words rattle around my mind. My hand reaches for my Chesterfields and I light a cigarette. I take a deep breath and watch the smoke spew forth and add to the hazy gloom of the bar.

'Did you hear me?'

'I heard.' I flick the ash into the tray. My words tumble out uncensored. 'You can't have it.'

'Obviously.' In the moment it takes Margie to light a cigarette, a wave of relief washes over me. 'That's why I'm here. I need your help.'

'What do you need? Money?'

Margie's face goes bright red and she hisses into my ear.

'No. I need you to get rid of it.'

This is not how I expected my night to progress and I struggle to arrange my thoughts.

'I'm not that kind of doctor.'

'But you must know doctors who can . . .'

'Ask around the nurse's quarters, or some of your female friends. Some of them must have been in a similar situation.'

Margie's chest heaves and she wipes her cheek.

My compassion overrides my panic as I hear her sob. I lean back into the chair and wrap my arm around her shoulder. She leans into me while playing with the gold band on her finger. Margie's emotions settle and she regains her composure. I remove my arm and we sit in silence smoking cigarettes and sipping our drinks.

If I can't be the one to do it for her I should at least pay for it to be done. I delve into my jacket pocket and retrieve my wallet. I'm glad I went to the bank after my shift, in anticipation of enjoying a night out with Margie. I withdraw a five pound note and rest my hand with the money on her thigh under the table.

'I don't know whether it's enough, but it's all I have on me. Let me know if you need more.'

* * * * *

I HAVEN'T SEEN MARGIE FOR SEVERAL DAYS. Ordinarily I would be unconcerned. Sometimes our shifts don't coincide, but I have a niggling feeling something is wrong. I dismissed these feelings for the first two days. It's day three now, so I discreetly check the nurses' roster. My tension eases as I see Margie has had two days off and is due on shift this evening. I'm tending to a young woman who received burns to her legs when a bomb went off and splattered her legs with factory chemicals. As I cleanse the wounds and remove grime, my eyes dart back and forth to the door. Finally shift change is apparent when an injection of nurses burst into the ward and swap notes with the nurses about to leave.

I can't see Margie.

I'm familiar with most of the faces and some of the names, but don't feel confident to ask any of them about Margie, except maybe Esther Dancovitch. She's a quiet girl who keeps to herself and isn't likely to gossip. I continue washing my patient's wounds while watching Esther and waiting for an opportunity. Esther collects medical equipment to be sterilised and takes them to the dirty utility room. I gather the bloody gauze and used bandages together in a heap, excuse myself from my patient and follow after Esther.

Nurse Dancovitch is sorting through dirty equipment. I dump the bloody gauze into the bin and the bandages into the linen basket. I need to sound casual.

'I haven't seen Nurse Connor for a while. I thought she was supposed to be on shift tonight?'

I hear a clatter of equipment fall to the floor. I turn my head to Esther.

'She's been unwell for the past few days, Sir.'

'Nothing serious, I hope?' It's a strain now to keep my tone light.

Esther collects the items from the floor and reorganises them. She's shifting her weight from foot to foot and opens her mouth a couple of times to speak, but bites her lip instead.

I wait. I want answers.

'She has a fever and some abdominal pain. My uncle thinks it's the flu.'

'Dr Dancovitch?'

'Yes. I was worried when she wouldn't come down to dinner. Marg– er . . . Nurse Connor wouldn't let me send for help, so I asked my uncle to come and review her.'

Shit. Dancovitch isn't an idiot. He'd know it isn't the flu.

'Is she still in the nurses' quarters?'

'No, my uncle took her to the Royal. He was worried the staff would be too distracted if she was here.'

'And he is absolutely correct. Perhaps I'll send flowers. Nurse Connor should know we're thinking of her. Let me know if you hear any news.'

'Yes, sir.'

Esther's face is unreadable and I can't keep up this charade any longer. I give her a nod and turn back to the ward.

* * * * *

LAST TIME I WAS IN THIS BAR, Margie was sitting beside me. Now I'm alone, apart from the uniformed soldiers who appear never to leave. I look into my pint glass, straight through the dregs of amber liquid to the wooden bar. I could have done more. I could have asked around maternity for a doctor who was willing to help her. If I had done some research I'm sure I could have found some medication or herbs that could bring on a miscarriage, but instead I gave her money and hoped for the best.

Ava must be looking down on me with fury for not taking care of her friend.

'Hello.' The voice comes out of nowhere. I turn to see Margie standing before me, neatly dressed in a black dress and a fur lined coat.

'Margie!' I gesture to the empty seat beside me. Margie seats herself and reaches for my packet of Chesterfields. I delve into my pocket for my lighter and hold the flame steady as she draws her first puff.

'I heard you were sick. I was planning to visit you at the hospital.'

'Probably best you didn't.'

'What happened? Are you still . . .?'

'No.'

'Did the police make enquires?'

'No.' She drew on her cigarette. 'We're in the clear. Maybe they've got more pressing matters to attend with a war on. Dr Dancovitch referred me to a colleague of his, an old friend who he said would be discreet.'

I inwardly chuckle to myself. 'His friend will think it was his.'

'He's married.' Margie looks almost offended.

'So am I.'

'You don't act like it.'

'I'm unhappily married. Is it wrong to look for comfort in the arms of another?'

'It is when it's your mistress's best friend.'

The accusation stings. I don't have to explain myself, but maybe I'm trying to work it out for myself.

'I never thought of her as my mistress. Our relationship was more than physical. She was my sweetheart. I was planning to leave my wife after the war ended.'

Margie shakes her head. 'They always say they're going to leave their wives. Most never do.'

'Well it doesn't really matter now, does it?'

'No.' Margie exhales a breath of smoke and flicks ash into a nearby tray.

'I'm sorry, Margie. For everything.' It seems inadequate, but I can think of nothing else to say.

'What do we do now?' Margie's face is composed and hard to read.

I sit and consider for a moment. My heart still feels heavy with the burden of Ava's death, and though Margie is a comfort, being with her fills me with guilt. 'We go back to being colleagues, maybe friends. We keep patching up soldiers until this hell is over.'

No flicker of emotion crosses her face. She stubs out her cigarette and picks up her purse and walks through the smoky haze, past the rowdy soldiers and out into the street.

Author's note:
Want to know more? Look out for the full length novel from Ava's perspective – *Death's Captive* from online bookstores.
Instagram: @authorscarlettreed

THE TRANQUIL REALM OF SILENCE
Amy Capstick

TRANQUILLITY. A peaceful realm of tranquillity. The soothing aquamarine world around her finally calmed the girl's tortured mind. The slow movement of the water incorporated with the sparkling surface created a heavenly atmosphere right in the depths of her backyard. Silence. Deafening silence shrouded all possible sounds. No more howls and cries from the ghosts and monsters above the surface. The serene laconism of the depths surrounding her was the only thing that could sedate the haunting screams in her dark mind.

For the first time in months, she calmly lay, engulfed by the warm, silky water facing the ever-deepening pastel sky above her. Flowing, shimmering streaks of golden, rosy-orange light painted the magnificent sky; so vibrant, yet soft in illumination. The final rays of afternoon sunlight sliced through the surface of the crystal-clear water, glittering and sparkling across her still, dull body. Her long, chocolate hair flowed around her as rainbow refractions of light rippled and quavered along all the surrounding walls. It confused her how such a magical world could so starkly contrast the agonizing pain of her mind and body. A corona of ashen grey and charcoal clouded her, her body limp and permanently damaged, her sad eyes dull with remorse.

For months she has tilted back and forth from the verge of taking her own life. There is nothing left for her to live for. There are no more dinner dates, dances or drunken parties ending in both of them passing out together on the couch and awaking to the sight of each other's morning faces. There are no more late-night drives with perfect friends to far away mountain tops where the stars shine brighter or adventures full of laughter or happiness or kisses or comforting embraces, or love or . . . her entire life is gone.

Looking up at the radiant sky, the girl reminisces back to the day it all began. Back to when her thoughts were as bright and colourful as the atmosphere around her . . .

He entered her life two years ago. He was different to the others she had met, sometimes quiet and insecure and other times outgoing with the most amazing personality and the best sense of humor. He was different though she loved him with all her heart. She couldn't imagine ever being with anyone else. She loved the face she came to know better than her own: the crooked front teeth, the same chocolate brown hair as her own that draped over his forehead when he needed a haircut, the dimples that came out of hiding when he smiled his true smile and his amazing deep brown eyes, one curious and the other filled with love.

Countless memories of him began to dance in her mind, appearing and disappearing, flashing before her eyes before being replaced with a new one. Their first kiss, the first time they said I love you, their birthdays, the first Christmas they spent together, Valentine's day, his tear-filled graduation, the drunken parties, Netflix naps together on the couch and night drives under shining stars. She could hear laughter, his laughter, a sound that lit up the world around them. One by one the visions infinitely appeared in her daydreaming mind, whirring in circles faster and faster clouding her vision . . .

Her eyes flashed open. The memories vanished. All was silent again. Still, she lay in solitude as the water gently rippled around her body and the vibrancy of the cloud's colours began to wash away. The wind picked up and signs of the creeping darkness began to return. She could imagine the whoosh of the wind through the swaying trees, the frantic calls of birds and animals as they prepared for nightfall. Yet she stayed in the silent realm of tranquillity.

As the final rays of sunlight withdrew from the water, the girl reminisced again. But now all she could see was blood. Crimson blood and flashing lights red and blue. The frantic commotion of people. The shrapnel of car pieces. She could still clearly hear the deafening screams of sirens echoing through the warm summer air. And she could still remember her silent screams and cries that choked her. That night, her worst nightmares came to life. Her heart was ripped from her body and splattered across the ground joining his pools of blood. She will never forget that feeling. The feeling of knowing the soul which filled her heart would never again be with her.

Her eyes pooled with tears, something she had become very familiar with over the past three months. Even underwater, they left their salty imprint on her cheeks. The ominous burden of solicitude had sunken the girl to her breaking point. What began as a cold, insignificant thought had over time magnified into mental, minacious clouds of hollowness and fear, gripping her with cold fingers, becoming more and more real every day. Atramentous agony as black as ink had allied with the sustained screaming, slaughtering her solemn mind. The apparent mental torture had evidently taken its toll on her. Every night for three months she lay crying herself to sleep. She fought an internal battle with the gripping blades of depression, leaving lines on her arms and legs, the thought of never seeing him again still resonating ever so clearly in her ruined mind and scarred body.

She lay unmoving, allowing the water to flow through her fractured veins and seep into her ajar mouth.

For a long time, she had suffered. Some nights were worse than others as she screamed into her pillow on the verge of ending her pain. Sometimes a sharp knife hovered over her wrists. She gripped it so tightly, her knuckles and face as white as a ghost, her body violently shaking. The girl would press the cold blade to her skin but could never bring herself to slice it. She would sit in the dark like that as if she was standing on the edge of the cliff for hours trying to force herself to end the pain, knowing that if she just jumped it would all be over. She had tried to search for a bright light, for a ladder to help her out of the hole she had dug herself into knowing confidently that every second would deepen the sunken place...yet there is no bright light. There is no ladder. There is only the reality of knowing he's gone and never coming back, knowing that she will never see his face again, touch his cheek, run her fingers through his hair, hear him laugh.

The girl looked up at the darkened sky once more, the first stars beginning to sparkle. The temperature of the water around her was rapidly dropping. Her skin became cold to touch, sending shivers even through the souls looking on as the damp night air was cooled by a calm breeze. She cannot breathe here yet she does not feel suffocated. She hadn't been breathing over the last three months. She cannot move any longer, yet she does not feel trapped where she is. She cannot speak, yet she does not need to anymore...it was all about to be over. She couldn't bear to think of him anymore. The memory of the crash and the abrupt destruction of the car clashed with his beautiful smile and the perfection of his charisma. It caused her so much pain...too much pain.

She imagined herself standing on the edge of the cliff looking down at pointed rocks below before glancing back up at the sky. She could see him looking down at her in bitter disappointment, eyeing the selfish act of cowardliness which would ensue in front of him. Her eyes blurred as tears streamed down her pale face. She held her shaking body tightly.

"I'm sorry,' she whispered to him. Heat from her gut boiled to a magnificent crescendo and as her last act of defiance, she began to scream.

'I'm sorry! I can't do this anymore!'

With the only energy she had left, the girl edged her toes closer to the rock face before dangling them over the cliff side. Her breaths shortened into quick raspy gasps. She closed her eyes, took one last breath to fill her defeated lungs, and jumped.

As she fell, she finally felt free. Each second she plummeted closer to her death, more and more of the formidable reminiscence from those painful nights lifted free from her body. As the end of her life appeared closer and closer the girl anticipated it even more. She had waited for this moment as if it was promised from birth and now it was finally happening.

Back in reality, water creeped into her mouth, slowly at first and then faster until the water was rushing in like a gushing stream. The water found its way to her lungs, filling them up with liquid rather than air. It seeped through every vein in her body, through every crack and every crevasse until there was no air left. Her vision gradually blurred, and her heart beat slowed. And just like that, her heart stopped. The water that engulfed her comforted the girl like a blanket.

Black. Darkness. But there was no pain.

Silence and tranquillity. Finally, pure silence and tranquillity.

ABOUT THE AUTHORS

David Bell has had an interest in words for as long as he can remember. His results in English at high school were not very good but he improved over the decades. His appreciation of the power, expressiveness, and subtlety of good communication grew. In the past 40 years, he has created essays, sermons, and poems, many heard but few published. He enjoys poetry and hopes to continue to do so

Amy Capstick graduated from Year 12 at Albany Creek State High School, north of Brisbane in 2018. Amy was placed second in the annual WAG/ Peter Campbell Memorial high-school-short story contest for *The Tranquil Realm of Silence*, reproduced in this anthology.

Pauline Davies completed her Bachelor of Arts degree, majoring in English literature/writing and composition in 2018 and writes and edits technical documents. After six years of study, Pauline has been enjoying the indulgence of reading for pleasure. Aside from the tribute to her mother-in-law, Pauline has taken a break from writing. Instead, she is editing the work of a local writer, Scarlett Reed, whose first novel, *Death's Captive* is shortly due for publication. In her spare time Pauline enjoys theatre, travel, scuba diving, and the dubious pastime of pub karaoke.

Bernie Dowling is a Pine Rivers journalist and author. His books include fiction and non-fiction. His novel, *Iraqi Icicle* introduced neo-noir detective Steele Hill who returns in two stories for this anthology.

Karine Dupre spent the first 20 years of her life traveling through books giving her ideas on how to behave and where to go next. Since then, her train has been hijacked by guerrillas in Mexico, she almost froze to death in a Finnish lake, found a dead body in Prague and got sunstroke in the Australian outback. Reading helps her breathe and plan her next adventure. Writing releases the overflow of her emotions.

Ronald Holt retired from the Queensland public sector in 2006 after more than 40 years. He wrote numerous reports and is now applying those skills to his love of creative writing. Ron has edited five anthologies in 2007, 2009, 2011 and 2013, and 2015 for the Arana Writers' Group. A regular contributor to the Fellowship of Australian Writers Queensland publications, AWG and WAG anthologies, Ron has had short stories published on Anzac Cove and global warming.

Caryn Jacobs is an adventurer into the world of writing after parking a career as an occupational therapist. Her concern about the increasing problem of loneliness in our society, as well as her exposure to the fascinating minds of people with autism spectrum disorder, brought the two characters in this story together. This is Caryn's first submission of creative fiction for publishing, which she hopes may lead to the need for her own website and an impressive social media profile.

Kenneth J Johnson was born in Coventry, England. He has published more than thirty short stories. His work has been published in an Australia-wide literary quarterly and he received a judge's commendation for the second chapter of his unpublished novel in the inaugural Roly Sussex Short Story Competition. He has worked variously as a milkman, postman, merchant seaman, computer programmer and a classical guitar teacher before retiring to write full time. Currently he is polishing his first novel for publication.

Ann Lewis has been weaving words in stories, poems and quirky puns for the amusement of family and friends for as long as she can remember. Ann's current mission is to write a book that her two children might actually read without protest. In addition to trying to share her passion for all things literature with her young family, Ann has recently begun to look for opportunities to grow and develop her talents as an author of poetry, phrase and prose.

David MacLaughlin began writing for a staff magazine when he came fourth from world-wide entries for a travel article. Writing took a back seat as David became active in choral and Celtic choirs and musical theatre. After that it was time to give writing its proper priority in things cultural. As a member of Arana Writers' Group, David has contributed to the group's anthologies with articles factual, humorous, some fiction and travel tales.

Virginia Miranda began writing in high school and was first published in the Brisbane State High School Year book, 1966.
Virginia is a member of Byron Writers Festival, Brisbane Writers Centre, Brisbane Writers Festival, and The Society of Women Writers Qld. She is the Secretary/Treasurer of the Fellowship of Australian Writers Qld. In 2014 Virginia self-published her first book, *Flash Fiction Volume One*, a compilation of thirty-seven stories each no more than 500 words.

Vera Murray was born in Allora, Queensland. She has been writing since her school days. Vera is a former Pine Rivers Shire Councillor and she had edited a magazine overseas. While running the Writer's Circle group in Pine Rivers, she edited and published three anthologies. Her book *Move Over James Bond and Other Stories* and her first novel *Leap Year: Blood Lust* were recently published. Her latest book *Move Over plus Humorous Verses* was released in 2014.

John R. Nolan received Acquired Brain Injury, after a new Valiant car in which he was he was travelling hit a telegraph pole at 144km an hour. He awoke a month later with amnesia in an alien world. He has lived with a serious brain injury ever since. John learned to write every step of his day down. John lives in Elimbah Queensland, Australia, with his wife, five chickens, and a fistful of dreams.

Lorraine R. Noscova has published short stories in anthologies and has published her book *Memoirs of a Vigilante*. Attending many writers' groups she wondered where did all the stories and poems go after they were read out at meetings. Hearing that writers had trouble having their work published, in August 2012 she created the monthly enewsletter *Writers' Grapevine* with the 1st edition being released September 2012. The *Writers' Grapevine* continues to this day and gives writers an opportunity to have their writings placed for other writers and readers to enjoy. For a free email subscription, email Lorraine at: writersgrapevine@yahoo.com

Jeanette O'Hagan first spun tales in the world of Nardva at the age of nine. She enjoys writing, fiction, poetry, blogging and editing. Jeanette is writing her *Akrad's Legacy* series—a Young Adult fantasy fiction with adventure, courtly intrigue and romantic elements. Her recent publications include novellas: *Heart of the Mountain*, its sequel *Blood Crystal*, and short stories, *The Herbalist's Daughter* and *Lakwi's Lament*. Jeanette lives in Brisbane with her husband and children.

Anne Olsson is a remedial therapist living and working in Pine Rivers. She has been an enthusiastic actor on the amateur stage and, in recent years, an eager world traveller. Anne's poetry and articles have been published in newspapers and magazines.

R. William Penshorn has travelled the world but still calls Australia home. Now retired and still touring, he spent most of his working years involved in surveying and civil engineering projects. Ray has written several movie scripts. His interests include comic collecting, classic automobiles, rock 'n' roll, art, surfing, and, of course, writing. His Tonka Toys collection were on display in the Queensland Museum's *Collectorama*, of 2014.

Raelene Purtill has, in her imagination, a husband of more than 20 years, three teenage children and a suburban existence, north-west of Brisbane. In the real world, she writes. Short stories are Raelene's preferred medium although she has produced plays and poems. She is a member of two writing groups, Strathpine Writers Group and Vanguard Writers, a group formed following a course at the Queensland Writers' Centre. Her blog is raelenep.blogspot.com.

Chris Radge is an Australian novelist based in Brisbane, where she writes fulltime and is a part-time NanMa. Her published works include *Smithy*, in 'Stories of Mystery and Crime', *Tinsel Fructify* in 'Stories of Forests and Fantasy' and *Ghost Writer* in 'Stories of Ghosts'. She is writing the YA Urban Fantasy *Elder Scale* series and Children's picture books *Where the Lost Things Go* and *Sneezes*. Chris represented Qld for 11 years in bowling. Contact chris.radge@bigpond.com

Scarlett Reed's short story is a standalone flashback scene that complements her novel, *Death's Captive* due out soon. Scarlett grew up in the Pine Rivers/Moreton Bay Region. She attended both Bray Park Primary and High School. After several years of working as a phlebotomist, she is now only weeks away from completing her Bachelor of Nursing degree. Scarlett Reed is a pseudonym.

Bakthi Ross is an author and has written many books. She started her writing career as a children's book author and progressed into writing about evolution. Her observations of evolution branched into many other books that are relevant to evolution. Her most interesting book is about how there are stars in everything. It is online. She lives in Morayfield, Moreton Bay Region, Australia.

Jae Salmon is an aspiring novelist who has spent most of her life dabbling in the written form. Jae has a keen interest and a bachelor's degree in social science. She writes short stories, poems, zines and songs which centre on existential themes. She also enjoys live music and has long been associated with community radio station 4ZZZ, writing countless live music and album reviews. Jae lives in Brisbane with her three adult children and grandson.

K.J. Sauffs - known as Jane to her friends - has been writing as a hobby for most of her life. She likes to read a variety of genres and that has carried over into her writing. She has hopes of completing a fantasy novel in the not too distant future. Jane is the author of *Off The Record: Case Files of a Psychic Detective*, published by White Bud Press. After moving a few times due to her husband's Army career Jane, and her immediate family, settled in the Pine Rivers district of Australia in 1994. When not reading or writing she likes to do beadwork and cake decorating.

Sonya Simonds, currently in year 12, likes writing novels and has been creating stories since she was three. She enjoys stories that are wholesome and child-like. Next year, she is planning to publish a novel, and in the future she might write a novel of *The Cat on the Ship to the Edge of the Earth*, with each chapter also being a story on its own. Sonya won the 2018 WAG Peter Campbell Memorial Award for high school story-tellers.

Jenny Woolsey writes stories and blogs. Jenny is a primary teacher and youth worker, and a strong advocate for people living with facial differences, mental illness and disabilities. In 2017 she was keynote speaker at Queensland's Down Syndrome Association Her three children have disabilities. Jenny's heart is for children and teens who struggle to cope with the hardships in their lives. Jenny's published novels are *Ride High Pineapple*, *Brockwell the Brave*, and *Land of Britannica*.

Printed by Libri Plureos GmbH in Hamburg, Germany